Giving my Heart to an Atlanta Street King

Londyn Lenz

1,000 53

400
100
500

400.00
109.00
509.00

- 1391.00
509.00
782.00

British Noel

It was Saturday night and I was in the mirror checking myself out. As I turned from side to side I was pleased with how I looked. My body snapped back all the way for someone who just had a baby nine-months ago. I was thicker than a fucking snicker with a big booty that these Georgia guys wanted as soon as they saw me.

I bent down to fix my strap on my Jimmy Choo heels and adjusted my nude bodycon dress. After fixing my dress I sprayed some J'adore by Dior on, and ran my fingers through my long hair. I decided to wear it curly tonight like my husband likes it. I was getting ready to go to dinner with my husband Derrick.

We have not been on the best of terms for a while now. Lately, he had been trying to make effort to show me he has changed but in my heart, I feel like it is too late and we should just separate.

I would be lying though if I said I did not still love him and wanted our family to work. We had a baby girl named Jaxon. She was the light of our lives. Jaxon is the happiest baby ever and I could not be more blessed to have her.

I looked in the full-length mirror and saw my husband, through the reflection, leaning on the doorway staring at me while biting his bottom lip. I winked at him and he walked over to me and put his hands around my waist.

We looked at each other in the mirror and I admired how handsome Derrick was. He was brown skinned, 6'1" with a nice body. No six-pack or anything, but his form was solid and sexy in my eyes. He was bald with a full beard and had a set of thick eye brows.

"Bae, you smell so good I could stand here holding you like this forever," he said as his lips kissed my neck and ear making me blush.

"Thank you. You smell good yourself. Now stop kissing on my spot before we not make it to dinner," I told him trying to break free from his hold but he held tighter.

"Sounds like you feel how I feel. I really want to show you off tonight so let's go so we can make our reservations." He kissed my neck and walked out the bedroom. I shook my head smiling and turned off the light, walking out the room.

**

The summer night was warm with a light breeze. Valet opened my door to let me out while Derrick slipped a $50.00 bill in his hand. He took my hand and we walked into the restaurant.

Bone's restaurant was a nice spot for a wine and dine evening. The nice hostess greeted us and showed us to our table. I noticed how he kept looking at me but I paid it no mind. Derrick is not the jealous type or at least if he was he never showed it.

Once we were seated, we looked our menus over.

I decided to get the shrimp scampi with Caesar salad and Derrick ordered the porter house steak with mash potatoes and corn on the cob.

"Hi, welcome to Bone's. I am your waitress Marie can I start you off with anything to drink?" she asked us but her eyes stayed on Derrick, which annoyed me because women always act like they did not see me with him.

"We will have water and a bottle of your finest white wine on ice please. Also, me and my wife are ready to place our orders," he said to her, wiping that smile right off her face.

We placed our orders and shortly after, she returned with our water and champagne.

"I would have been fine with the water, "I said watching him pour us some wine.

"I know bae but tonight I wanted to do things a little different. I appreciate you accepting my dinner invitation, I really wanted to talk," He said as he placed the bottle back in to the ice bucket.

"Ok, I am listening Derrick." I set back and let him have the floor, ready to finally address our issues.

"Bae, I know things have been messed up for the past three-years. But I am ready to get myself together, and be the husband you married four years ago. I let my success and money get to my head. Women started coming to me more than before and I fell into temptation. I am standing before you to tell you that I have changed," he paused.

"For the past two months, I have only been about you and Jaxon. I want you and need you in my life. I promise you British I am ready to do this the right way. Please, just stop acting so cold towards me. Come back and sleep in the same bed with me and give me your heart again. I can feel you slipping away from me and that scares me. I cannot be without you or Jaxon."

He looked at me with puppy dog eyes. The same eyes he has given me the last time he promised to change. Things have gone from good to awful in a course of three years.

"Derrick, I do love you and you are a great father. There has been so much damage that you have done to me emotionally.

If I keep letting you do this it will mess with my mental and physical being. If I am no good for myself then I am no good for Jaxon or you. The cheating is not the only area we have problems in. Whenever you get upset with me you want to throw in my face how you took care of me while I went to school.

Do you know how many times you did not come home? You would tell me you were working late and I knew it was a lie. I have cried so many late nights while you slept like a baby. You have lied so many times to my face that I have lost count.

I've questioned myself so many times, trying to figure out why you cheated. Am I not enough, am I not thin enough, could it be that I'm too dark? It's been driving me crazy.

I understand you say you have changed but you have given me two months of changed behavior. I have given you three-years of being a good wife and you constantly shit on me. I need some time to get myself together.

I have to fix my heart and focus on myself. Not who or what my husband is doing. If we were to try this again we need to start slow and my way." I looked him in his eyes the entire time so he could see how serious I was.

"British I promise you I have it right this time. I can be this man you see before you forever. I was stupid and do not want anything out there. I will take things at your pace and will not pressure you. I apologize for all the hurt and pain I have caused you. I only want to see that beautiful face smile. I never want you to question if there is something wrong with you. I am the one to blame. Can I have a kiss to seal the deal?"

He smirked at me biting his lip. I smiled and nodded my head. My smile left my face as quickly as it came. Behind Derrick I could see a woman marching towards us looking pissed off. He saw the look on my face and looked over his shoulder, to see what I was looking at.

"Well, look what we have here. Look who is playing the perfect husband. Meanwhile just two months ago you were in my bed," she said to him as she read the bottle of wine he ordered for us.

"Wow Derrick. You really know how to pick through the trash. Get this bitch away from me before I mop the floor with her ass," I said before hopping up, ready to smack her ass. She took a few steps back,

"Bitch I am not trash. Your husband is the trash and you are the fool to stay with him."

"Niecy what the fuck are you doing here?! Go the fuck home. Like you said I have not seen you in two months. Whatever we had is done! This is where I want to be," he said while grabbing my hand and I smirked at her.

Seconds later, the waitress showed up with the manager.
"Excuse me Miss but I am going to have to ask you to leave." Niecy gave us a dirty look before she finally walked off.

"Take me home. I do not care about the food or anything. I am ready to go, "I said to Derrick while grabbing my clutch, getting ready to make my way towards the exit.

I was not worried about seeing Niecy if she was outside. As mad as I was, whooping her ass would help me release some anger. I needed to stick to my decision and take some time apart from Derrick. I was drained by all this drama and I gave it three years. It was time for me to live for myself and my daughter.

Derrick Noel

All I wanted to do was have a good night with my wife and get back in her good graces. But Niecy had to bring her rat ass out sniffing for cheese and fuck it up.

I met Niecy almost a year ago at Magic City with my boy Eric. She danced there and I wanted her chocolate thick ass. I did not think I would get addicted to her head game and sex skills.

Now do not get me wrong sex with British was good as hell but she had limits. I could not nut on her face and she would not let me invite another woman in the bedroom. You tell me what man does not fantasize about that? If you are my wife we are supposed to please each other on every level.

With Niecy, I could do any and everything I wanted she was down for it all. Niecy was a stripper and had the stripper body. Her attitude was nasty as hell though. She wanted the treatment I gave my wife but that would never happen. No woman would ever get treated like my wife.

I knew all these women saw dollar signs when messing with me but it was not happening. British was the first woman whoever required me to do for her. She had me recognize birthdays, couple holidays and Christmas. I should have been done messing with Niecy, considering I never really wanted to hurt my wife. British meant everything to me.

You see me and British met seven years ago. I wanted her when I first saw her. But she was not trying to entertain my ass because I had a girlfriend. Because of that, I wanted her even more. British had me going through loops to get her.

I even broke things off with my girlfriend but British still gave me a hard time. This woman wanted to be friends first then date me. That was new to me, because any relationship I had been in was always based on just sex. Dating wasn't my thing. We would chill and watch TV or if my family had a cookout I would bring them but that was it.

But, when I got with British, she introduced me to a whole new world and I loved it. I was all hers and she was mine. I had to be the happiest man in the world when she said yes to being my wife.

Our first year of marriage was great. I spent that year getting my business off the ground. I was an Architect and I had owned my own company with my business partner/best friend. We started from the ground up and now we have high clientele.

The only downfall was women came flocking more than normal and I was not able to fight temptation. I started with just one chick and I thought my wife would never find out. But one turned to three and three turned into one of them falling in love.

The chick had the nerve to approach my wife while she was out with her two best friends at the mall. They beat that girl up so bad she moved out of the state. That was when all my dirty laundry fell out. The look my wife gave me will never leave my memory. I had truly hurt her. That should have made me get my shit together but naw, it didn't. I kept up the cheating and tried to do a better job at hiding it.

When we found out she was pregnant I was on cloud 9. I have always wanted children, and Jaxon came and made my life even better than what it was. There is a saying my mother used to say. *A child comes out looking like the person the woman thought of the most.*

Well British must have never thought about me. Our daughter was a spitting image of my wife down to the pretty brown skin. British wanted a stress-free pregnancy so for 10-months she showed different behavior. She did not argue with me nor did she wait up on me if I came home late or claimed to work late.

When Jaxon was born I almost missed it because I was with Niecy getting some head from her. I rushed down to the hospital right when British pushed my baby girl out. I thought I would never hear the end of it.

British never even said a word about me missing Jaxon's birth. We took pictures of our baby and celebrated her arrival. It's like it made her no difference if I was there or not. That's how I knew this was the start of my wife being fed up.

The only time I see her being her normal self is when she is with our daughter. Or her friends and family. The way she looks at me emotionless, hurts. She still cooked and kept the house cleaned. She just stopped doing the little stuff like fixing my plate when she cooked. Or running my shower when I got off work. I knew I was llosing her and I am a brother who is useless without his wife.

My wife loved attention from me. That girl was into holding hands, late night talks and all the other mushy stuff women love. Now we do not do any of that stuff. I mean I was not too upset about it because I hated all that shit. I did all of it because it's what she loved. Now that we don't do any if it I kind of miss it.

Not once has she come to me to complain about my lack of romance or anything. The shit had me thinking she was getting it from somewhere else. Just thinking about her with another man pissed me off.

I looked over at her and she was staring out the window in deep thought. Our daughter was with her parents tonight so Jaxon would not distract her from me tonight. I was getting my marriage back on the right foot tonight. I hate to sound like an ass hole but she had no choice but to come around because I would NEVER sign divorce papers.

Shortly after, we pulled into our driveway, and British got out before I had a chance to open the door for her.

We walked into the house, and British took her shoes off by the door. She hadn't said a single word to me since the restaurant and the silent treatment was killing me. I watched her as she washed her hands at the kitchen sink, wondering if I had truly lost her this time.

"Bae, I swear I have not---" she held her hand up to shut me up.
"It does not even matter D. I'm tired of all this shit. I need a minute to think things through. I think separating is best for us," she said, giving her undivided attention to the carton of ice cream she was now eating out of. She didn't look at me or anything.

"You can stop talking like that right now because I am not going to let you leave me. I know the shit I did to you was fucked up but I am not losing my wife. Hell no!" I did not mean to yell at her but this was bullshit. All I need is a chance to make this shit right. She had to have someone else if she was just willing to throw this away so easily.

"British do you have someone else? Tell me the truth."
She stood up and slapped the hell out of me. The shit stung bad as hell.

"Why the FUCK would you think I have someone else?! Oh, I see because you took the easy way out of problems and got under some new ass. Well I am not you! Once I found out I was bringing a baby into this world that became more important. Not whose dick I can hop on just because my husband is unfaithful!"

She let tears fall from her eyes and that hurt me. I hated seeing my wife cry. Lately all her tears were of sadness and it was my fault.

I stepped closer to her and put my hand on her face. I wanted to wipe her tears away but she smacked my hand down.

"If you can look me in my eyes and say that you want to leave then I will let you go. You and Jaxon do not have to leave our home. I will leave." I stood there waiting for her to answer. British kept her head turned to the right as more tears fell from her eyes.

I reached out to touch her again and this time she did not slap my hand away. I turned her head in my direction, wanting to look into her eyes. But she avoided eye contact with me.

"Look at me bae, please. I promise you this is the new me. I am changed and no matter what your decision is I will still will only want you. Let me make love to you, it has been so long," I said before I leaned in to kiss her.

I was shocked when she kissed me back. My wife had some of the softest lips ever and I loved kissing her. I deepened our kiss I pulled her body to mines as if I was trying to make us one person. Just as I was getting more into it my phone started ringing. At first, she ignored it and kept kissing me so I followed her lead and kept going. Then it rung again. This time she pulled away and picked it up from off the counter and looked at it.

"Your bitch is calling you. Better answer," she said before placing my phone face up, and leaving the kitchen. I heard her grab her keys and I took off out of the kitchen just to catch her opening the front door.

"British where the hell are you going? It is late!" I pushed the door back closed and stood in front of it. I was not about to let her walk out of here. Even if the sun was shining. She was staying here. Hell, we said for better or worse and this was the worst.

"Derrick move out my way," she said calmly putting her keys in her other hand. I shook my head no at her.

"DERRICK MOVE OUT MY FUCKING WAY!" She shouted pointing her finger in my face.

"NO!" I shouted back. Before I could block her, she kneed me hard as hell in the balls. Her knees felt as hard as a brick and she put force with it knocking my oxygen out my body. I couldn't stop her. She ran out the door slamming it while I was kneeled over on the floor.

"BRITISHHH!" I yelled her name but she was already leaving. I heard her car screech out the drive way. I can promise you this. Once I regain some strength I was going to get my wife back home with me even if she was kicking or screaming.

British

The next morning

"Let me get this straight, his side bitch showed up at the restaurant and acted a fool! Why didn't you call me and Kori you know we would have turned Bone's out in a minute girl?" Ashley said while she poured her some coffee.

I was sitting at the kitchen isle shaking my head stuffing my face with brownies she cooked yesterday. I left my house last night and came straight over Ashley's house. I knew she would let me sleep and drill me in the morning.

"Girl that bitch was scary. I stood up and she took several steps back away from me. Her ass got escorted out and that was when I told Derrick to take me home. I was so ready to tell him that I wanted to separate. Of course, he started talking and telling me things that sound good and I lost all train of thought. Ashley, I am so drained from him but I still love him. Why?" I tried to stop the tears from falling but I could not help it.

"Brit, you cannot fault yourself for loving someone you knew for seven years. You're married and have a child together. It would be inhumane not to love him. Your heart is good boo and you see the best in people. Don't get me wrong, Derrick is a good guy.

He provides, has your back when it is against the wall and is a great father but he has infidelity issues. You know I would never tell you to just up and leave your husband. But I do want you to do what is best for you and Jax. I am down for whatever you want to do. You know me and Kori got the both of you." She hugged me and made me smile.

I loved both of my girls. We met nine-years ago when I was a newly high school graduate. I had a mini fashion show at the community center and needed models, and Kori and Ashley came to audition. We hit it off and the rest is history.

"Thank you so much boo. Ok enough about me. Tell me what happen when The Game came into your shop for a haircut." I asked wiping my tears from my face, getting excited.

"Girl! He came in the shop yesterday because he saw me on TV cutting some celebrities hair. He said he wanted to get his shit cut by the best. Dude is married so you know I am not interested. But the pictures do him no fucking justice! He is so damn sexy in person!" She bragged making her light skin turn red. I could not help but fall out laughing.

"Bitch I'm sorry but I would have at least touched it. You never know he might be into red heads. I wish I could have been there but I saw his pictures on his Instagram. He tagged you and shit with heart emojis. I am so proud of you!" I jumped up and hugged her again.

Ashley was the best barber in Atlanta. Two years ago, she opened her own shop named Bladez. Baby girl was the shit and her client list was crazy long. Besides her being a cold ass barber she was sex on a stick. Ashley was a thick red bone with fire engine red hair. The thing that set her off from the rest was her fresh ass side cut and a face beat by the Gods.

"Where the hell is Kori ass? She said she would be here in twenty-minutes and that was an hour ago," I annoyingly said walking out the kitchen into the living room.

"Girl I don't know. You know she is talking to Chuck ass now so she is probably with is him. This heffa kept Aron for me while I worked last night and let my baby stay up until 1am. I had to shake my baby awake this morning. She'd let him get away with murder." Ashley shook her head laughing while sitting down next to me. Aron is her 2yr old son. He is adorable and between me, Kori and Ashley's mom he is spoiled rotten.

"That's how she does when she keeps Jaxon. Her clothes are always a mess because she has eaten everything from candy, to juice." We both set there laughing. A knock came to the door and we both could see Kori's red Lexus in the drive way.

"Hoe use your key!" We both were too lazy to get up and let her in. Kori used her key and opened the door.

"Lazy sluts!" said Kori as set her purse on the table and plopped down on our laps making both of us yell at her ass.
"Kori get your crazy ass up!" I said, laughing at her goofy ass. Ashley started smacking her on the booty.

"I am light as a feather bitches. Anyways listen I got some good news," she said before she got up and set on the love seat in front of us.

"My job is sending myself and two-guest first class all expenses paid to Jamaica! We each have our own suite and the trip is weeklong! Ok, you may now praise me," she said before her cocky ass took a bow.

Ashley jumped up, and started to dance excitedly, "Hold up bitch! This cannot be real! Hell yea I am down!"

"What about you Brit?" Kori asked with a hint of doubt in her voice.

"Yesss girl I'm in! So, when is the trip?" I asked eagerly ready to get out the country. The drama with Derrick was starting to really take a toll on me and I was in dire need of a girl's vacation.

"Ahhhh! Yes bitch! We leave in two-days so get your sitters together ladies! We gettin' some international dick!"

We all started laughing at Kori silly remark. I know the last thing I want is another man to cause more problems.

"Umm Brit have you been on Facebook today?" Ashley asked with her eyes wide looking from her phone to me.
I hesitantly shook my head no afraid of what she was about to show me.

"That hoe from the restaurant has posted some pictures and text messages between her and Derrick. This dusty bitch has tagged you in them," said Ashley as she placed her phone in my face.

The amount of anger I felt should not be humanly possible. I snatched the phone from Ashley's hand not to be rude but to get a better look at the pictures. There were pictures of them in the bed with her on his chest while he was sleeping. She even made him breakfast and took a picture of the plate of food, and of him eating it too!

Obviously, this bitch did not care about her image because there was one where she was kissing his dick while Derrick stupid ass was asleep. This bitch really went there with one of her kissing my name that was tattooed on his arm.
I was so in shock that I literally started to laugh. Ashley and Kori looked at me like I was crazy.

"What the hell are you laughing about?! Let's go drop this hoe!" said Kori's little ass, as she jumped up and took her earrings off.
Ashley followed and went to her hallway closet to get a bat. I kept laughing and shaking my head, not even wanting to go there.

"Wait besties. I do not want to fight her or him. Look, I am just as angry but fighting and wasting energy is not going to solve anything. How many stakeouts have we done at bitches' houses? How many girls have approached me about fucking MY husband? How many times have I kept you guys up crying over this? Too many to count, the one thing I have learned is Derrick is going to do what he wants. He is fully aware that this shit is hurting me. I can look at him and see that he is ready to change but the shit does not work that way. The only thing I want to do right now is go see my baby girl and get ready for our trip. I know you ladies love me so you hurt when I hurt. Trust me I want to fuck some shit up to, but it's not worth it."

They both walked towards me and hugged me. For once I was not crying. You ever become numb to shit to the point when tears will not even come out? That is how I felt at the moment.

Knock Knock Knock!

We all looked at the door when we heard the knocks. Kori went to look out the window.

She turned back at us with a nasty look on her face, "Oh, hell no! What the fuck is Derrick doing here?"

Derrick started talking through the door and hearing his voice immediately made me frown.

"British baby I swear I did not know she took those damn pictures. Please open the door and talk to me. I know you are in there because I see your car parked out here." He knocked again but with more force.

"Derrick get your ass away from my fucking door! Go hump on your slut!" Ashley yelled picking up her phone. I knew she was thinking of calling the police.

"Ashley, you and Kori mind all damn business! You two just want British to be lonely like y'all! British nobody said this road would be easy. But if you do not woman up and face this shit with me then you will be just like your girls! I been telling you I am a changed man," He yelled through the door.

How dare this nigga say that shit to me? I would rather be alone then deal with this. Suddenly, I closed my eyes and saw all the bullshit Derrick has put me through. The crying, sleepless nights, stress and heartbreak. Three years of pain that I endured dealing with him.

I snapped out of my thoughts, and snatched the bat from Ashley's hand and swung the door open.

"British—

Before he could even get any more words out I hit him in his leg with the bat. I did not want to break his leg just distract him so I could get to what I wanted. His fucking car!

"UGH SHIT!" He yelled out from the hit.

I did not even look back at him I just went straight for his precious Maybach. Call me petty or whatever you want to. I was a fed-up bitch and this was my way of releasing my frustration.

Envisioning all the arguments we had about him cheating, took me over the edge! So, I hit his driver window busting it on impact.

SMASH!

Glass shattered everywhere.
And then when I thought about him being laid up with one of his bitches while I was in labor, I totally lost it.
I took the bat and slammed it right against the passenger side window.
SMASH!

"BRITISH ARE YOU FUCKING CRAZY," Yelled, Derrick emerging from Ashley's porch towards me.

He saw the look on my face and stopped in his tracks. Smart move because I probably would have hit him again only this time I would have tried to do some serious damage to him.

"SHUT THE FUCK UP AND STAY THE FUCK BACK!" I yelled at his stupid ass.

SMASH! SMASH!

I hit his back window twice because the glass was thicker. I hit two big ass holes in it. I saw me and my girl's fighting that bitch that came up to me describing my husband's body and I had to beat her ass.

SMASH! SMASH!

I completely shattered his windshield. I left the bat in the third hole. I was breathing hard as hell but my adrenaline was pumping so hard, that releasing all of that pent-up frustration felt wonderful.

Kori and Ashley were on her porch with their mouths opened wide as hell. Ashley neighbors were outside looking as well. Derrick looked at me with so much anger in his face. I did not give a fuck—I felt good as hell.

I walked up to Ashley and Kori and hugged them, "I love y'all. Thank you for letting me stay here Ash. I am going to see my baby girl but I will see y'all tomorrow so we can shop for our trip."

They hugged me back with the same shocked look on their faces.

"Bitch you are crazy but I love it," Kori said laughing making me and Ashley laugh too.

"I love you boo and do not worry the police will not get called my neighbors know you are his wife," said Ashley as hugged me again before I walked off her porch.

Derrick was still giving me the death stare. I smirked and winked at him. I then hopped in my truck and headed to my parents' house to see my baby Jaxon. This Jamaica trip came just in time. I needed some time away from drama and men.

Terrance "Terror" King

"Fuck! Suck that shit bitch," gripping her dreads in a ball I was shoving my 11-inch dick in her mouth. Making her gag and tears fill her eyes.

I was a nasty nigga so sloppy head was the only way to suck my dick. These females today had to be taught how to get nasty on a dick. Being the nigga, I am, I only fucked with bad bitches. The problem with that was the pretty ones never wanted to suck dick right. They be so worried about staying pretty while dropping that dome. Fucking with me, I would break a pretty bitch in and have their mascara running.

"I got some nut for that throat bitch. SHIT," I said just before I came all in this bitch mouth.

My head fell back on my seat while she leaned out of the car to spit my nut on the ground. I reached over and grabbed her some napkins from my glove department to clean her mouth with.

I was so turned off by her wack ass not knowing how to suck dick. She did all that sweet talk in the club but when it came time to put in work she fell flat on the job. I should not be surprised. Most women would sell a kidney to fuck with me, my brother Ty or my nigga Ronny.

"Damn baby, you dropped buckets in my mouth," she said in her thick Jamaican accent while fixing her makeup. See what I mean about them pretty bitches.

I mugged her ass, "Hurry up and get the fuck out my car. You did all that teasing in the club but came out here and sucked my dick like you were retarded. Get yo' ass out my shit."

I usually was not that rude but she was pissing me off.

"Fuck you Terror!" She yelled before she jumped out and slammed my door. I didn't even give a fuck. As long as she got out my shit. I fixed my jeans and headed to my crib.

Let me not be a rude nigga and introduce myself. I am Terrance King known to all as Terror. If you even think about calling me Terrance you will catch a bullet before you get my whole name out your mouth. My dad gave me that name Terror because I was always getting into trouble from the time I started to walk.

I was born and raised in Detroit, MI but moved to Atlanta when I was 12 years old. I have a younger brother named Ty. The phrase "My brother's keeper" was made for the two of us. We were mad close and ran our multi-million-dollar business together. Before you think we are some average hood niggas that do not know shit think again.

Our parents have been together since they were fourteen years old. Daniel and Stonny King raised their boys to be educated business men. Our parents were judges and well respected in their field. They put nigga's like me and my brother away all the time. Myself and Ty took advantage of our parent's wealth. We both graduated from Clark Atlanta. I have my masters in finance and Ty has his bachelor's degree in business.

We decided to take the illegal route when were thirteen, that is when we met Ronny. That crazy nigga was from Jamaica and him and his parents moved to the states when he was 12. When he was 20 years old he decided to move back to his home town Kingston Jamaica. The three of us did a run for the local drug dealer at the time.

We would drop a duffle bag full of guns and drugs to one spot and wait for it to get picked up. Soon we got a handed some guns and a whole territory and the rest is history. Our boss at the time put us on pay roll. We were making so much money that at seventeen we had our own place. Pops and Ma were not too thrilled but they respected it mainly because we did go on and finish college. Now selling drugs and weapons to every big organization across the globe. Life was looking sweet as hell.

I drove up to my beach house I brought a few years ago. Me and my brother are always coming to Jamaica for pleasure and business. You'd be surprised how much Jamaicans love their weapons and drugs. So anytime we came to Jamaica we eft with a few millions, yea I said millions!

Walking into my all white marble kitchen I was high as hell and hungry as hell. It was late so I settled on a burger and some chips. I normally would cook a feast but I was in the mood for something quick. I wasn't like the typical nigga who did not know my way around a kitchen. Our pops taught us at a young age how to cook. He said a bitch would give up the pussy quick if you feed her.

Walking out of my kitchen with my food I went into my living room and turned on my TV to watch some sports highlights. My phone started to go off and I knew it was a booty call because my brother beach house was next door so if he needed me he would just pop up.

I looked down at it and saw it was my bitch ass ex Sheena. I hurried up and hit ignore and blocked her number as well, tomorrow I was for sure changing my shit. That bitch had been calling me trying to get back with me for a few weeks now.

She thought she was slick. I knew that nigga she cheated on me with had played her ass to the left. That hoe can suck my nuts if she thought I would take her nasty ass back. You wanna hear some funny shit? They have a new born baby boy. A fucking baby boy! I was walking around like a sucker ass nigga thinking I was about to be a father.

I pop up at my girl's job to surprise her with some food. I got the surprise when I saw her and a nigga in the lobby arguing. I thought some fool ass nigga was fucking with my girl. I walked up ready to give dude the hands. I got the shock of my life when dude tells me he been fucking my bitch for a year and that was his baby. I started beating his ass to a bloody pulp.

I didn't give a fuck who was around or who recorded the shit. You sit here and tell me you been fucking my bitch and our baby was yours! Oh, yea you are definitely getting these hands. I was the type of man to only pull my gun out if it was necessary. Trust and believe I keep that thang on me always though.

Any way Sheena had a DNA test done while she was pregnant and just like dude said the baby was his. I beat his ass again and put that bitch out my shit. I invested three years with her ass. Sheena was a silver spoon fed girl who never worked a day in her life. She has a real-estate company that she decided to open last year. Guess who paid for her classes and gave her start-up money. That would be me.

I would be a liar if I said she did not hurt me with that shit. I did not eat or sleep for a few days then I just got depressed and drowned myself in my work. I think I was more depressed about not becoming a father. I did love Sheena but I knew the kind of love I was supposed to feel for a woman who was about to be my wife. I just did not have that for her, I felt like something was missing.

I worked so much after the break-up that my family started to worry about me. Besides our illegal shit, me and my brother own a casino and five-star hotel. We have a club opening up soon called Kingdom. Now it had been five- six months and a new house later and I was past ready to move on and put it behind me.

There was no way in hell I would settle down again or get my feelings involved with another bitch. I was 27 years old, wealthy and hung so any bitch I run into could not get more from me but a wet ass and a mouth full of this thick dick. Fuck love!

***

"We need to get going so we can close this deal," my brother Ty said as we loaded the last of our shipment into the truck. We had a four-million deal to close with these Kingston niggas who need a reup.

Once we are done with this deal we were heading to Ronny's house. His ass was throwing a party on the beach tonight. That shit was going to be lit as fuck with all the bad island girls there. I needed at least two thick pieces to go to the room with me. Myself, Ty and Ronny never let a bitch come to where we lay our heads at.

Dumb mistake number one for a boss nigga. Everyone should not know you home address. Back in the states we have pussy pads we take bitches to. Anytime we are out of town hotels were like a second home when we need to get in some wet wet.

"Terror, nigga can your ass not act like a fucking asshole tonight?" Our nigga Sleez said to me from the back of my Escalade.

Sleez been rolling with us for four years now but we still did not let him completely in to our business. Plus, him and Ronny really did not get along. Ronny would swear that it was something fishy about Sleez. Even though he has never done shit to question his motives I still made sure I was paying attention to his moves.

"Hell yea bro. Your rude ass makes all the bitches stay clear from us as if we got a mouth full of dog shit. Attempt to act like you a cool dude." My brother agreed and passed me the blunt.

"First off fuck both of y'all niggas. I do not need no one on one etiquette class from you two dumb asses. Y'all better be happy I am coming because the bitches flock to us like mosquitoes to blood." I laughed at these clowns while I was driving.

"Get the fuck out of here! You be looking like the devil and shit then you spit venom when you speak to hoes." Ty ass was laughing getting hype and making Sleez laugh and agree as well.

"Yea but who goes home with two or more hoes every time we go out? Huh? I can't hear y'all niggas?" I laughed because they were quiet as hell. Not to diss Ty or Sleez because they pull hella bitches. But even with my nasty ass attitude, the ladies still hop on my dick like first draft pick.

We walked out of the warehouse with our four-million and went to drop Sleez at hotel. He did not come to Jamaica as much as we did so he did not have a house out here. I told his ass we were going to Ronny's crib but he said he wanted to go to sleep before tonight. Nigga better be happy I pass that shit on the way because I was not going out of route for his ass.

"Aye do we need to cut Ronny in on this deal? We are the ones who made the drop so why the fuck is he getting a mill?" Sleez asked while drinking his beer. This is the shit right here that makes me think Ronny is right about Sleez.

"What the fuck are you talking about nigga? Just because you do not see shit does not means it is not happening. You already know we all put in work. Chill with that shit." Ty told Sleez turning his nose up at the stupid shit he was saying.

"I'm just saying all he does is fuck hoes and eat off our hard work." Me and my brother looked at each other and decided to ignore what Sleez ass was saying but he would not let it go.

"I been talking to some of his crew members and they would not mind if he was taking care of--- Before he could finish I snapped at his ass.

"Nigga what the fuck is wrong with you?! Why would you talk to one of his members about this shit?! You gots be the stupidest muthafucka walking! Ronny has been around longer then you so if anybody needs to be reevaluated it is your ass! Killing for no reason is one of our rules we do not break Sleez! And trying to take out Ronny is killing for no reason! That nigga not above any of us! He not our boss or connect! We are our own connect! So, kill that shit nigga before I drop yo' ass!" I meant that shit to. Ronny was like our third brother and he has never showed signs of disloyalty. He even did a three-year bid for our organization. Sleez better dead that shit before he be in a deep hole.

"Man, y'all niggas scared," he mumbled but not low enough because I heard that shit. Big mistake! If you are not God or my mama I do not fear shit so for him to say that was a disrespectful move. And being disrespectful is one of my pet peeves.

I swerved over to the left lane and hit the brakes. Sleez or my brother could not even regain their composure before I jumped out my front door. Swinging open the back door where Sleez was. I grabbed him by the foot and yanked his ass out my truck. I was delivering blow after blow fucking his eye and nose up with my closed fist. I was a big nigga so I knew I broke his nose. They didn't call me Terror for nothing.

"Ok bro that's enough!" Ty yelled and grabbed me off Sleez. My anger was the worst out of all of us. Once I am mad there is no calming me down. I did not fuck with disrespect and fucking with my shit.

"Nigga don't you EVER fix yo' mouth to say I'm scared of shit! Ronny never done a damn thing for us to just take him out the game! You on that other shit and been on that other shit for a minute now!" I yelled at his ass while my brother was holding me back.

It took someone big like myself to hold my ass back. Truthfully if I still wanted to get to Sleez ass I could. Ty was a big nigga but I had him by some pounds and muscle mass but I figured he got the picture to not talk that shit again.

"Damn Terror nigga you broke my nose." Sleez was on the ground trying to get himself together to stand up.

"Nigga walk your ass back to your hotel." I jumped in my truck with my brother getting in the passenger seat and I pulled off. Fuck that nigga, I had been having an itch about him for a few weeks now.

When he said he had been talking to some of Ronny boys and they were having problems with him too that fucked with me. I do not know if Sleez is lying or not but I was going to get to the bottom of this shit soon. I would hate to kill Sleez but I will and I won't even lose sleep over it.

Let me let you in on some shit. Sleez had a fianceé two year back. Dude was straight in love, Tameka was the real deal to. Sleez found out she was expecting their first child. The nigga was ecstatic. We were happy for him because Tameka was a good fit for him. Sleeze did not have a lot of family. Just his grandma and his auntie, he just brought them a big house. One-day Tameka was coming from the store on a rainy day. A semi-truck collided with her car killing her instantly.

Sleez was fucked up so bad he started drinking bad as hell and started using heroine. Usually we kill anybody in our crew who starts using. No excuses or questions. I always felt you would do anything for that next high.

That alone made you unpredictable and I cannot have that. I bent the rules for Sleez because of his situation and he was becoming family. Ronny was ready to murk his ass on sight. Sleez checked into a rehab and has been clean for ten months. I still kept eyes on him though. He didn't know certain shit about our business.

**

Ronny's mansion was made of bullet proof glass. He had it built on top of a hill overlooking the island. You could see straight through his shit. If ever he was getting it in with a bitch and you pulled up while he was smashing. Your ass was going to get a free show. I didn't think he was crazy for the shit because nobody was stupid enough to fuck with us.

I do not give a fuck what country we were in. Our name spoke volumes everywhere. Walking to the door four of Ronny's goons opened it and dabbed us up. Any other time they would pat a nigga down before they even stepped foot on the property. Me and Ty were above that rule though. The same was for Ronny when he came to the states to visit us.

"What's up mon! How are my brothers doing?" Ronny came from his kitchen to greet us with his heavy Jamaican accent. We showed each other some love.
"Shit we can't call it nigga. Ready for your crazy ass party tonight," I told him giving him his duffle bag with one-million in it.
"Hell yea. I am ready to get into some dark skin that only Jamaica can deliver." Ty smiled and said after her dabbed up Ronny.

"The shit is going to be crazy. I am thrilled y'all could make it. Where is boy at?" Ronny asked referring to Sleez.

"That nigga had a headache, "I said to him. Ty looked at me then we both looked at Ronny. He looked down and saw my bruised knuckle on my right hand.

"I feel that. I will just say this though. That nigga got one time with me. Feel me mon?" We nodded at him and followed him to his basement. That was the only part of his mansion that you could not see from outside. He had it blacked out. This nigga basement alone looked like a one-bedroom apartment.

It was dark blue and red with a stage and three stripper poles on it. He had a fully stock bar, two pool tables. A few arcade games and a 96-inch TV on the wall. He had two bad ass bitches on stage dancing and making their fat asses pop.

"You know we have another deal to close in Russia as well in another couple of months?" Ronny told us as he poured us a shot of patron.

"Yea I know. That shit is only going to take four days though. Six-million will look nice," Ty said taking his shot to the head.

"Hell yea. We don't even need that shit but I am not turning down no money. I'd be a fool to ever say I had enough." Ronny and Ty nodded in agreement.

"Good looking on that airport hook-up bro." I slapped hands with Ronny to thank him. He made sure our shipment could get to Jamaica without running into trouble with customs. He also took care of them rude boy niggas once we got our money and left.

We made them boys think they were buying from us. Soon as we pulled off Ronny's crew filled them with led. They took our shipment of guns and drugs back from them along with another four-million. They had to die after I found out they planned on setting Ronny up here.

It would have been a matter of time before they tried to set me and Ty set up as well. You see now why I was pissed at

Sleez for trying to take Ronny out. Sleez thought Ronny did not put in work for this deal but he did not know what the fuck he was talking about. Like I said earlier I let Sleez know what I want him to know.

"No problem. Any threat must be handled with. Like we say, we never kill without a reason.

So, is your mean ass going to be nice to me island girl's mon?" He looked at me and asked.

"I told his ass." Ty pointed to me with his thumb while looking at the strippers.

"Here y'all go with this shit. Worry about y'all fucking self." I laughed shaking my head. They started laughing as well. We heard some heels clicking down the stair. Ronny's girl Lizzy came down in a long silk see through robe with a black lace body suit. Ronny's bitch was bad as hell, like a Jamaican Jessica Rabbit.

"You are always handling business when you are supposed to be handling this pussy," she said with her hands on her hips and that same Jamaican accent as Ronny.

"Take yo' ass upstairs and I will be there in a minute. You bein' rude to me guest mon," he laughed while pouring us another shot.

"Well since you are taking forever I need something to play with." She walked towards the stage where the girls were dancing at. The bitch with the Jamaican flag on tatted across her fat ass booty looked at Ronny's girl seductively. She licked her tongue across his bitch lips.

Lizzy grabbed ol' girl by the neck and tongued her down. Then she stuck her finger in the stripper pussy and licked her fingers when she pulled them out. We watched the free freak show like dogs in heat.

"We will be waiting on you Big Daddy." They walked upstairs and Ronny laughed and shook his head.

"Damn bro. I was deprived of that for three years' nigga. I am ready to go back to my old ways," I said and downed my shot.

"Shit every woman in Jamaica will be at the beach party tonight. You know the bitches love Terror," Ronny said and dabbed me up.

"Aye Ronny, that nigga Jerome is here to see you." One of Ronny goons stood at the top of the steps and yelled down.

"Bring him down," Ronny said walking around from his bar. His goon came down with a big trash bag. He went over to Ronny's furnace and opened the bag.

"Put that nigga in there and melt his ass." The goon pulled dude's head out first and threw it in the furnace. One by one he pulled the rest of dude's body parts out and burned them.

"Y'all know we do not kill for no reason. This nigga was working for those rude boys we shot up at the warehouse earlier. He thought I did not know. He tried to play me mon so he had to go," Ronny said to us taking himself another shot.

"Hell yea nigga! If it was not you who killed him then I would have got to him," I said turning my nose up at the furnace that the nigga was burning in.

"So, we need to get ready to head to Russia to close this deal. This shit is worth six-million apiece. We already have more bank than we know what to do with but I'm never turning down no money." Ty laughed and said.

"They want exclusive ass shit. The weapons alone are worth a couple million. They know fucking with that black-market shit is a big risk. The Russians are smarter than that," I said while looking at my phone.

Some random bitch sent me a pussy picture. I shook my head and placed my phone back in my pocket. Hoes do not know that none of that shit makes me run and drop dick in their panties. I like to seek bitches out. Random pics made them look thirsty in my eyes unless you were my bitch.

"Ronny, we about to head out of here. I need to get some sleep before the turn up in a couple of hours. I won't be getting any sleep tonight with all the hoes I am taking to the hotel. There won't be none left for you two. Looks like y'all will be using ya' dick beaters." I clapped my hands together because I was laughing so hard.

"Nigga shut the fuck up! You been talking king shit since you been back on the hoe scene. Pity fuck is all these bitches giving you." Ty joked with Ronny joined him and dabbing his ass up.

"Tell this nigga Ty! He thinks he can take all me girls mon." They fell out laughing teasing me because of my old situation. Any other niggas I would have been shot. But these my bros and we always clowin' each other with no limit.

"Fuck y'all bitches." I laughed while getting down from the bar stool.

"Aight brothers, I will see y'all tonight." We slapped hands together with Ronny and left. My eyes were heavy as hell. If I was doing any turning up tonight I needed to dick my bed down.

British

Fighting Temptation

We walked in our hotel and my mouth hit the floor. It was beautifully surrounded by palm trees and green grass. The inside was all white with turquoise blue color scheme and furniture.

"Look at this hoe. We have not been in Jamaica for an hour and she has already found her next nut." Ashley said pointing to Kory. This bitch always found her a nigga within five minutes of being in a room. Most of the time they scoped her ass out first.

"He is fine though damn. Those long black dreads are working with his dark skin. Look how she is smiling, cheesy bitch." I teased but it was all love with my babies. We knew Kory would be the first to get a nut anyways.

"Here she comes all floating and shit." Ashley laughed making me join in.

"Don't hate hoes. Even in another country they come to me. His name is Ronny and damn he is sexy," Kori said biting on her tongue and flipping her hair.

"Well you must have made one hell of a mark because he is staring at you like the last piece of jerk chicken. His ass better poke those eyes back in his head," I told her as Ronny looked at my friend with lust biting his lip.

Of course, this bitch not having any chill looked back. And for the first time she blushed, smiled and dropped her head. Kory never did that, she was a nigga at heart and never showed anything on her face other than lust.

"Bitch look at you are blushing and grinnin' let me find out you caught feelings." I teased her while giving the bell boy my bags.

"Whatever bitch. Listen he invited us to his beach party he is having. I told him we just got here so we will play it by ear." See I told y'all. This bitch was a straight nigga, now why couldn't she just accept the man's invitation.

"We don't have shit planned this first night so we are hitting that party up." Ashley said as we walked to the elevator.

Kori's job hooked us up with penthouse suites. All our rooms were next door from one another which was fine by me. I did not need to hear whether one of these bitches getting dick down while I try to get some sleep a few inches from their bed.

"Oh my gosh Kori I am selling my business and working with you at WKBA! This shit is beautiful!" I was in awe as I walked around the suite.

It was so big and beautiful. I had a sitting area, a large chrome appliance kitchen and a spacious master bedroom with a king size bed. I opened the door I saw in the sitting room and it lead to another door. Asley opened it with a big grin.

"This shit is all the way live! I am never going to want to leave Jamaica!" She screeched and started twerking.
"Bitches, did my job hook us up or what!" Kori opened her joining door that led to Ashley's suite.

"Ok we have about three-hours to whine down and get ready for tonight. British yo' ass better wear what I picked put for you. Remember you are not a mom and you damn sho' not no wife during our entire stay here." She pointed her finger at me like I was a child and I got in trouble.

"Hell yea bitch loosen up these next seven days." Ashley agreed and pointed her finger at me also.

"Ok are you two done or can I get ready." I was annoyed because they made it seem like I was so lame. So, what if on a Saturday night I loved going to Target to look at their new comforter sets. Hell, I know I am not the only one who loves new sheets.

"Don't be mad boo it's all love." Ashley said poking her lip out into a sad face. I smiled and shook my head.

We went into out rooms and chilled for a while. I showered and let my hair hang wet with a part in the middle. I applied some mouse to it so the curls would stay. I took out the swim wear Kori picked out for me and I just shook my head. Please do not get the wrong idea about my baby Kori. She liked Derrick and respected our marriage when he was making me happy. Now she still respects him but she could not stand his guts. Ashley felt the same way as well.

I looked at myself in the mirror and loved what looked back at me. How Derrick could cheat on this is totally beyond me. Kori did her thing picking out my swim wear. She had me looking all fast with a two-piece bikini the colors of the Jamaican flag.

It came with a long sleeve fish net top that stopped right over my ass and it hugged all my thick frame. I put some hoops on and my black sandals. I put my room key in my risk wallet along with my iPhone 7 and walked out the suite.

Kori and Ashley were waiting on me. They looked like they were straight out a magazine. Ashley had a blue one piece with a short wrap showing her thick thighs. Kori slayed the all-white two-piece with thong bottoms.

"Yassss bitch! I am so happy you did not chicken out and you wore what I picked out. I told your ass I would have you looking sexy and comfortable at the same time. Next time just trust a bitch." Kori gloated while we walked to the elevator.

"Next time I will hush because I must admit I look good. Hell, all of us look good! I would fuck us." I jokingly said.

"Ugh hoe Kori like's that shit not me." Ashley laughed as we walked off the elevator.

**

The beach was set up nice as hell. There were black gazeboes with cream chairs inserted all over the beach. Five bars were set up there also next to the DJ booth. As we walked to the entrance of the beach the men were on us. These Jamaican men were very forward then the men back home.

"Damn you looking' good as fuck me want you bad mon." Some fine Future looking dude with shoulder length dreads grabbed my hand.

"Umm no she good. Let her dangle first damn." Ashley aggressive ass snatched her hand from the strangers. I laughed because sometimes these bitches acted like my nigga instead of my friends. It was all out of love though because I was the same way about them.

"Look there goes an empty gazebo that is a good view of all the action." I pointed and we rushed over there before someone took it. The DJ played some hot tracks and we danced in our seats for a few songs while we watched the party.

"I need a drink and since we all cannot vacate this spot I will be right back. I already know you want a sex on the beach and Ashley you want a long island ice tea." They smiled and nodded to me.

The crowd was so damn deep I thought I would never make it to one of the bars. There was every liquor you could imagine against the wall. I was going to try something new but then I decided not to experiment and get what I knew. A Bacardi Pina colada.

"Excuse me, I would like to place an order please." I smiled at the bartender. His rude ass looked at me and went back to talking to smiling in the bitch face he was in. I stared for a minute then I cleared my throat.

"Umm excuse me! I said may I place an order please!" I was looking as mad as I felt. This rude nigga sucked his teeth and still did not move. What the fuck did I do to get rude service?! F.Y.I. I looked way better than the bitch face he was in.

"Aye nigga! Didn't you hear her say she wants to order a drink from your bitch ass?" I heard a forceful voice that was so loud it boomed over the music.

I looked up next to me and saw a chocolate Hercules. This man was so fine it should be against the law. He had a body filled with muscles I could climb. I quickly imagined me soaking up his beard with my juices from Miss. Kitty. He had a sleeve of tattoos on both his arms.

"I-I heard her I was j-just getting to her." The bartender looked like he saw the devil in the flesh.

"And her drinks are on the house." Rude ass bartender smiled nervously at me. My hero had him so shook that he dropped one of the glasses breaking it soon as it hit the ground.

"Calm down nigga! Make her shit right and all her drinks are coming out of your pay all night. Next time act like you got some home training slimy ass." My hero grabbed the drinks from the bartender with flared nostrils turning me on. Finally, able to find some words I spoke.

"Thank you for helping me with that rude bartender. I have no idea what his problem is," I said while looking everywhere but him. For some reason, he had me feeling like a nerdy school girl talking to the star quarterback.

"It's all good mama. His ass will be fired after tonight," he said while we walked through the crowd. I felt like I was with a celebrity because people were moving out the way for his ass.

"I can carry the drinks from here. You do not have to walk away from your section." I did not need him coming back to my table with my crazy ass friends.

"Naw it's good. What kind of nigga would I be if I just walked away from yo' fine ass." I smiled and kept looking at the crowd. We made it back to the gazebo and these girls were not even there. Thank God, nobody took our spot. He placed our drinks down and to my surprise pulled up a chair and set next to me.

"You know you are the finest bitch at this party. Not saying that you are a bitch. Ya' feel me?" I nodded because I really was not offended.

"Thank you, I'm sorry I never got your name."

"It's Terror," he said looking at me. Finally making eye contact with him he had some deep brown eyes.

"Terror? Can I get a government name?" I looked at him with my nose slightly turned up. I hate when a guy gives me his street name.

"No, you cannot get a government name. Terror is my name. If you cannot call me that then you need to not call me at all." My eyes grew big and I arched my eye brow.

"Ok well I choose the second option. You can get up and leave," I said as I took a sip of my drink. I was serious as hell, rude ass nigga.

"I ain't going nowhere. I am going to sit right here and finish talking to you until you bore me and I WANT to leave." He set back and looked my square in my eye.

"Nigga then sit here all by your lonesome." I got up and walked away from him. So far, I am not feeling any of the dudes in Jamaica. *Where the hell are these bitches at?* I thought to myself.

"British!" I looked in the direction I heard my name. I saw Ashley and Kori on the dance floor dancing. The guys they were dancing with looked good as hell. I am happy these two were having a good time because I was not.

"Where the hell you been?" Kori asked while she stopped dancing to come towards me. Ashley followed. I told both of them about my little distraction with Terror.

"Fuck that nigga. Do not let him fuck up your night, dance with us." Ashley said as she rocked her hips back and forth to the reggae music.

I tried to hide my smile but it came out anyways. In no time, I was dancing with them and having a great time. Terror was completely pushed out my mind. Murder She wrote by Chaka Demus came on and everybody started moving their hips and dancing sensual.

I felt a pair of strong hands slide around my waist. I kept dancing with my booty pressed all up against his groin. I pressed my back against his chest and I was pleased to discover it was hard and chiseled. I looked back and it was my admirer who grabbed my hand when we first arrived. He was a hottie with his hazel eyes and he was working the hell out of his body as it intertwined with mines.

"Dance for me baby." Between the music, the alcohol and his Jamaican accent I was feeling so good.

We danced together for a few songs then I was ready to sit down. I noticed Kori dance partner was Ronny, the guy from the hotel. He was all over my girl as if they were a real couple. I had to admit they look good together.

"I am going to go take a rest. Thank you for the dances." I walked away in to the increased crowd before he could object. He was fine and all but I did not want this to go any farther than the dance floor. Getting back to our gazebo I was happy it was empty, no Terror.

The next morning, I woke up to a massive hangover. I had shots throughout the night and danced my ass off. We did not get back to our hotel until 2am. I hopped out of bed and went to handle my business in the bathroom. I had no idea what my girls wanted to do today but I wanted to go for a run on the beach. After I put on my workout clothes I knocked on Ashley's door to see if she wanted to join me.

"Good morning sun--- "Ugh!" I stopped mid-sentence once I got a look at Ashley's appearance. Her red hair was all over her head. She had eye boogers in her eyes and one lash hanging off.

"Shut yo' cheery ass up. And before you ask no I am not going running with you." She crawled back into bed and put a pillow over her head. I plopped down on the bed next to her.

"Come on! I do not want to run alone plus it is 9am so that's a strong seven hours of sleep you should have gotten," I said laying my head on her side. Kori's joining door opened and she came walking in with an oversized t-shirt on and her purse.

"Look at this hoe doing the walk of shame. Did Ronny rock yo' world girl." I laughed teasing her. Ronny was all over her all night so I knew they were going to hook-up.

"Yes he did bitches. I did a three-way with him and his chick. Well he kept telling me that she was not his girlfriend but I beg to differ. Anywhooo, the night was amazing. He ended up telling her to leave after round one which was only me and him while she smoked and watched."

"Wait a minute, he told her to leave before the three of ya'll even got down!? Bitch that's not a three-some. If he just threw her out then maybe that is not his chick after all," I said while still laying on Ashley who had not come from under the covers.

"I guess you're right. He didn't even want me to leave this morning. He insisted I put on this big ass shirt so no dudes would he staring at me. I think I like him." That confession made me sit up and Ashley as well.

"Eww bitch what happened to you?" Kori said making the same face I made at Ashley earlier.

"Fuck y'all! So, did you just say you like him?! Oh my gosh hell must have frozen over." Ashley teased and I laughed with her.

"Aww our boo caught feelings and it only took a nigga from another country to bring it out of her." I stood up off the bed.

"Damn British how can you even be in a workout mood after the shots you were throwing back?" Kori said as she climbed into bed with Ashley.

"It makes me feel better. Let's explore Jamaica today?" I said before I was about to leave.

"Cool. Ronny's boy is taking his boat out today and he wants us to come. He has two best friends and I have two best friends so why not put y'all together." Kori always tries to play match maker.

"Ok that's cool, I'm about to go run before the beach gets crowded bye babies." I blew a kiss and headed for the beach.

*

After stretching and waking up my muscles I put my Bluetooth in my ears. I chose Toni Braxton Greatest Hits playlist from Spotify and began my run. The beach was gorgeous with crystal blue water. The sky was clear and the sand felt like plush under my gym shoes.

I was on a runner's high as the cool breeze hit my skin. Slowing down I caught my breath and did a couple of squats to keep my ass right. When I was done I took off my shoes and socks. I decided to put my feet in the water and take in the lovely view.

I thought about my life and how the past three years have been. I thought about my family, friends and my beautiful baby girl and how I will raise her to have zero tolerance if someone cannot love you right. I never want her love for two. Being the emotional person, I am, I felt a single tear slide down my cheek and I wiped it away.

"Whose ass do I need to whoop for making you cry?" I looked up to see Terror standing next to me shirtless and with some basketball shorts on. *Damn!*

Terrance

The bright ass sun hit me in the face burning the fuck out of my eyes. I rolled over and grabbed my cell phone and noticed it was after 6am. I sat up in the bed and looked around trying to figure out where the fuck I was.

I looked in the bed I was in and there were four girls laying down sleeping with that "got dicked down face." Memories of last night came back and I remembered meeting these freak ass friends. All of them wanted a sample and I was glad to give it to'em. I left a stack on the counter, got dressed and headed to my beach house.

The way my body felt I could use a run. If my ass hurried I could get it in before the beach filled with people. I went home and changed into my grey basketball shorts and my grey Nike running shoes. Deciding to run shirtless I grabbed my iPhone armband I headed out the door.

While running I had Kendrick Lamar DAMN album blasting in my ears. A little while in my running I see a sexy ass figure ahead of me. I could not see her face but that body was bangin' she had on these black and red stretch pant with matching sports bra.

All you could see was ass moving up and down as she ran. Baby girl was the kind of thick I loved. She had a little meat on her stomach that I could grab while I ate that pussy out from the back. Then she stopped running and hit a couple of squats and it seemed like the ass got fatter with each one she hit. *Fuck! I got to hit this bitch guts this morning.*

I thought to myself. I watched ma take her gym shoes and socks off and take a seat in the sand. She must be thinking or some shit. Well I am about to fuck her whole mind up with this dick. I walked closer to her and I noticed she looked familiar. Then it hit me, this is the attitude bitch from last night. Her stuck up ass dismissed me because I would not give her my government name.

I should kick sand on her ass but I ain't that nigga. As much as I hate to admit it I thought about her fine ass ever since she walked away from me. I wanted to play with her insides all last night and wake up to her not them four hoes. I watched her pretty ass a few seconds.

Baby girl was in deep ass thinking because a tear slid down her face. I have no idea why I got so mad and felt like killing something for making her cry. This was not even my bitch for me to feel like this. Suddenly I softened up and walked up on her.

"Whose ass do I need to whoop for making you cry?" She looked up at me with her hand above her forehead to block the sun in her eyes.

"Oh no, what is your mean ass doing out here," she said standing up and wiping sand off that juicy ass of hers.

"The same thing you were doing, going for a run. Why are you crying ma? Who fucked with you?" I watched her scan my body from head to toe with them hungry eyes. I had to smirk because women thought just as nasty as men.

"Umm, I was just lost in a thought that's all." She gave me a weak smile and I could see straight through that fake shit. I knew someone had hurt her, that was a heartbroken tear that fell from her face which furthermore pissed me off.

"So, how long has your husband been fucking up?" I looked over at her punk ass wedding ring again. I saw that shit before I stepped in with the rude ass bartender nigga yesterday. I had peeped her fine ass when she walked on the beach. I saw that ring on her finger but I did not give a fuck. I wanted to smash her brown skin ass.

"Why do you get to ask personal questions about me? But when I ask something simple as your name I get the run around?" She gave me a look of annoyance with one hand on her shapely hip.

"Don't beat around the fucking question. I knew you were married yesterday. Judging on the fact that you came on this trip without him. And you sitting here crying and shit tells me ol'boy fuckin' up. How long you been letting him treat you like shit?" I asked her. Looking straight in her eyes.

I wanted to see if she was going to lie. We as men only do what women allow us to do. When a woman shows us she will not tolerate our fuck ups that's when we either get our shit together or we bounce. I believe every man can be a good man but only for that one woman. If he keeps treating you like shit then you are not that woman. Some women are just to blind or don't want to accept that fact.

"What do you mean by letting him?" Astonishment was written all over her face with wrinkles in her forehead. I did not give a fuck though I was always real about my shit.

"Just what I said. We only do what y'all allow so again I ask. How long have you been allowing fuck boy to fuck over you?" I was getting annoyed myself because she had no reason to be ashamed about the shit.

I liked a woman who would put up a fight for her nigga. When I decided to make a woman my wife she will not have to fight for my heart. She would have it way before I made the decision to propose to her.

"Fuck you, asshole." The look on her face was filled with rage and anger as she turned and walked off. I must have struck a nerve.

Not ever being the nigga to chase after a bitch I shook my head and walked off in the opposite direction. I was not even in a workout mood anymore. She had pissed me off to the point I was ready to fight. I hate a runner, stand there and face yo' shit. I know we are strangers but I wanted to know why was she crying. Fuck it! Hopefully I do not see her ass anymore while I was in Jamaica.

**

"Aye I want to invite some girls on the boat this afternoon that's cool, right?" Ronny asked as he blew on his hookah.

"Yea that's straight nigga but yo' ass know how I feel about females on my boat. But you my nigga so it's cool. I trust theses some bad females or you would not be fucking with them." I put out my blunt and picked up a missile and placed it in the box. We were in my living room smoking and getting ready to ship out some hash and weapons to a buyer for a quick three-million.

"I met her when she was checking in with her girls at my hotel. Ma was fuckin' fire mon I had to have her. I had her spend the night at my crib after the party, get this shit though. Lizzy showed up at my crib while me and Kori was just about to get down. I'm thinking shit about to pop off. Naw not at all, Kori looks at Liz and licks her lips and wants Liz to join us. You know I'm down. They get to kissing, licking and shit but my eyes could not leave Kori's body. I tell Lizzy to leave and I will get at her tomorrow. After she storms off I get in Kori's pum-pum all night into the morning. Shit is crazy." He had us laughing so hard my side was hurting. Ty was falling out the chair from laughing.

"Hold up nigga, you put Liz out with no dick!? I know she was ready to kill you," Ty said through his laugh.

"Damn nigga so you whipped off a bitch you just met." I teased him while still laughing.

"Fuck you muthfuckas I am not whipped! Liz know not to show her ass in my house mon." Ronny started getting serious which made us laugh even more.

"Shit I gots to see ma and her girl's now! If you bringing bitches to your house and putting your old bitch out for the new." We continued packing up weapons and drugs while smoking. We loaded the truck up and sent them on their way by our driver.

I have always loved boats from when I was a boy. Me and Ty use to say we were going to build a better version of the Titanic when we grow up. Having a boat in Jamaica only made sense. I named my boat Stonny after my mama. I felt at ease when I as on the water that's why I never allowed bitches on my boat. This was my sanctuary and bitches fuck shit up. Sheena never even been on my boat.

All day my mind been on thickums and our run in on the beach this morning. I just can't shake this girl from my dome. All I see is her smile and her sadness when she was crying. I am a natural protector.

The shit I was feeling for baby girl when I saw her cry had me want to hunt her punk as husband down and beat his ass. I know I needed to slow my role because she could be a thot and played ol'boy first.

She don't look like the type to be a dirty bitch. Hell, Sheena did not look like she would be a dirty bitch and look how that turned out. I just needed to push her big booty ass out my mind and focus on these girls Ronny got coming. Nigga better know this is the only time I am allowing this shit.

"Aye they are coming up the dock right now," Ronny said as he went to go meet them. I went downstairs of my boat to grab some glasses for the wine and grab some more napkins for the food I cooked. Your boy loved to eat and my pops always taught us every woman loves a man that can cook.

When I surfaced back up top I almost dropped the glasses. Thickums from this morning was standing next to two other bad girls. Now what type of shit is this?! *What are you trying to tell me about this woman God?* I thought to myself. I played it cool and so did she, baby girl was looking so damn good. I wanted to kick everybody off my boat except her.

She had this short strapless one-piece on looking good as hell. It was hugging her thick ass body. I looked down at her feet and just like before they were done up matching her nails. I loved a woman that kept herself up. I don't mind a woman having off days but keep them nails and feet together and we cool.

"These are my niggas Terror and Ty. Niggas, this is Kori, and her homegirls British and Ashley." Ronny introduced us as he took Kori's hand and they had a seat all cheesin' and shit.

"We actually met already at the beach party. This is rude ass with the name problem I was telling y'all about," British said pointing to me.

"Oh, so you are the one who was being rude to my besty!? Well, be nice today please this vacation is really for her." Redbone with the red hair said to me. Now normally I would cuss a bitch out for trying to tell me what to do. But I remembered British face on the beach and I punked up.

"I got you lil' mama. I'll be nice." I went over to my boat and started steering it.

I had my co-captain on the boat as well so I would not have to be stuck steering and can't entertain my date.

I watched the view for a minute so I could soak up God's art work in the sky. My eyes kept deceiving me and looking at British. I was happy as hell to know her name finally. I called my co-captain up here to take over the wheel while I grab something to eat.

I had my speaker playing Pandora on 90's R&B. I fucked with some new shit but give me some 90's early 2000 music any day. Ty ass did not surprise me when he eye fucked Ashley. Nigga had a thing for a red bone. I saw him look at British first but I would hate to have to dig in my baby brother's ass.

"You not hungry?" I asked as I stood next to British with a plate for me and a plate for her. This woman was so fine to me. I just wanted to feel her naked body against mines.

"Yes, thank you. I was just about to fix me a plate after I texted my parents." She smiled at me and took the plate. I took that as an invitation to sit down next to her.

"You have to tell me where you ordered this food from. Who sautéed this shrimp and lobster tails, might have a faithful customer for the next five days," she said as she put another shrimp in her mouth. British had these nice full lips that I just wanted to kiss on so fucking bad.

"The chef is right in front of you baby girl." I held my arms open and smiled at her. She gave me one of the biggest smiles and said.

"Wow! A brother who can cook, that is rare. Well my compliments to the chef. You have a talent on you. This is five-star restaurant worthy. Even your presentation is beautiful." I smiled at her and laughed to myself. I already have two restaurants one in Atlanta on Ferry Rd and one in Downtown Detroit on Monroe Ave.

"Thank you so much British I appreciate that. Maybe I can bring you to my beach house and make you dinner while you are here." Yea I put that shit out their just like that.

I just wanted alone time with her to see what type of woman she is. I need to understand why would her husband hurt her in anyway.

"That sounds nice. Surprise me with what you are cooking. I pretty much eat anything except brussels sprouts." She laughed and said. I laughed also because I did not eat them either. They smell like funky ass feet.

"I love your boat to. It's beautiful. Must be very peaceful to come out here. With no distractions from the world and only the sound of the water." She looked straight ahead when she spoke. For a split second that sad look was on her face again. Instantly my mood changed from relaxed to anger. She shook it off and turned her attention back to me. I needed to cheer her up.

"Come here." I stood up and grabbed her plate and put it in top of mines. After placing them on the table I went over to my co-captain and told him to take a break.

"Step in front of me." She did as she was told. I grabbed her left hand and placed it on the wheel and I did the same with her right hand.

"See how simple it is? Your sailing the boat." I whispered in her ear. My body was pressed against the back of her body. This girl felt so good and she smelled even better, like peaches.

"Oh my goodness! I'm sailing!" British had a huge smile plastered on her face. Her eyes had a sparkle that in my opinion represented happiness. The fact that I put that shit there made me feel on top of the world.

"Terrance. My real name is Terrance," I said against her ear and her neck.

"Nice to meet you Terrance," she replied in a sexy low tone.

"Anytime you are with me I only want to see this face you have now. Come back to my beach house with me when we dock." I lightly kissed her neck.

She bit her bottom lip making my dick jump against her ass. Hearing our friends come from downstairs brought me and her back to reality. For the rest of our boat ride we all laughed and talked.

We found out all three of these females were on their grown woman shit with their successful careers. British and Ashley were mothers and damn good ones from the way they made it seem. I was happy as hell they lived in Georgia. The phrase small world had never been so true. Me and British were stuck together like glue. I was either holding her hand or putting my hands around her waist.

When we docked British told her girls she was riding with me and she would catch up with them later. These girls must really be close because they drilled my ass about taking of their girl. I reassured them that she was in good hands.

"If you don't mind me asking what is it that you do for a living." British asked me as she walked around my big beach house.

"Well I have a few businesses. Restaurants, A casino, a club that I am about to open up and two tattoo shops." I set down on my kitchen stool and pulled her between my legs.

"Ok, well how did you get start-up money for all of that?" I let out a low laugh because I knew where she was going with this. Usually I will tell a bitch none of her fuckin' business. But I feel like British does not deserve to be fed bullshit.

"I sell weapons and drugs." I looked at her and she looked back at me.

"Thank you for being honest. No judgment this way." That was some real shit she said. The sincerity in her eyes made me believe her.

"You know I cannot stop thinking about yo' Yummy ass since the beach party. That attitude stuck to my ass and so did you." I had her facing me while my hands were around my waist and I rubbed her lower back.

"I did not have an attitude. You were being rude." She jokingly rolled her eyes.

"So, are you ready to tell me what is the sad shit about." I could not let that shit go. I needed to know the type of woman she is matches how I am feeling. I do not have time to fall in love with a hoe again. Not that I was falling in love. Hell no!
"Well I have been married for four years now and three of them have not been the best." She went on to tell me about their fucked-up relationship.

She got a little emotional while she talked. Anger built up in me when she cried again. Ol'boy is a real fuck nigga and does not deserve British or the life she gave him.

"Damn mama that is some heavy shit. You strong ass hell. I apologize for how I came on you at the beach this morning. Nobody can fault a spouse for trying to save their marriage." I squeezed her tighter while talking to her.

"I accept your apology but you were not 100% wrong in what you said earlier. Derrick did what I allowed." She shrugged her shoulders. I got a little in my feelings when she said that nigga's name I can't front.

"What about you Terrance? What is your relationship status?" I told her I was single and about me and Sheena fucked up relationship.

"Wow. Looks like your just as strong as me to bounce back from that mess. I'm sorry that happened to you." She rubbed the side of my face. I never let a bitch touch my face. I used to get annoyed when Sheena would do that shit. My mama used to tell me that was one of the quickest ways to break out. A person's hands carried all types of germs.

"Let me kiss you British." She kept her eyes on me as I leaned forward and put my lips to hers.

British had some of the softest lips and her mouth tasted yummy as hell. I slowly inserted my tongue in her mouth and she did not object. Our tongues danced around and my hands moved from her back to her fat ass booty.

It was as soft as hell like and expensive pillow top. British breathing changed and she put her small hands on my big ass arms. This kissing' shit had my dick about to buss through the seam of my pants. British must have felt the same because she pulled away.

"I have never been kissed by another man since I have been with my husband. It's only been him since we met. I don't want you to think I do this sort of thing all the time." Every word she spoke I believed and hung on to.

This fuckin' girl had my ass even if I tried to deny the shit. I wanted British and when I say I want her I mean I want her to be mines. As far as I was concerned her punk ass husband had fucked up.

"Your kisses taste so yummy. That's what I am going to call you, Yummy-Yum." I bit my bottom lip. She blushed and looked down.

"I am about to taste you. I promise I will not penetrate you." I kissed her again and placed her on my kitchen counter.

The sight of her thick pretty brown skin ass on my counter with lust in her eyes made my mouth water. I went back to kissing her hard as hell. I unzipped her one-piece from the back and slid it down. British had the sexiest strapless lace bra and thong on. Her titties were sitting up looking luscious as hell. I slid her thong off and a pussy was staring me in the face.

"Damn British baby you have the prettiest pussy I have ever seen." She smirked at me and I kissed her again.
British lips were so soft and I felt something weird when we kiss but in a good way. I sucked two of my fingers and inserted them in her honey nectar. Her pussy muscles latched on to my fingers like a magnetic force.

I could only imagine what it would do if I was to put this 11-inch in her. She had her back arched and was looking in my eyes. I bit my lip and looked at her. Working my fingers at just the right speed I took my thumb and massaged her clit making British moan in pleasure.

"Ssss shit." Her voice was so fucking sexy. My dick was pleading to come out and meet her pussy. But I knew she was not ready for that. I slowly slid my fingers out and licked them bitches clean, ya' boy was a nasty nigga.

"You taste so good Yummy-yum, let me make you feel good. Even if it's while you are in Jamaica. No strings no fucking drama. Just me pleasing you and showing you how to feel." She was breathing as if her breath was caught in her throat. I started licking and sucking on her neck while she was squeezing my arms.

"Ok Terrance, I am down for that." She smiled while looking at me which made my huge ass bust open a grin. I went back to kissing her and dropped to my knees with her pussy in my face. I pulled her a little forward and dove head first in.

British tasted so damn good the name Yummy-yum fits with nobody but her. Her pussy juices were definitely going to play dress-up with my beard. I was going to feast on this pussy. I did not want to use my fingers I just wanted to eat that muthafucka. I wrapped my lips around her clit and drunk her juices up like it was a faucet. I started swirling my tongue around that bitch. I almost made her fall back on the counter.

"Damn Terrance! Mmm hmmm baby!" She didn't know it but all that moaning made me do was eat her ass up even more. I changed my mind and decided to add some finger work. I took my face away from her stick pleasure for a second and sucked on my two fingers.

I slowly slid them in and started slowly flickering my tongue over her clit. I dug deeper and started fucking with her g-spot while I massaged her clit with my thumb.

"Oh Fuck baby I'm cummin'! Ughhhhhhh SHIT BOY!" British came long and hard. I cleaned all them sweet ass juices up. She had her thick legs wrapped around me like a knot. I detangled them and kissed her thighs and belly then made it up to her face with a mean mug.

"Who the fuck you callin' a boy British? Don't ever let that shit slip out your mouth when you talkin' about me. I know this is new to yo' ass but this here is a MAN," I said pointing to myself. Her sexy thick ass smiled and bit her lip.

"Yes sir," she said that shit so shy but seductive as hell.

"Take your Yummy ass up the stairs and strip so we can shower. You ain't about to get tha dick we only about to chill and talk." I helped her down and watched as he she picked up her shorts and thong.

I grabbed that thong out her hand and put them in my pocket. She smirked at me and walked up the stairs. Her ass moved in rotation with her hips and thighs with each step she climbed. I watched her sexy ass body climb each step.

I had no idea what I was getting myself into. I only know this woman was on my brain ever since the beach party and now her ass was about to be in my bed. At first, I just wanted to fuck and move on but her features just kept coming in a nigga's dome. Shit like her smile, smart ass mouth and lips would fuck my head up all day. I just have to make sure I'm careful and leave this shit in Jamaica. I shook my head and headed up stairs to my Yummy-yum.

Derrick

It had been days since I talked to my fucking wife. The only thing I knew for sure was that she was in Jamaica and due to come home tomorrow. I swear I called her phone at least ten times every hour on the hour.

Her ass had me blocked! Her friends had me blocked and they blocked me from their social media accounts. I made fake accounts but they had their pages set as private. British profile picture was her and her girls on a boat so I knew she was fine. I just needed to talk to my wife, this shit was annoying me. When I found out Niecy bitch ass posted those pictures and text messages on Facebook I panicked.

I knew she was not over at Kori's house because I traced the phone and it pulled up Ashley's address. I had always watched my wife and went through her phone when she was sleep and her laptop.

B was not a sneaky woman she did not hide shit from me. I was always paranoid she would one day retaliate on my ass and get her a nigga. The only thing I ever saw was thirsty dudes sliding in her DM but she would never respond.

When I pulled up to Ashley's house and they looked out the window at me I knew all three of them knew. I wanted to explain to B that I had not been fucking with Niecy for two-months now. This shit has spiraled way out of control.

All I wanted to do was take my wife out to a special dinner and win her back. The shit went from a romantic night to British fucking up my car with a bat. I have had no other choice but to drown myself in my work. Me and my team were building a new club in Atlanta called Kingdom.

We have yet to meet our clients, we have always met with their assistant Debra. This is my biggest account yet and I am very proud of myself and my best friend/business partner Eric. We met freshmen year in high school and have been cool since.

"Man this shit is so fucked up. British still has me blocked. Her smart ass even blocked my work number and your number.

Then Niecy keeps blowing my phone up which at this point I do not have shit to say to her. How would you handle this shit?" I looked at Eric and asked him. We were in my office going over the final touches on the club. We were supposed to meet the owners after.

"I would have been checked Niecy's ass the minute she put those pictures on line. That bitch specifically wanted your wife to see. I do not play when it comes to home. Any bitch I run across knows I will beat her ass if she tries to fuck up what me and Sheena has. After the drama we went through with her ex! I be damned if a bitch tries to fuck our shit up. You should see why the fuck she keeps calling you that way you have a reason to see her and set her ass straight. You feel me?" I nodded my head and agreed to what he was saying.

Eric had some hard times to with his girl. When they met she was in a relationship. Sheena was always telling Eric that she was unhappy and her boyfriend was always in the streets and she was lonely. He ended up knocking her up, this nigga was ecstatic and even planned on proposing to her.

He went up to her job and got a surprised when her nigga popped up as well. They got into a fight and Sheena left her nigga for Eric. Eric was like me, unfaithful but loved his home and wifey. Sheena gave birth to their baby boy Eric Jr. and they were happy.

"I feel that man and you are right. I need to handle this shit before British gets back. She got both feet out the door and I cannot have that." We went back to work and finalized the plans for the third floor of the club.

The shit our clients wanted was exclusive as hell to get. From flooring, walls, ceilings and bathroom designs. This was a million-dollar deal and we could not wait for the grand opening.

"Aye let's roll so we can finally meet our clients. After I can handle this fucked up shit in my life." We left out my office. I checked with our staff to see if they needed us to sign or go over anything before we stepped out.

Eric pulled up behind me in his red Corvette. We both stepped out and walked to the front entrance of the club. While we waited on our clients we were looking at the outside of the building and I was pleased with our work. This was my skill since I was a little boy. Taking shit apart and rebuilding a better version.

If possible, I would rebuild the twin towers in New York. We both looked up when we saw a black Phantom pull up. Once parked a big nigga stepped out the driver's seat and went to open the back seat.

Two older people stepped out. They almost put you in the mind set of your parents or some shit. My first thought was to laugh because these could not be the people who owned this club. We installed stripper poles and "special V.I.P." sections on the third level of the club for discreet shit to happen. I guess you make money whatever way possible.

"Hi. I'm Derrick Noel and this is my business partner Eric McKnight. We are the owners of Noel and Knight Architects." We both shook their hands and the older man spoke.

"Hello. I am Daniel King and this is my wife Stonny. We apologize you were supposed to meet with our sons but they are still on business. I assure you they will be here for the grand-opening." I nodded in agreement and we walked in the club.

As we walked around myself and Eric explained each room from top to bottom. I had my business iPad out showing them the designs their assistant sent us. We stayed true to every detail.

"Well I am very pleased. Our sons will approve this without question. Me and my wife are more like silent partners so we will not be at the grand-opening. We will leave the partying to you young folks." We all laughed and walked outside. We talked about a few more details and then the Kings got in their car and left.

"This grand-opening is going to put us on the map even more. The news will be here and that is free publicity," Eric said and I nodded in agreement.

Don't get me wrong I was happy as hell. I just needed my personal life to catch up with my professional life. My phone started vibrating. I pulled it out hoping it was my wife but I frowned when I saw it was Niecy.

"Let me bounce so I can handle this crazy ass bitch." Me and Eric dabbed each other up and we went our separate ways. I was heading to Niecy apartment so I can set this shit straight with her stupid ass

*

I parked my car in front of Niecy's complex. Niecy was a stripper and she made bank doing it so her complex was really nice. You know the saying *You can take the girl out the hood but not the hood out the girl.* Well that was how she was, Niecy could live in an upscale estate and she still would behave like a loud, ghetto ass thot. I do not know why I ever started fucking with her country ass.

I knocked on her door and she yanked it open with an attitude as usual. I looked her up and down remembering how I got wrapped in Niecy's life. She was bad as hell; her skin was a milk chocolate without a blemish in place. Now her body was not as thick as I liked it but her had ass and long legs. This bitch had become my weakness out of all the hoes I fucked with.

"Oh so now you want to show your fucking face. I been calling and texting you for days D!" she yelled at me and I just rolled my eyes and walked in.

"Aye shut the fuck up, that's why you are cut off from my dick now. You run your mouth too much. Now listen, why the FUCK did you post those pictures of us on Facebook and then tagged my wife. Are you trying to make me fuck you up?!" I had my fist balled up out of anger not because I was about to hit her.

"So, it's ok for her to jump towards me and talk shit? You did not even defend me!" there she goes with that yelling again.

"Bitch is you fucking stupid?! Defend my side bitch against my wife? What type of shit are you smoking!? Look I am working shit out with my wife and it would be nice if you would step the fuck off Niecy. Please do not make this bad for you." I looked her dead in her eyes so she could know I was serious.

"D, baby why is you talking like this? Me and you were ok with our arrangement and you just switched up on a bitch. I do have feelings to you know, your breaking my heart." She walked closer to me until she was in my face.

There was no denying Niecy was a bad bitch, but she had nothing on my wife. British had body, looks, a career and smarts. Niecy started rubbing my chest, then my arms then my face. My dick betrayed me quick as hell and she noticed it.

"Somebody does not want to leave." She stood on her tip-toes and whispered in my ear then licked it. I still was giving her the same mean mug while she kept kissing and sucking on my ear and neck.

"Niecy, stop. This is not why I came over here." Who the fuck was I kidding.

I could have stopped her if I wanted to but my little head was taking over my big head. I picked her up roughly and slammed her on the wall. Her strap on her tank top slid down her shoulder showing me she did not have a bra on. I popped her titties out and started sucking on her chocolate ass nipples. While she moaned for me to fuck her.

I was just about to whip my dick out but my phone started ringing. I knew it was my mother because of the ringtone. My phone ringing brought me back to reality and I looked at what I was doing. I was about to fuck another woman after promising my wife that I had changed.

I looked at Niecy and she was breathing hard biting her lip. She looked at me like she wanted me to murder her pussy. My dick was about to break the fuck off. I bagged away and shook my head while fixing my clothes.

"Baby why are you stopping? Come get this pussy." She opened her legs and lightly hit her fat pussy with her hands. As much as my dick was pointing in her direction my big head spoke loud and clear this time.

"Stay the fuck away from me Niecy. That is my final warning." I started walking out the door before she said some shit to shake my world.

"Derrick I am pregnant!" For a moment, I felt like I left my body. This bitch could not be pregnant. She is just saying that to get me to stay.

"Very fucking funny Niecy. Don't play like that ma." I was about to slap the shit out of her for acting so desperate.

"I am not fucking playing. I will be 11 weeks Tuesday, I went to the doctor already. Here." She opened the drawer next to her and shoved a manila folder to my chest and went to sit down on the couch.

I stood in place and opened the folder. Niecy had her proof of her doctor's appointment. She had paperwork with all the doctor information on it. There was a positive pregnancy test in there with some ultra-sound pictures. This shit could not be happening.

I always strapped up with every bi—then I thought back to a few months ago. I ran into Niecy in Ohio while she was dancing at my frat brother's party and we fucked in the closet without a rubber.

"FUCK!" I yelled making her jump. There was no way British would stay with me if another woman is carrying my child. I would lose her forever and then what the fuck would I do.

"Get rid of it." I looked at Niecy and said. Tears started falling down her face but I did not give a fuck.

"Wait a fucking minute! I am not good enough to carry your child but I am good enough for you to fuck UNPROTECTED at a bachelor party! Yea nigga I know exactly when this baby was conceived! You must be worried about the wife. Well what about me Derrick? Huh? I am NOT getting rid of my baby." She wiped her face and folded her arms. I had nothing else to say to her rat ass. I had three-grand one me so I pulled it out my pocket.

"Handle that shit." I threw the money at her and walked out slamming her door.

"DERRICK!" I could hear her screaming my name. I made it to my car and pulled off. As I drove the freeway I just thought back on the last three years of my life. All I had to do was be faithful to my wife and be a good man. Now this bullshit is catching up to me and I was paying for all my fuck-ups. Damn!

British

In a few hours, me and my girls would be leaving Jamaica. These have been the best seven-day vacation. Jamaica is beautiful with some good ass food, fun outdoor activities, good clubs and fine as men. Speaking of men Terrance, Ty and Ronny had me and my girls on a fucking high.

Kori barley stayed in her suite because she was always at Ronny's place. Ty wore Ashley's tuff ass down and was with her every day. I can tell when we get back home they were still going to see each other. I was happy for both my boos. Me and Terrance were trying to keep things light and no attachments.

When we would be apart all we did was text each other. I didn't even give him any cookie, we only kissed and some oral on his end. I am happy that we have not fucked because I think I would have even more feelings for him.

I have never been with a guy like Terrance as far as him being a thug. Don't get me wrong he is book smart with a degree but he also is very street and talks street. The shit turned me on, he is aggressive and ruff which is new to me. My ass was eating it up! Derrick was a clean good guy who knows nothing about street life.

There was nothing wrong with that he just is not as aggressive as Terrance is. Derrick was to worried about me doing some cheating. Like he thinks I do not know he goes through my phone and laptop while I sleep. Terrance is aggressive and does not ask to touch or kiss me, he just does it. When we look at each other I see him. No guilt or deceit just him. It is refreshing and scary because I know I must let this go. I am still someone's wife.

"Thank you for making my visit to Jamaica be a memorable one," I said to him as I laid on his chest in my two-piece bikini. We had just gone for a swim and we were now laying in his beach chair in front of his house.

"You're welcome Yummy baby. No need to thank me. When you plan a visit here or anywhere again hit me up and let me know. I can make that place memorable as well." He cockily smiled. I set up and looked at him laughing.

"Shut up! You are such a smart ass, Jamaica will be our spot." I got up and he pulled me back down.

"Did I tell you to get up off me? Fuck over here." See what I mean about his aggressiveness! My pussy started pulsating.

"I have to go get ready to go to the airport you know that." I was laughing because he still was not letting me get up.

"I know what you have to do. I won't have you late just chill with me for a second." He started playing in my hair.

"What are you mixed with?" He asked me.

"My grandfather's mother has Indian in her blood. All of their hair touched their asses and I guess it passed on to me." I stared at the water while lying back on his strong chest. This is how we spent most of our time, talking, chilling and laughing.

"Who has this pretty ass skin you have and long eye lashes?" That made me chuckle because everybody loved my skin complexion.
"Well, my mama has pretty coco skin and so does my grandma. And my long eye lashes come from my daddy. Thank you for the compliment." I looked up at him and kissed his lips.
Before I could lay my head back down he stopped me and pulled me up and gave me a deep kiss. Every time we kiss I get lost in the moment. My body gets to tingling all over. I just want

him to take all of me all night long. He pulled my strings to my bikini top loose and pulled it off.

"I love your skin on mines." He looked at me and said then went back to our kissing fest.

His big hands felt so good as they discovered my body. His touch was so ruff but soft at the same time. It was like he was using his hands to verify I was real. While he is talking about my good hair, him and his brother had pretty hair as well. Ty wore waves and Terrance had a mini curly fro.

He had that beard that was all over his face but it was soft and so sexy. How I have enjoyed covering it up with my juices with his head between my legs.

"I am going to miss you Yummy. Think of me ok because I will be thinking of you." He looked at me and said. I nodded my head and we just looked at each other for a while. You ever looked in someone's eyes and they tell you all you need to know? That is how I felt looking in Terrance eyes. I know he wants this to go further but because he does not want to get hurt he will remain silent.

"I am going to miss you too Terrance and don't worry you know I will think of you." I smiled at him went back to kissing him. I have no idea why I even opened this door when I know it is going to take an army to close it.

*

A week later. (Atlanta)

Tuesdays are usually slow for Slay. It works for me and my staff because that was when our shipment came in. I put a lot into this store, a year ago we started getting local celebrities. Then Rihanna came in here because she saw a fan have a pair of our boots on at her concert.

She told her she brought them from here. Rihanna almost brought our store out! She shared all of it on her Instagram page and tagged our store Slay in all the pictures. We have blown up since then. We even have had more celebrities come. I almost shitted bricks when the incredible Mary J. Blidge came a few months ago.

I was in my office on the second floor going over some paper work and yapping it up with Ashley. Her shop was not very busy either so she had some time to gossip with me. Plus, she still was talking to Ty. I was using my boo to see about Terrance. I would bring him up every so often.

As much as I hate to admit I missed him. I tried to not think about him or day dream about his head between my legs. The shit was hard as hell to do. I have had some solo moments imaging him while in the shower and playing with myself. I wanted to text him so bad but I knew that would be like opening up Pandora's box.

"Do you know what would make me love you for life British?" I playfully rolled my eyes and shook my head. I knew this girl wanted something.

"What would that be?" I responded with humor.

"I have a date tonight with Ty. The problem is I didn't realize I said yes on the same night my mama plays Bingo. Wouldn't you love it if your nephew came over and kept y'all company? Please Brit I will treat you to lunch and pay you." I almost hung up on her.

"Bitch don't do me. You know damn well I would never charge you. Aron is no problem he is a good baby. Pack him a bag he can stay the night." Her happy ass squealed in my ear like a mouse.
"Thank you boo I love you forever."

"Bitch I want that lunch date though. Olive Garden please." I teased her and we both laughed.

"Oh shit Kori's show is on." Ashley reminded me while turning her radio on. I turned the music on and had my girl's show playing through the whole store. Everybody loved her show so no one was tripping.

"Ok so today in Kori's Korner we are talking about three-somes. Do they make or break a relationship? Let me tell y'all about my Jamaican mix I had while on vacation. You have not lived until you had some Island love between yo' legs! Mmm-hmm I am here to tell ya the shit is fire.

The whole store was laughing hard as hell. She got into details about her and Ronny freaky week. Then the really funny shit came when she started accepting callers. One caller tried to shame her for being into three-somes.

Kori chewed his ass up! This crazy girl told him his wife was cheating on him with a man and a woman because he was so boring. This bitch was nuts and she had my whole store in tears from laughing.

"I swear that girl has no filter. She can talk all that shit she wants on the radio but Ronny has her acting different. Like she cakes with him all day and she rarely goes out. Do you know she told me she is spending Fourth of July in Jamaica?" Ashley said with happiness in her voice. I was smiling from ear to ear.

I liked Ronny and I could tell he was feeling Kori. That bitch is hard to tame and his ass was doing it from another country. Me and Ashley talked for a few then I got back to work. I unpacked a couple of boxes and was pleased with the pieces. My designers I worked with really did there the damn thing with this collection.

I heard my phone go off on my desk but ignored it. I figured whoever it was would call my store if it was important. After a few minutes, my phone went off again. I stopped hanging clothes up to see who was texting me. My heart hit the bottom of my feet when I saw Terrance name on the screen.

Terrance: I need to see you Yummy.

Terrance: Do I need to pay your store a visit?

I laughed at his last text but knowing how aggressive he is I knew he was not playing. I didn't want him coming to my store and having my employees be all in my business. I decided to text him back with a huge grin on my face. I felt like the fucking joker.

Me: Hey Terrance. No, I am not ignoring you lol I was busy at work. I do not need you up in my store distracting my employees.

He texted back after a few seconds.

Terrance: If yo' ass was ignoring me I would I have paid you a visit. Distraction or not I don't give a fuck and you know I don't. Look I need to see you. Think of some shit to tell dude and meet me at Carrabba's at 7.

Me: I can't tonight I am keeping Ashley's son for her. I am free tomorrow night though.

Terrance: Bet Yummy! Look sexy for a nigga to.

Me: Lol! Goodbye Terrance.

Seeing he did not text anything back I went back to work. For the rest of my work day I had a smile on my face. I did not know what the fuck I was doing seeing another man. Only thing I knew for sure was I missed him. As long as we are in a public place and not secluded we should be good.

The rest of the day went by quick as hell. I picked Jaxon up from my parents' house and took her home. Derrick and I have been staying in the same house but he has been sleeping in our guest room. I had a condo I was waiting to hear back from any day now. Even though I have no idea if I wanted to stay married. I knew for sure I needed some space between me and my husband.

Terrance "Terror"

I could not wait until our club Kingdom grand-opening day. We had a few months until the day but from what our assistant Debra told us things were looking good. Me and my brother decided a few years back to open a night club. Atlanta is a hot ass spot to open up a club! We started putting our plans in affect just last year.

Having money gave us the advantage to do shit our way and on our time. Our illegal affairs always kept myself and Ty out of town. That's why our personal assistant and our parents stepped up and took over.

All we did was tell them what we wanted and give them the designs our sketch artist drew. Pops told us he found a great architect to do this project and because we trusted our pops decisions we were good to go. This was easy money! No matter what people are going to always want to party and have a good ass time.

Once this takes off and become successful me and my brother are going to open one up in Detroit. The D was our home and we always wanted to show love in anyway. We weren't like the other muthafuckas who moved out the D and didn't fuck with it. Naw, Detroit would always be home.

"Aye bro, yo' ass not even paying attention to the video pops sent us. What the fuck you over there chessin' about like a school girl nigga?" Ty punk ass tried to take shots at me. We were in his man cave watching the video our pops sent us. It was designs for the bathroom and different floorings for the club. Ty was right, my ass wasn't paying attention.

Our top security guy and friend Mike was with us as well. Mike been down with us back when we started when we were teenagers. He wanted to get paid but did not have much street smart. He was just a 6'6" big black nigga who could fight his ass off. Mike really did not talk much. He only nodded his head, smirked or gave yo' ass a look. It usually meant he was about to beat yo' ass or kill you.

His dad was into karate and that taekwondo shit. When we saw him in action we decided to hire him as muscle. That was when we were little nigga's. now we have a security team a mile long and Mike oversaw all of them.

"Fuck you bitch. I ain't chessin' at shit. And I was paying attention. I like the gold flooring for the bathroom." Ty fell out laughing.

"Nigga ain't no gold flooring! Damn bro what bitch got you in la la land?" This nigga kept laughing at me pissing me off. Mike smirked while rolling his blunt up.

"Aye nigga chill with that bitch shit. This British nigga so pick your next words carefully." This fool looked at me with shock on his face.

"Wait, I thought y'all agreed to leave that shit in Jamaica? Don't tell me she gave you a Love Jones in only a few days bro." Ty shook his head at me.

"How the fuck can you even come on me like that!? Nigga Ashley yellow ass got your nostrils wide open. You going on dates and already trying to baby proof your house. Don't nobody want yo' creepy lookin' ass around their child." I started laughing. His ass was just like me. He could dish the jokes but could not take them.

"Fuck you bro." That was all he said making me laugh harder. Mike ass smirked harder and shook his head.

"Sensitive bitch!" I yelled as he walked out the room.

I can't front though, I was geeked as hell when British texted me back. We did agree to leave our thang in Jamaica. At first, I was cool with it but I started missing the shit out of her. I never been a nigga scared of rejection so I decided to shoot her a text. If she didn't respond I would have personally made a trip to her store.

Even though I was not scared of rejection at all but when it is done to me I hated it. I don't know what the fuck I was feeling for British sexy ass. All I knew was I wanted to be near her.

As I thought about our dinner date tomorrow my phone alerted me I had a text. I thought it was from my Yummy pretty ass but it was from Sleez. He asked if he could meet up with me and Ty. My brother walked back in his man cave just in time.

"Sleez just hit me up and asked if he can slide through. You cool with that?" I asked my brother taking the blunt out his hand.

"Shit I'm cool. The nigga been M.I.A. since you beat his ass." Ty laughed taking a seat in his recliner. We were about to finish watching the video on the projector pops sent us.

"All this sneaky and odd behavior shit is done after today. I swear bro I will gladly out a bullet in Sleez head. His mood swings and beef with Ronny is getting squashed today. I am going to have a few of our guys keep an eye in him to." Ty nodded in agreement.

We smoked and played the game for a few minutes until Ty surveillance video showed up on the TV screen. It alerted him someone was at his gate. Ty got up to let Sleez drive in.

"T bro I just got this carpet installed. If you have to blow this nigga brains out yo' ass is paying to have it shampooed." Ty had a serious expression on his face. I chuckled and agreed.

My plan was not to put one in Sleez but if it came down to it then so be the shit. I have never been afraid to pull the trigger. Exclude children, I would drop whoever I had to drop.

Mike went and let Sleez in while me and Ty stayed in the man cave smokin'. Sleez walked in first with Mike behind him. I laughed to myself because I always told him to never give a nigga yo' back. Not unless you ready to die.

"What up Terror. How you been?" Sleez tried to show me some love with a dab. I left his ass hangin' and stood up. Mike was behind him leaning against the entrance.

"I'm good nigga. So, what's the word? Wat'chu need to holla at me about?" I did not want to do no small talk bullshit. I put my blunt out and waited for him to talk.

"Look, I was trippin' in Jamaica. I apologize for comin' at you the way I did. I been on some other shit lately but I got myself in order man. For real I just want to be back down with y'all." I looked at him then glanced at my brother. He nodded his head and I went back to looking at Sleez.

"We good my nigga. No bad blood this way, I do think it's best if we part ways though. We don't need that type of shit around our business. This wishy-washy behavior is shit I don't even deal with from a bitch." I had my nostrils flared while I spoke because I wanted to beat his ass again. Sleez looked at me then looked at Ty.

"Ty come on bro, talk to him. I'm good now! I admit I was trippin' and shit but I swear I'm good." He pleaded with Ty.

Everybody always thought Ty was the nice one between us. People had shit fucked up because he is the crazy one. I just physically look like a mean nigga because I was bigger. Ty was the loose cannon.

"Nigga I don't have to talk to my brother about shit! He right here and he can hear yo' ass.

The answer is no, get the fuck outta here Sleez. We are bending the rules for you yet again. Any other muthafucka would leave in a body bag." Ty was squeezing his handle on his gun waiting to pull it out.

He had a craze look in his eyes and his mouth was twisted up See what I mean, the nigga crazy. He will be paying for his own carpet to get cleaned!

"So, it's like that my nigga's? Fuck--- before Sleez could even get his words out Mike hit him square in his throat and head knocking his ass unconscious.

"Damn Mike nigga. Is he dead?" Ty asked looking down at Sleez laughing.

"Naw, I hit the nerve in his head that puts you to sleep for a while." He picked Sleez up like he was some damn groceries.

"Kill him?" Mike looked at us and asked. My brother looked at me. I knew if it was up to him he would. I thought about Sleez grandma and auntie.

"Naw, drop his ass off at his crib. We will keep an eye on him in case he tries some shit. Mike nodded his head and carried Sleez out the door.

"Nigga yo' ass quick to have a heart but the first to destroy some shit." Ty joked while lighting up the blunt again.

"You talk a lot of shit. What up with you and Ashley nigga? Y'all been chillin' together since Jamaica?" Just that quick we moved on with the shit with Sleez ass. Ty smiled big as hell when I mentioned redhead name.

"We cool bro. I'm feelin' the fuck out of her but she got guards up and shit.

Her baby daddy played her and their son to the left. Now she think's all nigga's the same. I'm down to show her ass I'm different though. You know she still ain't gave up the pussy! I never even been to her crib or seen her son. Only pictures of him on her Facebook and Instagram." He shook his head while passing me the blunt.

"Nigga any good mother will be careful of who they bring around their child. Don't fault her for that. The not giving up the pussy is the same thing as well. Females know that is our goal anyways. Some niggas are up front about the shit and some beat around the bush about it. The longer they make us wait the more they feel they in control.

Niggas who want to hit and quit will move on and say fuck it. A nigga who is trying to build will be up for the challenge. Just prove her ass wrong about you like you said. Fuck her mental first bro." He nodded and I passed him back the blunt.

"What up with you and British? I knew y'all was not gone drop that shit in Jamaica! Yo' ass caught a Jones for her thick ass?" He laughed and turned in the game.

"Ain't no Jones caught this way nigga. I just can't shake her ass. I think it's because I don't know what the pussy is about." Ty shook his head.

"Hell naw bro. I know yo' ass, you feelin' the fuck out of British. You just faking for the crew because of Sheena dirty bitch ass. I told you to pop her and that nigga she was cheating with. I like British though, she a good girl like her friends. You see me and Ronny locked it down. Don't tell me you trippin' about her wack ass husband." He smirked at me. Any other nigga would have got these hands for even thinking I had worry in me.

"Ty don't make me fuck you up. I don't give a fuck about her bitch ass husband! You know that shit. But if British is loyal to his ass then I am not about to put my feelings out there to get played. I will kill her husband in a minute.

I don't know why I can't shake her man. I wasn't like this with Sheena." I confessed. My brother had the same stupid ass smirk on his face. He picked up his game controller and passed me the other one. We played the game and smoked the rest of the afternoon.

*

Tonight, was my date with British. We had been texting all day until we both had to get ready. I was glad she kept her word and was meeting me. I have no idea what the fuck I wanted to come out of this. I just know I need to see her and be around her pretty brown ass.

I sprayed some of my Givenchy cologne on and looked myself over in the mirror. British was always rubbing and touching on my arms so I made sure to have them on display. I had some Cavalli jeans on and some grey Yezzy's on. My shirt matched my jeans with the grey logo on it. Satisfied with my look I left out my bathroom and headed down stairs out the door.

I walked out my crib towards my Mercedes Benz G-Wagon. On the drive, I couldn't even help being excited about seeing British. I had thought about her a lot even before we had our time alone. It was just something about her that stuck to a niggas dome.

I was playing Jay-Z new shit 4:44 album bumping that fire shit. I pulled up to the restaurant and stepped out and walked into the entrance. The hostess and greeter eyes almost fell out their heads when they looked at me.

"Umm hi welcome to Carrabba's. Will you be dining alone or waiting for a party?" The greeter talked to me but eyes were all over my body. I chuckled at her young ass.

"Naw ma I'm waiting on someone." As I spoke I saw British sitting at the bar. My dick jumped at the sight of her gorgeous ass. She hadn't noticed me yet as she set there sipping on some wine.

"Actually, I just spotted my date. You can get us a table for two ready." I winked at the young girls and left them drooling. I walked towards British direction and lightly placed my hand on her lower back.

"What's up Yummy baby," I whispered in her ear. She looked at me startled.

"Boy, you were about to get a glass of wine thrown in your face. You scared me." She smiled and turned on the stool.

"What I tell you about that boy shit? Fuck over here and hug me." I pulled her by her arm into me. That familiar peach smell invaded my nostrils. We hugged for a minute then we pulled away. She was smiling from ear to ear making that brown skin glow.

"You look good as hell Yum damn!" I bit my lip looking at her fine ass.

She had these skin-tight jeans on with a silver shirt that was off both her shoulders. Once again, her feet were done up matching her nails. She had these sexy ass heels on making her feet look even more sexy. I never been a feet nigga! Her hair was straight with some up in a ponytail and some down.

I loved how long and thick British hair was. I had no problem with a woman wearing weave. It was just something about that natural shit that turned me on. Long or short as long as she made it look good I loved it.

"Thanks love. You are looking good as hell yourself." She smiled at me while looking at my arms. I smiled because she was always looking at my arms or messing with my beard.

"Excuse me, your table is ready." The young ass hostess let us know. We followed her to our table. I could not stop touching British. I had my hand on her lower back as we walked. Her pretty ass was blushing and smirking.

"Your waiter will be with you shortly." The hostess nodded at us and walked away.

"So, thank you to agreeing to have dinner with me." I set across from her in our booth. I could tell she was nervous. She would only look at me for a quick second at a time.
"You're welcome Terrance. I did not want to cook tonight anyways." I nodded my head at her statement.

"Is that the only reason you came out tonight? You could have got some quick ass take-out," she laughed.
"No, I wanted dinner. You were a bonus." I smiled at bit my lip.
That shit always made her wet and I wanted her pussy drenched by the time our food came. I noticed she would not give my long eye contact like we did. She would look at me and quickly look away.

"Why you not looking at me long British? You scared of a nigga or something? Look at me Yummy." She cleared her throat and looked at me. I know I'm a dick for feeling this way. But I love how nervous I made her. The fact that she did feel nervous told me her feelings were just as strong as mines were.

"I am not scared of you Terrance. You just like messing with me." We both laughed. The waiter came and we placed our orders. I got the Tuscan-grilled sirloin. British ordered the lobster ravioli. We both ordered some wine as well.

"What made you agree to meet me? You missed me like I missed you?" She smiled and looked down at her lap. Looking back up at me my heart jumped this time. British was so fucking sexy! Her eyes just wrapped me around her finger more and more every time I looked in them.

"Well your invitation kind of left me with no choice. You threatened to come for me if I didn't." I could tell my aggression turned British on to the max. It's all in her body language.

"I wasn't bullshitin' either. I will always come for yo' pretty ass if you try to block me." I loved turning her on. She did the cutest shit to me when she was in heat. One of them being when she clears her throat.

The waiter came with our food and we talked while eating. I had her cracking up telling her some of my childhood stories. British got to telling me about her background. I loved how close she was to her family. Then she told me how she met her crazy girlfriends.

I liked their bond and the fact that they did not have drama. Most female friends secretly hated on one another. Slept with each other's man or prayed on your downfall.

I loved her stories of her being a mother. Her daughter was not even a year yet. But British took pride in being a mother. It was like her daughter made her stronger. Before you knew it, we had been sitting talking for two hours.

"Can I get you guys anything else?" Our waiter came and asked. I took it as order something or get out. But if ma valued her life she better use her good customer service.

"Yes, can I have another glass of wine." British gave the waiter her glass.

"All this wine you are ordering. Don't make me take advantage of yo' fine ass," I said to her. She acted like she was clutching her pearls.

"You wouldn't dare. I'm a married woman." I laughed at her ass.

"You know that *never* stopped me before." I can tell the wine was kickin' in because she became riskier. She bit her lip and started rubbing my leg with her foot. I looked at her. We had a full-blown stare down. I don't know what the fuck this woman is doing to me but I was feelin' the shit.

"Yo' ass has had enough to drink. Come on let's bounce." I stood up and pulled her chair from under the table. I tipped the waitress a bill and paid our check. We left out the restaurant hand and hand looking like a couple.

"Excuse me, me and my co-workers think you guys make a beautiful couple." One of the workers said to us. We both smiled.

"Appreciate it ladies but I'm only her side nigga." All the workers even British mouth dropped. We turned around and walked out. British started laughing hard as hell.

"Oh my goodness Terrance! I can't believe you just said that shit to them. Did you see their faces?" She was holding her stomach cracking the fuck up.

"Fuck them. Give me yo' keys British. I'm not letting you drive home drunk" She looked at me to see if I was serious. I did not blink or smile at her ass. I was serious as hell.

"Terrance, I am ok. I have drove home a little tipsy before." This girl was dropping her keys and shit. Hell naw!

"Yum I don't give a fuck what you did before me. Today is a new day and you are NOT driving. Get yo' ass in my shit I'm taking you home." I grabbed her keys off the floor.

I put British fine ass in my passenger seat and buckled her in. I went back into the restaurant and told the hostess to give these keys to a big nigga named Mike. I told her to guard them keys with her life. If anything happens to them I would be back. She swallowed hard and agreed. I called Mike to come take British car to her house once I text him the address. I went back to my truck and British put the aux cord in her phone playing some girly ass music.

"What the hell you got playing in my truck?" I raised my eyebrow at her.

"This is Toni Braxton You're Makin' Me High. You don't know shit about this. This right here is good music." She was snapping her fingers to the music. I usually do not play about my radio in my shit. But I let her have her way.

"I already put my address in your GPS. I used to have this truck before I got my Escalade," she said and went back to listening to her music.

The drive was quiet because she was enjoying her music. Some shit she played I fucked with so I was not to annoyed. I got to her block and noticed there was no car in her drive-way or in front of the house. I turned the music down.

"I know yo' husband has a car. Y'all livin' in this nice neighborhood and you pushing a 2017 Escalade. Where is he?" She put her head down and un-plugged the aux cord from her phone.

My nostrils flared because she did not deserve this shit. Her loyalty to his ass turned me on and pissed me off. I opened my door and got out. I walked around to her door and unbuckled her seat belt. I gently pulled her out and closed the door. I leaned against the door and brought her in front of me with my arms around her waist.

"Look British. You get no judgment from me. It's easy for me to sit here and say fuck him do you. Clearly you still love him and you are loyal. I just never want you to think you the problem that nigga is being a bitch. You and your daughter are perfect and when the time is right I will step in.

Meanwhile I am on your dime. I can't shake yo' fine ass so whenever you can get away you let me know. You gotta bring baby girl with you then that's cool to. It's all on you. Just know it's only you who got my attention. Let a nigga show you how it is to have someone loyal and true to *only you.*" I looked at her in her eyes and got lost again. This time she looked back into mines without looking away.

"I can't shake you either Terrance. If we can do this without being messy then ok. No personal shit though. We can do dates but no home visits, only hotels. And no family introductions. Except Ty because I already met him. Deal?" I wrapped my arms around her tighter and kissed her.

I missed the fuck out them soft ass lips. Like I know she likes my hands roamed all over her thick ass body. Her arms were wrapped around my neck. You think I gave a fuck who saw us? I wish her husband would have pulled up and saw us. I would have beat his ass and took her and baby girl with me. Finally, she broke our kiss.

"Thank you for a good evening Terrance. I will text you tomorrow." She was still in my arms as she spoke.

"Hell naw, you textin' me tonight Yum." She bit lip and looked down. Cute ass!

"Are you going to let me go so I can go inside?" I shook my head no. I pressed my lips on hers again. We kissed long and hard again. Her tongue was so soft just like her full-lips.

"Night Yummy baby. Think of me ok." I pecked her a couple more times on the lips. She was loving that shit because she kept squeezing my arms harder.

I finally let her go and watched as she walked to her door. She turned around and smiled at me before she closed the door. I walked in my truck just as Mike pulled up with her car. He parked it in her drive-way and placed her keys in the mailbox. I texted her and told her. Mike got in my ride and we pulled off.

The ride home I thought about how I tried to leave this shit along. I told myself I could drop this shit in Jamaica and get another bitch. One who was available. It is just something about British brown skin pretty ass. I still think my first thought was right. I just need to get the pussy and I will be good. I can move on after I hit that shit. God I hope so!

Derrick

"Am I boring you daddy?" I snapped out of my daze I was in. Looking in the sexy brown honey that was making it clap in front of me. I remembered I was in Magic City with Eric wild ass. He was sitting next to me getting a lap dance.

"Nigga how can you not focus with her bad ass shakin' in front of you. Here ma, show my boy some titties." He handed her a fifty-dollar bill. She smiled and placed the money in her G-string. She slowly walked up to me while taking off her top and freeing her double-d titties. They were sexy as hell. She climbed on her lap and started grinding.

As good as it was feeling my mind still went back to my problems. Shit with British was a mess. Ever since she came back from Jamaica she was not fucking with me. I slept in the guest room every night.

The only time we would talk was if it was about Jaxon. She even slept with our bedroom door locked. Like I'm a fucking stranger in my own shit. Tonight, I decided to meet up with Eric for a beer.

Fucking with his ass always led us to a strip club. As bad as these bitches are tonight my mind would not let me enjoy myself. These hoes ran to us because we are regulars. They knew we were paid.

"Aye man I will be back." I nodded at Eric to let him know I heard him. When the stripper who was on his lap lead him towards the back. I knew he was going to get it in.

"Daddy I gots to do something to cheer you up. I usually don't give a fuck what a customer is feelin' as long as they pay. But yo' ass to fine to be lookin' all mean. Come on daddy." She took my hand and led me to the back. I knew this is the last place I needed to be.

"Hold up ma. I can't fuck with you like this. I'm married and I promised my wife I have turned a new leaf." She smirked at me but continued pulling me to the back. I know she not hard of hearing.

We walked in the back to the private room. She opened the black and red curtain and let me go in first. I walked in the black and red room. There was a red suede couch in with two poles and a touch screen TV in the wall. She came in once I set down and closed the curtain. I watched her touch the TV screen turning it on. Ma went through the music choices and picked Janet Jackson fine ass track Do you mind.

"What's your name? I'm Treasure." She stood in front of me looking sexy as hell topless with her red G-string on.

"Derrick. Look—she cut me off. "I know you are married Derrick and I heard you loud and clear. But still you seem stress and obviously the Misses is a problem. I just want to make you feel good. Like I said earlier, I don't do shit like this. Yo' ass is just to fine to not have anyone make you feel good. Let me dance for you and that's it." She held her hands up in a surrender way. I agreed. Hell, she is fine as hell and I could use this shit.

The music started and she went to the pole and started dancing. I usually don't like to see a bitch dance on the pole. To me it was a waste of time. Watching Treasure wrap her big ass cheeks around the pole and twerk was sexy as hell. She climbed at the top and swirled down the pole.

Like her body was a ribbon wrapping around the pole. She hit the splits and stood up all in one motion. Ma walked over to me with the hips moving like they had a mind of their own. She turned with her back facing me and started grinding on my lap like nobody's business. I think because she took her time seducing me made this shit so sexy.

Not like most strippers who dance and dip. Ma smelled good as hell to. She grabbed my hands and put them on her titties. Then she grabbed the other one and placed it on her pussy. All while still dancing in my lap. I know I should have stopped! But fuck it had been a minute since I felt some pussy. Hers was shaved, fat and wet as hell.

She leaned back with her head over my left shoulder. I was pinching her nipples making them hard as hell. I rubbed on her clit and inserted two fingers in her. Ma was tight as hell. In no time, my fingers were covered in her juices.

"Ssss just like that daddy." Her voice was so sexy. I looked at her pretty face on my shoulder. Her eyes were closed and she was biting her lip.

Between the shots I had, the music and her fine ass. I was feelin' the shit to the max. I kept working my fingers in and out her pussy while squeezing her titties. She was grinding her hips to my rhythm. After a few more seconds she came all on my fingers. Her shit leaked in my hand and on my leg.

"Fuck daddy! That was lit." She was breathing hard as hell. I was lightly rubbing on her clit making her jerk. I was rock hard and she must have noticed it.

"My turn," she said while getting up. I watched her slide between my legs and unbuckle my pants.

I wanted to stop her but my dick was so hard it was about to pack up and leave. She pulled my thick 9-inch out and stroked it. I leaned my head back and closed my eyes. Next thing I felt her wet tongue and mouth swallow my shit. Ma sucked my dick so good and nasty as hell. She even licked and sucked on my balls.

"Fuck ma!" I came all on her titties. The sight was beautiful to see! Her nasty ass rubbed it in and licked her index finger. I was ready to fuck!

"I don't want you to get in more trouble. Whenever you do want to be naughty call me ok." She pulled my cellphone out my pocket and keyed in her number.

Just like that she kissed me on the cheek and walked out. I felt drained as hell. Then the guilt hit me. I had to calm down because it wasn't like I fucked. I just got a little head. Shit a brother was about to explode with all that backed up nut in me. Not ready to go home I went to the bar of the club and had some more shots.

*

I felt the sun hit my face burning my skin. I cracked open my eyes and quickly shut them tight. The sun light was too sensitive for my eyes. I rolled over until the sun was out of my face. Opening my eye's, I looked at the white wall that was in front of me.

Where ever I was someone gave me a blanket and took my shoes off. I looked around some more until I saw a fireplace. Recognizing the pictures that were on it I realized I was on Eric couch.

"You finally up nigga? Here, I know you are not going to want to eat. Sheena made you her hangover drink." He set some red shit in front of me along with some aspirin. I took the aspirin and downed the drink. It wasn't too bad.

"Good looking man. I can't believe I got that drunk." I set up and realized I only had my boxer on.

"Where the fuck my pants at?" Annoyance was in my tone. Eric laughed like the shit was funny.

"Nigga you had some of yo' boys on the front of them. Sheena took your pants off and washed them. You better be happy you did not go home with that shit. British would have killed yo' ass." I laughed and quickly stopped. Oh fuck! I did not go home last night. I didn't even check in. I know British has blown my phone up.

"Aye man you seen my wallet and shit? I have to call B and let her know what's up. I know she is ready to kill my ass." Eric went to his dining room table. He handed me my keys, wallet and cellphone. I rubbed my hand over my face before I unlocked it. I blinked my eyes fast as fuck to make sure I was seeing what I saw. My wife did not call me not one time. I mean not one text, voicemail or phone call. That was not like her ever. If I do not come home she blows me up or shows her ass in the morning. Eric walked back in the living room with my pants.

"So, what's the damage? Do we need to fake a hospital stay again?" he asked me jokingly.

"Naw, her ass didn't even call me. No text or shit!" I looked up at Eric and his eyes were bugged out.

"Damn nigga. That shit is even worse. If her ass did not call then she is up to some shit. I hope for your sake when you still have a home to go home to." Eric was making me nervous as hell.
I don't know why I thought British didn't give a fuck. Her ass is probably fed up with my shit and left my ass. I hurried up and put my pants on.

"Chill bro, you might as well shower then leave. You smell like bitches and liquor. Whatever B gone do it's already done. As many time as you have talked her out of dippin' on you. Just do that shit again but this time have some jewelry." He started laughing.

"This shit is not funny E man! I can't lose my wife. Fuck! I keep fucking up. Her ass just been pushing me away with this sleeping separately shit. Now Niecy ass talking about she pregnant—he interrupted my rant.

"The fuck man! How and why the fuck did you knock Niecy up?! Tell that bitch to dead that shit!" He was hitting his fist in his hand getting hyped up like it's his life.

"E don't you think I told her that shit. That bitch is keen on having this baby. Said she don't care if I'm around or not." I shook my head at the thought.

"Well then there you go right there. What the fuck you crying for? She gave yo' ass the green light to walk. I say fuck her and that damn child. Put that shit behind you and save yo' marriage. Even though we do our thang I love B like a sister. You are not going to get another woman like her." I could not agree with Eric more.

He was right. Fuck Niecy and that mistake she carried. I needed to focus on my marriage and my ONLY child.

I showered and headed home. I stopped and picked up breakfast for me and British. I was ready to accept the consequences on whatever she had for me. As long as she did not leave me. I didn't mind being in the dog house. I stopped at IHop and picked myself up some buttermilk pancakes and bacon. British loved them strawberry cheesecake pancakes and strawberry crepes.
Pulling up into our drive-way I grabbed our food and walked to our front door. I was happy to see British truck in the drive-way. Knowing she was home made me take a deep breath. I prepared myself for the cussing out my wife had for me.

When I walked in the house it was spotless. The smell of that plug-in Hawaiian breeze smell hit my nose. British loved that smell good shit around the house. That shit annoys me because it smelled like fruity shit to me. I heard some music coming from the kitchen. I went in there and set the food on the counter. Seeing that B and Jaxon were not in the kitchen I walked out leaving the food.

I went up the stairs and heard British making Jaxon giggle. My heart warmed listening to my ladies play. When I pushed the door all the way open British was putting Jaxon dress on. My daughter looked so cute in the little yellow sun dress and black sandals.

B kept her looking so girly like herself. She was tickling Jaxon while putting a head band on her head. My daughter had a big curly fro at only 9-months. No doubt she was going to have long hair like her mama. I lightly knocked on the door. British turned around while holding Jaxon.

"Say good-morning daddy." She waved Jaxon hand for her. My baby girl laughed and spit everywhere. I stepped in the room and could not help but smile at the sight of Jaxon.

"Hey baby girl. You know I love you." She smiled big with four teeth. I loved my daughter.

I think I did not have that huge bond with her because she was a girl. Don't get me wrong I loved my baby. British just always had her with her. They went shopping together and had lunches. Jaxon was only 9-months and had already been to a kiddie spa. If I had a son then we would do father and son stuff. I think I just didn't relate to the girly stuff British and Jaxon did.
"Where are y'all about to go?" I asked British because she was dressed as well.

My wife was so fucking fine. Today she had on a long nude maxi dress. Her whole back was exposed making me annoyed. I loved how B dressed because she would wear the right clothes for her thick frame. But I also knew she was sexy as fuck even in sweats. These Atlanta niggas loved her pretty ass and it made me a little insecure.

"I am taking Jaxon with me to run errands. I smell Ihop, I'm starving. Thanks babe." She smiled big at me and kissed my lips walking downstairs.

I stood in Jaxon's room confused as hell. Where the fuck was the cussing out and throwing shit at me? She didn't even have anger in her face? That shit scared the fuck out of me. B would never ever not go crazy on me if I stayed out all night.

I walked downstairs and she was sitting on the stool next to Jaxon high chair. She put a piece of her crepes on Jaxon chair. Baby girl ate it up. British was eating and I just studied her for a minute. I knew this woman like the back of my hand. I can tell when she lies, or when she is angry.

I knew when she was up to no good and when she is hurting. This woman in front of me was emotionless. She ate her food humming and picked up her phone and scrolled her Instagram. I took my food out and went to the refrigerator and grabbed me some orange juice. Is set on the stool next to her and began eating. I still watched her out the side of my eye.

"My store on Instagram is almost at a million followers. My personal page is at 50k. That's crazy, right?" She looked at me smiling big. British looked so beautiful when she smiled. I just wanted to never make her sad again.
"That is amazing baby. Congratulations." We talked and laughed.
Jaxon was eating her crepes and I gave her some of my pancakes. Once they were done I watched B clean her up and clean our mess up. If my boy Eric was here he would tell me to relax and enjoy this new British. I just couldn't. I fell some kind

of way about her not reacting to me being one all night. Shit did she even care?

"Ok babe we are out of here. Have a good day today. I'm cooking stuffed peppers with salmon tonight," British said taking Jaxon out her chair. She kissed me and headed towards the door. Hell no!

"B hold up. What the fuck is going on? Why the fuck yo' ass ain't said anything to me about staying out last night? Do you even give a fuck? What type of game are you playing?" I was heated now. She stood in front of the door with a smiling Jaxon still in her arms.

"You stayed out late before Derrick. I figured you were with Eric or at work. Why are you so mad? It's not like you were at somebody's strip club doing something you not supposed to be doing. Stop stressing D." She smiled at me and walked out the door.

I stood there feeling like the biggest asshole. I don't know why I underestimated my wife. She knew all my hangouts and places I thought I she didn't even know about. I keep digging myself deeper and deeper in the hole. I have no idea how to get my ass out.

British

Me, Jaxon and Kori had been together the whole day. We went to Meijer's, Khols and Sephora. Jaxon never minds being out, if I had her stroller she was a well-behaved baby. I got stopped by people telling me how pretty she was. Also, how friendly and she was. Walking out of Sephora the sun was showing out today. I hurried up and put my shades on and pulled the visor down on Jaxon's stroller.

"I knew we should have went to Mac. Sephora never has the shade of blush I'm looking for," Kori complained.

"I told yo' ass. Do you need to go to another store?" She shook her head no to me. We got to my truck and Kori put Jaxon in her seat while I put her stroller in the trunk.

"Let's get my baby some ice cream. You want some ice cream Jaxx?" Kori asked Jaxon making her laugh.

"Don't be using my baby because your fat ass wants ice cream!" I teased he while putting my seat belt on.

"My ass is the only thing on my body fat punk. Tim Horton is down the street. You know they put a Cold Stone inside of it. We are getting' ice cream wasted ain't that right Jaxx?!" Kori turned around looking at Jaxon making her laugh so hard. My baby was such a blessing.

Playing Toni Braxton's Heat album, I pulled into Tim Horton's parking lot. I decided to leave Jaxon's stroller since they had high chairs in there. The heat was hitting us making sweat form instantly. Walking in to Tim Horton's the cool air hit us feeling so good.

I walked over to a clear booth and set down. Kori grabbed a high chair and opened Jaxon's diaper bag getting some disinfected wipes. She started wiping down the chair. I started laughing shaking my head.

"I swear sometimes you act like you are me and Ashley's baby daddy." She blew a kiss at me and kept wiping down the chair. I swear I have the best BFF's ever and I don't know what I would do without them. We build each other up and support each other. As Queen's, we adjust each other's crowns. I wish all women were this way towards each other.

"Fuck that, these dirty ass kids and all the germs they carry. No mam! My Jaxx is not catching shit." Kori took Jaxon out my arms and put her in the high chair.

She even went in her diaper bag and gave her a toy to keep her occupied. I laughed at Kori because you could not tell her Jaxon and Aron were not her children. Me and Ashley only carried and delivered them.

"Gone and put our order in. I got Jaxon, you already know what I want." This heffa dismissed my ass like I was her woman.

"Yes daddy, anything else?" Sarcasm was in my voice. I stood up and this goofy girl smacked my ass. I loved this crazy bitch with her annoying ass.

I walked up to the front and the three male co-workers were looking at me like they were stuck in a trance. They had to be 18 years old. I looked behind me just to see if it was something else that had them stuck on stupid like this.

"Umm hello. I would like to place an order please." They snapped out of it.

The light skin one stood in front of the register and cleared his throat. I smiled at him and he returned it. I could see how these women become cougars. All three of them were fine as hell and I could imagine the young girls went crazy over them.

"I don't mean to be rude but me and my friends think you and yo' girl are the sexiest lesbian couple. Like even y'all daughter is beautiful." He had an innocence to him. I could not help myself in being petty.

"Thank you so much babe. She a pain in my ass but that's my baby." I looked at Kori and bit my lip.

Her ass was busy playing with Jaxon. I ordered Jaxon some chocolate ice cream. I loved their cookie dough ice cream and Kori liked their cheesecake ice cream. Walking back with our ice cream I laughed because the young workers watched me like I was a porter house steak and they were starving.

"What'chu laughing at?" Kori asked digging in her ice cream. I put Jaxon jumbo bib on and let her do her thing with her ice cream. I swear those jumbo bibs were godsend.

"Girl the workers thought we were a couple. I told you yo' ass act like my baby daddy. I played along with it and said you were my boo thang." Me and Kori started cracking up. She looked back at them and they blushed. The shit was cute.

"Damn the dark skin one is fine. Bitch I might cheat on you." This bitch stuck her tongue out showing her tongue ring. I laughed and shook my head at her.

"Bitch I want a divorce," I told her. We were into eating our ice cream laughing at the mess Jaxon was making.

Two girls walked in loud as hell with some long ass braids touching their asses. They were the Alicia Key's braids from when she first came out. I can't even hate they were cute. They walked passed us towards the front of the store.

"Excuse me, both of y'all braids are cute," I said to them. They smiled big as hell and swung them to the back.

"Thanks girl!" The one with her dimples pierced responded.

"Yea thank you! Its rare women complement each other." The other brown skin one said.

"I know right. That shit is sad as hell." Kori chimed in. I nodded my head because the shit was true.

We were so busy hatin' on each other. Jaxon was done eating ice cream so I took her to the bathroom to clean her up. Because of her jumbo bib her dress was spotless. When we walked out I saw Kori on her phone.

This girl was smiling and blushing away. I was loving every minute if it because she claimed she would never get this way. I set down with Jaxon in my arms. My baby was playing with a plastic spoon having a ball.

"Ok Ronny damn I will come see you. I have to be back though because I have a grand-opening to go to. Ok baby I will talk to you later." Hanging up Kori smile was a mile wide. The shit rubbed off on me and I was smiling hard like her ass.

"Bitch you look like you slept with a hanger in yo' mouth!" We both burst out laughing.

We talked about her and Ronny and my boo was so smitten. It looked good on her. The girls with the braids were sitting down a few tables from us. We could hear a little of their conversation.

The brown skin one kept staring at Kori. I heard her friend say that is the girl from the radio. Kori was so engaged with Jaxon she didn't even know she had fans spotting her.

They got up and walked towards us.

"Excuse us again. Are you Kori for Kori's Korner on the radio" The one with the pierced dimples asked.

"Yup that would be me!" Kori had a glow on her face. She loved her job and loved her fan group even more.

"Told yo' ass that was her." She looked at the brown skin girl and said.

"I'm Alicia. This is my best friend Treasure. Can we have your advice about something." Dimples known now as Alicia asked Kori. This girl was too anxious to say yes. Other people's drama amused Kori.

"Sure, what's up," Kori said adjusting herself in the booth. I looked down and my baby fell asleep in my arms.

I laid her on my chest and waited for the story to start. My ass was nosey to!

"Ok, so Treasure is a dancer at a strip club. If paid right sometimes she will ya' know." Kori gave her a thumbs up to let her know she understood.

"Well like normal she gets a dude in the VIP section. Well not only she did hook him up for free! This silly ass girl likes him. Mind you they just met last night. Oh, and he is married! Can you please tell her how many levels is she being stupid." I looked at Kori and she looked at me. I knew this topic all too well. Only difference I was the cheaters wife and not the mistress.

"Ok, first off I will give you the wrong. You should have had his ass pay! No amount of like is worth your coins. You could have told him you liked him after the fact. It is nothing wrong if you find love in the club. The fact that he is married means he comes with some baggage. Did y'all talk enough to get his back story? Like is he getting a divorce? Separated from his wife?"

"No. We didn't talk about that. He didn't want to go to VIP because he said he told his wife he was done cheating. I don't know what it is about him I just was intrigued." She put her head down with a shameful look. Almost like her saying this story out loud. Kori picked it up to because she stuck her lip out making a sad face.

"Look, don't be ashamed for how you feel. I personally just would not waste my time. Nigga's are every fucking where. Hell, there are three fine one's behind the working counter over there." Kori pointed to the Tim Horton guys.

"Don't pick someone who comes with problems. You lucked up because usually we don't find out the baggage. Not until after we have invested out time and love. If he is married and he was at the strip club sounds like an ass to me anyways." Laughing Alicia high five Kori.

"Thank you! I told yo' ass to forget about that nigga." She looked at her friend who was still looking sad.

"Your right. We didn't even exchange numbers or anything. I need to just forget about Derrick." When she said that name me and Kori whipped our necks up like whiplash. I just know damn well she did not just say his fucking name. I pulled my phone and went to his picture.

"Is this your dream guy?" I held the phone up so she could see it.

I went to the picture of me and him. We were in bed and I took a selfie of us in the bed. We were naked but you couldn't see anything just our faces. When she looked at the picture her whole face and body language changed. Her friend looked at it as well and she shook her head.

"He is talking to you to?" Looking stunned she had even more of a shook when I held up my ring finger. Treasure looked at my 3-karat wedding ring set.

"We are way beyond fucking talking. You see this little bundle of joy?" I pointed to Jaxon.

"This is our fucking daughter. I would take Kori's advice and go find someone else baby girl. You do not want these problems." I looked her dead in her eyes.

"How the fuck are you going to threating her? Yo' husband is the one that is trifling!" Her little friend said. Kori almost jumped out her booth but I hurried up and grabbed her arm. Jaxon was still sound asleep.

"Get you and yo' fuckin minion out of here. Don't worry about my husband I got that nigga! Next time get money outta the nigga instead of a face full of nut." Treasure had tears running down her face as she stormed out the exit. Her little dog followed behind her.

"You should have let me beat her friend ass! That bitch talk too much." Kori had anger all on her face.

"Naw, my baby is with us. Any other time I would have slapped her ass." I rubbed Jaxon's back as she slept.

We got up and walked out of Tim Hortons. We were about to go to Kori's house and chill for a minute. I put on Beyoncé Dangerously in love album. I loved me some Queen Bey and all her music. But that first album is hands down the best.

We pulled into Kori's gated condo. I loved her place because it was different from her personality. It gave you a warm cozy feeling. Her decorum was beige, chocolate brown and white. It reminded me of some of the decorum's you see on Pinterest.

I laid Jaxon in the room her and Aron shared. Yes, this girl had a room split down the middle for Jaxon and Aron. One side for a boy and one side for a girl. It was filled with clothes and toys. Even a TV and DVD player in there.

As if me and Ashley split custody of our babies with her. We loved her even more for being an amazing God mommy. Me and Kori were chilled out on her couch shoes off and blankets thrown over us. We were watching Girlfriends show on her firestick.

"Bitch you seem calm as hell about what happened back at Tim Hortons. I been watching you and you really seem like it didn't faze you. I never seen you like that Brit. What's up?" She looked at me concerned.

I never told Ashley or Kori that I was back in touch with Terrance. Even though it's more to my actions when it comes to Derrick.

"Kori honestly I am just drained. Who is getting Derrick's dick off is the least of my concern. No matter what he just keeps fucking up. I do love him but I have no more fight left in me. As soon as this condo is ready me and Jaxon are out." She was slowly nodding her head. I hesitated then I spoke more.

"I umm also been talking to Terrance—"she cut me off.

"Bitch KNEW IT! I mean, what you just said I believe you meant every word.

But your mind seems to be somewhere else. Almost like you are unbothered by shit because you placed your happiness somewhere else. Sooo how long have y'all been back in touch?"

This silly girl was getting comfy waiting on my response. I laughed.

"Only a few days. I went to dinner with him and I enjoyed myself. We still have not slept together and I don't think we ever will. He told me he was on my time and he wants to keep seeing me." Kori looked at me smiling hard as fuck.

"Brit you blushed and smiled the whole time you talked about him. This is the most emotions I have seen you have. Aside when you are with Jaxon I never see you glow anymore. You know me and Ashley will be your alibi whenever you want to see Terrance. And what the fuck you mean you not givin' up no cookie! Bitch Terrance is fine, why the fuck not?" She turned her nose up at me.

"No, it will complicate shit. Right now, I am just enjoying his company and his attention. Girl when we kiss his big hands be all over me. He is so aggressive and street, shit make my pussy overflow." I bit my lip thinking about Terrance chocolate ass. Kori was rolling over laughing.

Jaxon woke up so I went to get my baby. Kori had some left-over lasagna and fruit salad. I fed Jaxon while Kori slept on the couch. After eating I set Jaxon on my lap and turned on Doc McStuffins. My baby loved that show so she was all in. My phone alerted me I had a text. I smiled when I saw it was from Terrance.

Terrance: Hey Yummy baby. I'm missin' yo pretty ass

I smiled harder and replied.
Me: Hey love. I miss you to □

I didn't have to wait long for his reply.

Terrance: I'm seeing you today (NOT a question) I'll be done handling business at 4

I couldn't help but bit my bottom lip. I love this man aggressiveness! I replied.

Me: How you on my time but telling me when I'm going to see you? What if I'm busy?

Terrance: I bet yo' ass meet me today! Just like I bet that pussy wet thinkin' about me.

Before I could reply to his nasty ass, he sent another text.

Terrance: Is it wet Yummy? Tell daddy?

I swear I had to adjust my body on this couch. I was beyond turned on when I replied to him. But I had to play it cool.

Me: Wouldn't you like to know. And who said you daddy?? Umm noo sir

I laughed quietly so I would not wake up Kori's nosey ass. He replied in minutes.

Terrance: Yea whatever woman. Meet me at the Four Seasons I got a suite for us. Send me a picture of your pretty ass face.

I smiled and did what he asked. Now I had a million selfies in my phone. But I figured he could get an original one. After I took it he replied with a picture of him. Damn Terrance is so sexy! I replied with heart emojis and he told me to have that same feeling when I see him later on.

Putting my phone down on the ottoman I kissed my baby while still smiling. Kori was still knocked out. Or so I thought! With eyes closed she spoke.

"Bitch that man got you gone as fuck. Looks good on you though. Leave Jaxon here while you go to the Four Seasons." She smiled big while her eyes still were closed. I threw her throw pillow at her making both of us laugh. Hell, if Derrick is still doing him maybe it's my turn.

Terrance "Terror"

I was leaving my restaurant to interview this new chef I needed to hire. I had him cook some of our dishes. Myself and a few of my other staff members were the tasters. He did good as hell; my entire menu was created by meals that I made. I just was in no position to be a full-time chef.

Not with my other business ventures needing my attention. The best decision was to hire two head chefs'. They could not get on my payroll until I tasted there cooking. I took time and made my entire menu up. I be damned if I my food tasted like a fuckin' microwavable dinner because the chef cooking is bad.

Once I finished up business I headed to the Four Seasons so I could meet British fine ass. I could have had her meet me at our hotel my family owned. But I took bitches there all the time. This woman was on my mind more and more every day. See the thing about this nigga here, I never get sprung!

I was with Sheena for three years and even though I did not cheat. I still was not sprung over her. When she used to throw fits, or try to whine I would just put this dick on her to get some act right. That shit worked every time. I never sat and just thought about her or any woman for that matter. I was going to marry Sheena because she told me she was pregnant.

We were not a bad couple, when shit was tight it was tight. Her pussy was good and her head game was good as fuck. I had to get her use to taking and sucking my dick. My shit was the biggest and thickest she ever had.

She used to run from this dick and choke every time she would put it in her mouth. We didn't argue much the most if we did would be because I was gone a lot. You see Sheena was spoiled and a brat. She always wanted things her way and what she wanted. Like I said before I did miss her when we broke up.

We spent three years together, I was more hurt about the baby. A nigga was looking forward to being a father. I was not like some of these men afraid if a bitch got knocked up. I figured if I stuck my dick in her raw then I am willing to accept the outcome.

I never ran from some shit that I did. I just wanted the right woman to carry my child. Which is why Sheena is the only woman I ever went in raw. That took a year for me to make that decision. Me and my brother did not play that raw shit!

We always kept magnums on us every time we walked out the house. Pussy was everywhere and because of who me and Ty were. Bitches would spread their legs to us in an alley if we told them to.

But like I was saying I never had a woman on my dome as hard as British. I knew she felt the same way because she would send random texts. They would always be asking what I'm doing or just some girly emojis. I welcomed that shit though because it means I was getting to her. I know I told British I was on her time. I did mean that shit but she would be on my mind so tuff I would text and call her.

I did not give a fuck about her husband. British never once said shit to me about calling and texting randomly. As long as she was cool with then I was cool with it. I could always tell when she smiled from hearing my voice.

I pulled in to the hotel and had valet park my truck. After threatening the young nigga who I gave my keys to I walked into the hotel. I walked to the front desk where two women were dressed in black. They smiled at me and of course had lust in their eyes.

"How you doing. I have a reservation for Terrance King." I gave her my I.D and she put some shit in her computer.

"I do see that Mr. King. I have you down for our luxury suite. You only booked us for a night? Would you like to upgrade for the weekend?" I told her no thank you. She smiled and went to get my room key.

"Here you go Mr. King you are all set." She gave me a burgundy room key with the work Luxury written in gold on it. I took the key and smiled at her.

"I have a guest coming. I told her to let y'all know my name. Have a key ready for her as well. Don't give my woman a hard time. Thanks beautiful." I smiled and winked at her.

I laughed to myself on the way to the elevator. I found it funny how these women went crazy over me and my brother. I made baby girls day I'm sure of it. Probably went to ring her panties out. Ha!

When I got to my door I put my key in and walked in. Four Seasons hands down had the best suites. They always made a nigga feel like the King I already was. I know I will have British with me for only a few hours. I still wanted to put her in some luxury shit. In my eyes, she was the Queen to my King. With other bitches, I booked simple ass hotel rooms.

The fuck I look like putting a bitch in a suite for a simple nut. Sometimes I didn't even do a hotel. I'd go to their spot, my truck or my club. If it was up to me we would be at my crib. But I know British wants to keep shit simple. I went to the living room and turned on the TV to ESPN. Watching some basketball highlights I heard a knock at the door.

Opening the door room service came in with me and British dinner. When dude brought the food in on the rolling table he set the dining room table up with our meal. I checked our food while he set up. I didn't play that under cook shit. I don't want to see any pink or somebody getting' a bullet.

The food looked good as hell and it was hot. I ordered us some steaks, asparagus, mash potatoes and shrimp. Room service put the Dom Perignon on ice with our glasses. I tipped him a Franklin and he left. I heard the door unlock. I bit my lip because I knew it was British sexy ass

She stepped all the way in and let the door close. I was in the dining room which gave me a view of the front door. She saw me and smiled big. Looking at her reminded me why I gave her the name Yummy. She had on a simple nude maxi dress all the girls wear in the summer.

When she closed the door, I saw her whole back was exposed. My blood went from my head to my dick. The nude color looked so good on her brown skin. I wanted to peel that dress up off her thick ass.

"What's poppin' Yummy baby. I missed yo sexy ass." I walked up to her and hugged her. My arms went around her waist. She followed by putting her arms around my neck. I inhaled her peach scent. The shit drove me crazy.

"I missed you more Terrance. You did not have to do all this love. I would have been cool with a basic room." She smiled looking around the room.

"You ain't no basic ass woman so no basic shit. Get that out yo' vocabulary." I grabbed her hand and sat her in the chair at the dining room table. I sat next to her and poured us some champagne.

"This food looks so good. I'm starved, and you got everything I eat." She smiled at me. British smile was so bright.

Her teeth were straight and white and her cheeks had them pretty creases when she smiled.

"I remember what you ate when we were in Jamaica. Plus. you told me steak and mash potatoes were one of your favorite meals." She opened both her eyes wide as if she was shocked.

"Well I am impressed! You actually listened to me wow." She started cutting into her steak.

"Anything about you has me all ears Yum." British looked up at me. Her face was so beautiful. I loved how she did not ever pack make-up on it. The most I ever seen her wear was lip shit and mascara. Her face was beautiful on its own. Something about when we have our staring sessions pulled me closer to her. Them eyes had me gone.

They were so honest with a bit of sadness. We finished eating and laughed like always. Our conversation was always on point. British was the easiest person to talk to. I opened up with her about shit that only GOD knew.

She never judged shit about me. I loved when she told me stories about her daughter, family or friends. It was a certain glow she had on her face. Like they gave her peace and comfort. I hope one day she can glow like that about me.

"Come lay with me and watch a movie. Yo' ass not leavin' me yet." I stood up from the table with her following me.

We went into the bed room. The suite was on the top floor. We had a huge window over-looking the city. The blinds were open and it was dark outside. I went over to close them but British stopped me.

"Leave them open Terrance. With it being dark plus the view, it looks amazing." She was right the shit looked good. I nodded and walked to the night stand picking up the remote. I turned the TV on and we picked out a movie. We decided to watch 40-year-old Virgin.

"Do you mind if I get some junk food from the mini fridge?" British asked me. I appreciate her asking but I looked at her like she was crazy.

"Yum baby anytime you are with me you don't have to ask for shit. Grab me something out there to." She walked out the room and in seconds came back.

Sitting the food on her side on the night stand she took her sandals off. I loved British feet because she always kept them up. I never smelled them and they were just pretty. I took of my shoes and clothes except my Versace boxer briefs. I pulled back the covers and got in the bed. I was sitting up in the bed with my back against the head board.

British was about to get in but I gave her a look. She blushed and playfully rolled her eyes. She came up out her dress revealing her sexy thick ass body. The type of bra she had on I had never seen. It covered the front of her titties but there was no back. The shit was sexy whatever it was. Her titties sat up even more looking good.

She had on a nude thong matching her dress. I wanted to make love to her all night with her looking the way she did. British climbed in bed and set up just like me. We started our movie after getting comfortable. She passed me a can of Sprite and some Lays chips. I watched her open her cherry Pepsi and hot Cheetos.

"What Terrance? Why are you staring at me?" She had her nose turned up. I laughed at her.

"Fix yo' ugly face woman. I was looking at you eat your hot Cheetos. You givin' me some too. Those my favorite chips." British smiled and smacked her lips.

"First off you know damn well I'm not ugly. Second shut up, I am not sharing my chips." Sticking her tongue out at me she put a chip in her mouth.

I laughed and shook my head. Opening my chips and drink we played our movie. Me and British laughed so hard at that movie. The shit was funny as hell. The part where he took this drunk bitch home and she threw up on him! I laughed so hard my sides were hurting.

We continued watching it and still eating junk food. British was drinking her Pepsi and when she was done she let out the loudest burp I ever heard. I fell out laughing and she started punching me in my arm.

"Damn woman! That was a manly ass burp," I said still laughing. She laughed and hit me in my arm again.

"Shut up, that shit was sexy. Stop laughing at me Terrance King!" She faked pouting. I still was laughing sitting like her. I pulled her into me and put her between my legs. Wrapping my arms around her I whispered in her ear.

"That shit was mad sexy Yummy baby. Forgive me for laughing at yo' manly burpin' ass." She started laughing and so did I.

I loved our chill time because we had fun. British never acted like she had to be perfect with me. I loved how ditsy she was and how she would eat a burger and have a beer. It was like we were friends who just happen to like each other.

Still between my legs and in my arms, I tilted her chin back. I brought my lips to hers and we kissed for the first time today. Our tongues played tag with each other and my hands went all over her body. She loved that shit because her moans while we kissed told me.

"Next time I see you yo' ass better hug and kiss me. Don't make me wait that long to feel them lips." She looked at me biting her lip and nodded her head. When our movie went off she wanted to watch another comedy. It was a little after 10 and the night was still early for me.

"You staying the night with me Yum?" I saw her on her phone texting. I tried not to get annoyed because I knew she was married.

"Yup. I was just texting my girl to make sure my baby could stay the night." She placed her phone back on the night stand. I looked at her for a moment. Knowing her smart ass mouth I chuckled and explained myself.

"Before yo' ass ask why I am staring at you I just like what I see. When we were in Jamaica and we ran into each other on the beach running. I remember seeing tears fall from your eyes. I saw sadness and pain in your face. Knowing what that looks like on you and seeing you now makes me feel good. You look happy and I know I have something to do with it." I sat back down on the bed next to her.

She looked at me then climbed on my lap. Straddling me she kissed the fuck out of me. Pulling and sucking on my lips. Had me feeling like a bitch the way she switched it up on ya' manz. I never seen her this aggressive. She pulled away and looked at me. Her eyes filled with tears.

"It is because of you. I had an annoying day and besides my girls and my baby. You have made this day a good one for me." She gave me a half smile. I wiped her face and gipped her waist tight.

"What happen today baby." I rubbed the side of her face gently. She had her hair down so I ran my fingers through it. She got to telling me the story that happened to her at Tim Hortons. Although she did not shed a tear telling me the story I still wanted to beat her husband ass. How the fuck do you keep fucking over something so beautiful. No fucking way if British was mines would I ever hurt her. Especially over and over again! The shit had me on fire.

"That shit is tuff as fuck to go through. I wanna tell you some shit. I don't want you to get afraid when I say it. But I wouldn't be me if I didn't keep shit hunnid." British nodded her head. We continued looking at each other as I began to speak.

"Don't ever hesitate to call me if you need me. I don't care the day, time or season. You and baby girl never have to feel stuck in shit. I know you independent and got yo' own bread. I admire that about you. But if shit ever gets out of hand or you need an ear. I'm right here. Always baby. If you feel scared or whatever, I'm right here. British I need you to understand if it ever came to it. Your husband will disappear if you ever do have to call me on some serious shit. I hear all the time of these men hurting these women. The woman wants out and dude has it in his mind he wants to hurt her. Shit is crazy and I be damned if that happens to you or baby girl. I will personally chop yo' husband up in pieces and put him in my fireplace. You scared of me now?" I asked hoping she did not fear a nigga. She shook her head no.

"I'm not scared. I understand where you're coming from Terrance. Thank you." She hugged me and it was genuine.

I hugged her pretty as back. I kissed her hard as hell. My dick was so hard it felt like it was ripping my boxers. I wanted to fuck the shit out of British right then and there. I knew that would be too much for her. I only wanted to make her happy. Not confuse things for her. If she gets some of this dick, her head will be all fucked up.

I laid back with her on top of me. Without me telling her she took off her little bra and tossed it on the floor. British knew I loved her skin on mines. I had a hard grip on her soft ass. I moved my hands to her back, her thighs. Then to her hair and back to her ass.

Since I couldn't fuck her I wanted to eat that Yummy pussy she had. I ripped her thong off in one tear. My lips never leaving hers. She let out the sexiest moan against my lips. I'm starting to believe my street ways turned British on.

"Sit yo' sexy ass on my face. I want that pussy all in my face soaking up my beard." British did exactly as I said.

Her pussy looked so good coming down on my mouth. British thought I was playing. My mouth watered thinking of tasting her sweet juices. My mouth felt like it was made to be on her pussy.

I was tonguing her clit down. Going back and forth from swirling my tongue to sucking on her clit. British was going crazy. I had my hands griping her waist tight as fuck so she couldn't move.

"Oh my fucking God Terrance! Sssss shiiit" She moaned over and over sounding sexy as hell.

Shit drove me crazy knowing I was pleasing her so good. British makes the third woman I have put my mouth on. Hands down the taste of her pussy knocks the other bitches out the park. I gave her clit a rest and put my tongue deep in her hole. My tongue was long enough to get in that tight muthafucka. I made circles in her gushy walls. While fucking her whole with my tongue. I took my thumb and rubbed on her clit. Her ass lost it.
"I'm cumin' baby. Ughhhhhhhh!" Just like I wanted, my beard was soaked.

I pulled my tongue out of her walls. I went right back and attacked that clit. Her body was jerking making my insides smile. I knew her clit would be sensitive so I slowly licked it back to life.

Not being able to take it British fell back. I set both my legs up with my feet flat on the bed catching her.

That pussy was still on my mouth. I showed no mercy to her ass. All the shit she talked while we texted came back to mind. When I was done with British pussy her body was sweating. Baby came a total of four times. She tried to tap out but I was not having that shit. I made her stay on my face the entire time.

"Oh my goodness!" Having cum for the fourth time I finally let her fall back. She was breathing hard. Her brown pretty skin looked good sweaty. Laying on top of me with her pussy still in my face. I kissed it and sat up making her straddle me. I put my hand around her neck not squeezing hard.

"Whose daddy British?" I looked at her with a serious face.

"You are." She shyly said blushing and looking down. I bit my lip with my hand still around her neck. I brought her lips to mines. Kissing her sloppy and hard at the same time.

"Come on wit yo' Yummy ass. Let's take a shower." I kept her straddling me and carried her to the bathroom. I can tell right now I am going to have to turn into Terror about this woman. How tha fuck this happen!

A month later

I pulled out of La Parrilla Mexican restaurant. I had just had lunch with British sexy ass. It was almost two months since I met her and the shit been lit. I still did not break her off any dick. The shit was getting harder for me every day. And a nigga was not getting no pussy on the side.

I meant what I said when me and British talked at her house. I wanted to show her how it was to be a nigga's only one. I been fucking since I was 10 years old and could fuck until I am 100 years old. A month was not hurting me especially fucking with British. Bets believe I ate that pussy though every time I saw her. Unless she was bleeding. I would just hold her then and give her that cookie dough ice cream she loved.

I knew her husband was still fucking up or something. British saw me every fucking day and sometimes would stay the night. I told her if she ever needed she could bring the baby. She declined my invite which I understand. The way she was with her baby girl made me crave her even more.

We did what she asked, we went on dates and chilled at the Four Seasons. The staff there started knowing me and British by name. We did everything from bowling, golf, the movies, dinner and even laser tag. I was now on the freeway on my way to meet my brother. We needed to talk about our club we had opening in two-months.

Both of us have been so busy with our illegal shit we have not focused on The Kingdom. We had a huge deal with the Russians and Italians coming to a close after our grand-opening. We were able to move the drugs without any problem with the pigs. That was another easy million a-piece for me, Ty and Ronny. PnB Rock song Selfish came from my phone. I bit my lip because I knew it was British fly ass.

"What's up Yummy baby. You miss daddy already?" I knew her ass was blushing and biting that sexy lip.

"Not more then you miss me." I laughed because I loved her smart-ass mouth.

"You might be right about that." Before I could say more my other line beeped in.

"Hold on Yum this Ty crazy ass." I clicked over to my brother.

"Bro what's—he interrupted.

"T bro one of our spots been hit. Three of our guys were shot. I know Del and his two brothers were in the house. So far that's all I know. They took the dope and money that was in there." I was already re-routing myself to get to our spot in Bankhead.

"It's hot here bro so let's meet at Grady hospital," Ty told me. I could hear the wind on the end of his phone.

I knew he was already hittin' the traffic. I was once again switching lanes headed to the hospital. The young nigga's we had in Bankhead were good kids. They just hustled trying to feed their families like all of us were. All three of them just graduated high school. I was covering their tuition for junior college.

When I arrived at the hospital I saw Ty's white Yukon truck in the parking lot. I walked through the doors and I spotted Ty on his phone.

"What the fuck happened?" I was so heated! Who the fuck committed suicide by robbing us.

"Del, Troy and Drew were all in the trap. Them niggas blessed as hell that they did not meet our creator today. Whoever did this shit left them alive on purpose. Del was shot in his leg. Drew and Troy were shot in their fucking arm. They said the niggas were wearing all black with masks and leather gloves. Drew said he was looking for anything. He said them niggas even had their shoes disguise.

They ran out the back of our building on foot. Must have had a get-away waiting on them or some shit." Ty was shaking his head. My ass was in deep thought as soon as he said our crew was hit. Who the fuck robs a trap house and shoot niggas the way they shot Del and his brothers?

"Aye you think Sleez did this shit?" I looked at Ty and his face said it all.

"I don't put shit past nobody. But this is sloppy. Sleez knows how to shoot and aim is on point. I think this is some little amateur niggas. The niggas dropped a stack of money running out. I'm not scratching Sleez either though." I nodded my head.

Whoever the fuck did this shit was going to die. No questions asked, rather its Sleez or some amateur niggas. They were done for. After we went to visit Del and his brothers. I told the doctor I had their medical bills covered. I also talked to the brother's family. I let them know I was having one of my men drop a duffle bag off for them tonight.

Me and Ty walked out the hospital. Even though I was glad Del and his brothers were ok. I still was pissed. The change and small dope they took was not shit. The money was only 15 g's and the dope was only a few bags. The principal was somebody stole King merchandise.

"This shit is stupid as hell yo'. Maybe the niggas that did this has beef with Del and his brothers." Ty looked at me and said.

"That shit is a good ass motive. They purposely left them alive maybe thinking we would kill them." In the middle of me talking my phone started ringing.

My mind went to British. I forgot I had my bae on hold. It wasn't her ringtone so I knew it was not her. I saw it was one of the cops we had on payroll.

"Yo' Johnson what's the word?" I thought he had some news about the robbery for me. He had some shit much worst. As he talked my face felt like hot lava. I balled my fist up so tight my knuckles were about to pop out my skin. My brother was looking at me crazy.

"You good T?" I hung up with my face balled up.

"Our fucking warehouse was raided! They arrested ten of our crew member. The shit gets worst bro. The warehouse was fucking empty! They arrested our guys though because they had guns on them. Johnson said he can get the charges dropped. We gotta go pay the bail and pick them up."

"What the fuck is really going on bro?!" Ty was just as pissed as I was. The shit that was stolen out the warehouse was part of the Russians and Italians shipment.

We arrived at the police department and paid the bail to get our boys out. The money it cost to get them out wasn't shit to a boss. When we left, me and Ty talked to our crew. The shit they told us pissed me off. Some niggas in the same attire as the ones who robbed out spot did this shit as well. They didn't shoot anybody this go around.

These muthafuckas put our boys in one of the rooms in the warehouse. After they took our shit they left leaving our crew in the room. The police came rushing through later raiding the warehouse. In a way getting our shit stolen was good thing. The warehouse was empty but our crew was strapped and some had weed on them. Being a King and having this state in yo' pocket this shit disappeared like nothing happened.

"Nigga this shit is fucked up. The Russians and Italians are going to be expecting their shit in two months. How the fuck are we going to tell them half they shit been stolen? Good thing the other shipment came to Jamaica with Ronny," Ty said to me as we stood outside the warehouse. After we chopped it up with our crew they dipped out.

"We getting our shit back from whoever took it. We got two-months to handle this shit. I'm going to hit Ronny up and let him know what's up. Meanwhile yo' ass do what you do best. Put yo' ear on the street with Mike and his boys. I don't care who y'all have to kill to get information. Whoever you even *think* has something to do with this. Kill them! I don't give a fuck how they beg and plead. If they ever looked at us wrong in the past. Spoke bad on our name, kill they ass. After I handle shit at our hotel I will meet up with you. I need to get some blood on my hands to take out my frustration." Ty nodded his head.

We dabbed each other up and went our separate ways. On the way to my crib my phone rung. The number was private. I turned my nose up because I don't answer private calls.

"Who the fuck is this?" I roared in the phone.

"Shut the fuck up barking nigga! Did you and yo' punk ass brother really think y'all could cut me out?!" I turned my nose up because I knew this was this bitch nigga Sleez. I had a feeling his ass was behind this shit. Nigga was sloppy because he was back on that dope. I bet money he was.

"You a fucking dead nigga. I hope you know that shit! Get that shit all through yo' dome bitch! I am going to fuckin' kill you. I spared yo' bitch ass for your grandma and auntie. Now, I am killin' yo' ass slowly." I was heated as I spoke through gritted teeth. Sleez started laughing.

"You the one that's dead. You and Ty! Once them Russians and Italians don't get their shit. They killin all of ya'll. You ain't gone find me hoe ass nigga so don't try. Just know I ain't stoppin." He hung up in my face.

I sucked on my teeth and balled my phone up in my hand. I squeezed so tight the screen shattered in my hand. Shit turned up so many notches. I was going to get Sleez ass in the worst way. Starting with everyone who is associated with this nigga.

Sleez

I hung up the phone still felling the same way I did a few weeks ago. These niggas were my brothers. They been there for me during the toughest times of my life. That's why when they decided to cut me off I was hurt. I know I have been off my game lately but I lost my whole fucking family. Tameka was my fucking world for so long.

When she told me she was pregnant I felt so lucky. I knew when I first met her she was going to be my wife and give me kids. I was with Ty when I got the call. My world came crashing down when I found out her and my son died. Besides my grandma and auntie, I had no real family. When I met Terror and Ty a few years before Tameka I felt like I had brothers.

I fell off for a while and started using. But hell, I couldn't cope with losing my family. I knew them King brothers would have killed me if they knew I was using. There was a rule about using and being in the crew. Terror felt he couldn't trust a fiend. I knew then they were my real brothers when they spared me and put me in rehab.

Everybody was relieved for me when I got cleaned except that bitch nigga Ronny. Ya' see from the beginning we just did not get along. He judged me as soon as he met me. Terror had us chop it up and see what the problem was. Do you know this bitch nigga told me my name made him know I wasn't shit! From then on, we just tried to stay clear from each other. I tried plenty of times to set that nigga up. His ass was untouchable with the Kings and Jamaicans having his back.

After a while I fell back until a few months ago. One of Ronny's crew member caught up to me. He asked if I liked Ronny or if I had it my way would I kill him. At first, I thought the shit was a set up. Then dude told me a few of Ronny's Jamaican rude boys wanted him handled. Me and him chopped it up for a while.

I met him and the other guys who were secretly plotting against him as well. I didn't even want him dead to take over Jamaican turf. I just wanted him dead because Terror and Ty liked him more. They treated him like he was a King. He knew all their moves and contacts. I know they met him when they were kids but I was just as loyal. I was kept out the loop on a lot of shit! Even Mike Kung-Fu ass was treated like family.

Terror thinks I just started using again. Truth is, I never stopped I just hid it well. I was doing more the cocaine this go around. I was on pills and meth sometimes. I didn't want to be this way and fuck up my life. But this shit with Tameka and my unborn is fucking with me. I tried hard as hell to keep clean and just get money.

I knew my grandma and auntie would want me to stay right. Hell, nobody knew how the fuck I felt! I lost every fuckin' thing and people just went back to their normal lives. Terror and Ty tried to get me to get back out there and get some pussy. Yea I fucked a couple of bitches to get a nut. But my heart wanted Tameka and my unborn.

I was at my lowest I had ever been. That shit I talked about cutting Ronny out the deal in Jamaica. That shit was just me being high and yappin' at the mouth. For Terror to jump out his whip and start throwin' punches was unnecessary! Then we get back to the states and they stopped fuckin' with me. I figured I would let shit cool off. I fell back and chilled at my crib. Getting' high and fucking hoes was all I did.

Once I felt it was time I decided to meet up with my so-called brothers at Ty's house. I apologized for the shit in Jamaica. These stupid ass niggas looked at me like I was a fuckin' stranger. I felt the heat as soon as I walked in Ty's house. These bitches acted like they were about to kill me. Not only did they cut me off but our brotherhood was salvaged also! I felt like David Ruffin when he got kicked out of the Temptations. I have put my life on the line for them!

Every fuckin' drop I made. Every time I had to go through customs with dope in my bag! All the bodies I have dropped for them! They think they can just cut me the fuck off!? But keep that Jamaican burnt jerk chicken eatin' ass nigga Ronny on the team! Hell naw, I don't want to take over any fuckin' thing. I just want all of them to suffer! Ronny is the only one who I am going to kill. That nigga is as good as dead! Terror and Ty got a lot of suffering ahead of them! Dumb muthafuckas!

<u>Derrick</u>

I lit the candles on our dining room table. After I did that I poured some champagne in the glasses. Looking over the feast I prepared I had to pat myself on the shoulder. The food looked good and my presentation was romantic. I wanted to go all out for my wife tonight. I brought out the Lenox Westmore china set. Her parents brought us the set as a wedding present. I had a beautiful gold table cloth and expensive champagne.

I had her favorite singer Toni Braxton playing low in the background. I cooked a nice ass meal for her too. Ok so I'm lying, I didn't cook shit. But British didn't have to know that. I faked cooked a lot of meals for her and she never could tell the difference. I had a takeout order from The Capital Grille. My ass did not know my way around the kitchen beside cereal. I had lamb chops with raspberry mint jelly. Baby red skin potatoes with seasoned carrots. I had her favorite salad as well. Arugula with tomatoes and dried cranberries. I knew my boo would love this shit.

I had her pops keep Jaxon for us over night. British mom was visiting her mother for the weekend. I heard British pull into our drive-way. I checked the food and turned the dimmer down on the lights. I looked myself over and made sure I was tight. British loved me in sweats so I had some black sweat pants on with a black beater and my Nike slide-ins. I heard her key in the door and I grabbed the bouquet of roses I got her. When she walked in I just looked at her. British was so fine down to her pretty ass feet.

"Hey boo. How was your day?" I hugged her and placed the roses in her arms. She looked at them then at me smiling.

"Hey yourself. My day was pretty good. These are beautiful boo, thank you. You look good D." She kissed me on the lips and took off her shoes. Something was different about the way British kissed me lately. She used to never just give me one kiss. It was multiple kisses like she couldn't believe it was me. I pushed it out my mind for now.

"Thank you sexy. Come see what I did for you boo." I grabbed her hand and led her to the dining room. I saw her smile big as hell at the sight in front of her.

"Wow D! This is so sweet boo. What's the occasion?" I smirked at her and said.

"Nothing. Just wanted to do something nice for you." I pulled her chair out and she set down. Before I set I poured us both some wine. Sitting across from her I watched as she took a sip of her wine.

"When did you do all of this? Did you go to work today?" I smiled at her and nodded my head yes.

"Yup I went to work. I did a half day and came home to cook for you. Don't worry about the kitchen because I already cleaned it up." Surprised look on her face she smiled at me. I fixed both of us a plate.

We said grace and dug in. As usual we ate in silence. British looked different to me, almost like a glow. I knew she wasn't pregnant because we have not been having sex. Maybe she is just looking extra good to me tonight. We both cleaned out plates and I put the rest in the refrigerator. British went upstairs to take a shower and put her pajamas on.

While I straightened up I heard her come back down. I was just finishing putting the china back in the cabinet. British walked in the kitchen and I almost nutted in my pants. She had on these silk pajama shorts and matching top. British ass was so big it hanged out the shorts making my dick hard as fuck.

"You wanna go in the living room and watch a movie?" she asked me shocked the hell out of me. British has not asked anything of me since we went to dinner before Jamaica.

"Sure boo. You can pick." I smiled at her while wiping the counter off.

Once I was done I turned the kitchen light off. I went to join British on our sectional. She was sitting up on the lay-out part. I sat next to her and put my arm around her waist. This was the closest I had been to my wife in so long. She smelled so good and felt even better. I smelled her hair and it smelled like that fruity shit she uses. I never could figure out what made my wife smell so sweet. I watched as she went through movies on Comcast OnDemand.

"Let's watch How High! I feel like laughing," she said with excitement. I turned my nose up.

"Hell no. I don't want to watch a bunch of bums' smoke." I knew she was annoyed but I didn't care.

"What about Knocked up?" I smacked my lips at that choice.
"B how old are we?" She rolled her eyes and gave me the remote. I went through the movies and picked Hotel Rwanda.

"See, this is a grown ass movie." I put the remote on the table and got comfortable.

British got up and I knew she was going to get some junk food. I never understood people who couldn't just watch a movie. All that eating is a distraction from the movie. Then I bet you she is going to come in back with them damn hot Cheetos.

Walking back, I laughed to myself because she had a bottle of water. Those damn chips and a Reese cup.

"Why do you need all that to watch a movie? Now you about to be loud with the bag and smacking." British ignored me and opened her chips. I started the movie and we were into it. British of course was loud with her food annoying me. I didn't want to ruin the mood so I ignored it.

I got thirsty and went to get me something to drink. I opened the fridge and grabbed me a bottle of water. I heard British phone go off while I was in the kitchen. I looked at the time on the stove and it was past 10.

I figured it was one of her girl's or her dad. I knew I was wrong when I came back and British was blushing. I know my wife, no matter what. I know my wife! No matter how many times I fuck up. She would never cheat on me. Her heart and conscience would feel like shit if she cheated. It just was not in her.

"Who is that?" I asked standing in front of her. I watched her closely to see if she would get nervous.

"Just Kori telling me about her and her new boo. She is so crazy and a pervert." She smiled and shook her head. British set her phone down on the end table next to her. I continued looking at her. I knew firsthand what a liar and cheat looks like. I couldn't tell if she was lying. Which annoyed me even more.

"What the fuck is going on B? Don't fuckin' lie to me either. Everything about you is different." I stood in place waiting for her to talk.

"Derrick what are you talking about? Nothing—

"BULLSHIT!" I did not mean to yell but she is trying to play me.

"I know you. Better than anyone! You are different and I know it! So, what the fuck is up. If you open your mouth and speak and it's not the truth then just shut the fuck up." She stood up and folded her arms.

"The truth is I thought we could have had a good evening. Never mind the fact that you didn't cook none of the food you said you did. Then again why am I surprised! Every meal you claimed you cooked has been from a restaurant. I gotta hand it to you D, you pick some expensive ass restaurants. Then you always give me roses and tell me there my favorite. My fucking favorite flowers are tulips! My wedding bouquet was tulips! I buy them for the house all the time. You really don't fucking know me. I thought we would always learn about each other when we got married. I looked forward to that. You stopped wanting to know me when you started cheating." I had no words to say.

I stood there looking at her talk. She had no emotion, no tears. Not once have we ever argued and she not cry. It always showed she cared and was hurt. The woman stood before me had an expression on her face that I did not recognize. British called me on my shit and my lies. I always thought she was clueless about shit. Getting angry I was not about to stray away from the subject at hand.

"Fuck all that. What is going on with you? Something is up British and you need to just put the shit on the table. Woman the fuck up!" I was shocked when she started laughing.

"Nigga I will be a woman when I see a man in front of me. Where were you the other night Derrick? I know for sure you were not working or at Eric's house. You should change your spots up. I knew the strip club you were at. I tracked your car to the spot!" She walked closer to me with so much anger and hate in her eyes.

"What? Nothing to say? Well I have fuckin' plenty to say. You see I took our daughter shopping and out for ice cream. I was approached by a bitch named Treasure. Ring a bell? Well, she shocked me when she needed advice from Kori about some nigga whose dick she sucked and liked. You see she knew he was married! He even told her he was trying to do right by his wife this time. Yet, she still managed to get his dick in her mouth! So, you see Derrick. You don't ask me about shit unless yo' ass is clean." She walked away and stopped turning around and looking at me.

"I'm tired of this game. Me and Jaxon are moving out. As soon as the condo I purchased is ready we are leaving." My fucking heart fell to the ground. I rushed British and grabbed her arm.

"What the fuck you mean you and Jaxon are moving out?! No the fuck y'all not! British you are not leaving me and taking our daughter. Look, I don't know what the fuck happened but I don't know a Treasure---

"DERRICK SHUT THE FUCK UP LYING! That's all you do is lie! You lie to get out of trouble, you lie to impress people. Hell, you even lie to cover up the lies you already told! Just stop D, ok. Just stop." She snatched her arm away from me and walked up-stairs.

I stood there feeling like a damn fool. Anger and hurt ran through my body like the blood in my veins. I wanted to kill that bitch Treasure and every bitch that fucked my shit up. I took that shit out my mind. I had to figure out how can I get British not to leave me. I usually knew what to do to get her to forgive me. But this new woman up-stairs, I had no clue who she was. I know I need to do something fast or lose my wife forever.

*

Here my stupid ass was a few nights later at the strip club. I was no closer to getting British back on my team then I was a few nights ago. When I tell y'all she was distance as hell I mean that shit. I only saw her leaving or coming in from work. She would take care of our daughter day and night. She moved Jaxon in our master bedroom and kept it closed and locked. I didn't know where to begin with British. I knew she wanted the truth but I couldn't bring myself to say it. I promised her I changed and just kept fucking up.

"So, nigga what are you going to do? I told yo' ass about letting British have her own account. I don't play that shit with Sheena's ass. No bitch is going to have an opportunity to plot on me." Eric took his shot the bartender set in front of us.

"Man, I trust British. You know she got her store and Jaxon's account handled. I never thought about her plotting. Hell, she didn't have to plot. What B makes in a day at the store is enough to get a condo." I took my shot and asked for another one.

"Here comes you little stripper admirer right now. I'm going to get my dick sucked while you handle yo' business." I looked up and saw Treasure coming towards me. I dabbed Eric up and went back to taking my shots.

"What's up Mr. Faithful. What you doing back in here?" She sat down on the stool next to me. I didn't even make eye contact.

"Shit, I needed a drink and wanted to see some ass." She took one of my shots and downed it. I had three more so I didn't give a fuck.

"You didn't have to come here to get drinks and see some ass." I looked at her then. I couldn't deny Treasure's beauty. She had a good girl/bad girl look with some sexy chocolate skin. I knew playing with her would be trouble and I already had one crazy stripper on my hands.

"Look Treasure. You are sexy as hell boo and that head game is fire. But I really just came here for a drink. Nothing more than a drink, I can't get down like that again." She half smiled at me. Moving her long braids behind her thick body she stood up.

"Ok Derrick. I understand. Have a good night." She kissed me on the cheek and walked away.

I blew out hot air and turned to finish my drinks. I looked down and noticed a piece of paper next to me. it had Treasure's name and number on it. I looked at it and shook my head. For some reason, I didn't throw it out. I saved the number in my phone and went back to drinking. I had no intentions on using the number. I just felt it was no harm in having it.

British

"I'm proud of you boo. Ripping Derrick a new asshole the way you did was perfect! I wish I could have been a fly on the wall for that shit." Kori laughed and high fived me. Ashley chimed in laughing as well. We were in the nail shop getting the works done. Eyebrows, nails and feet.

"Girl the shit was crazy. I planned on having a mellow night but he kept comin' at me backwards. It felt good to get the shit off my chest though. The scary part is I'm not worried about him finding out about Terrance. I'm more concerned on moving on. Derrick and I relationship is destroyed beyond repairs." I kissed the top of Jaxon's head.

My baby was sitting on my lap while my feet soaked. Like always she was being a good girl. She even behaved while she got her feet polished.

"I feel you Brit. As long as you and Jaxon are happy then so are we." Ashley said pointing to her and Kori.

"Ok so after we leave here let's get something to wear and go out tonight. Nothing ratchet, just like a lounge or some shit. Y'all know I got the 411 on the hot spots. Let's get drinks and have a girl's night." Kori was so hyped she kept moving while the lady scrubbed her feet.

"I'm cool with it," I said and so did Ashley.
Leaving the nail shop we decided to go get something cute for tonight. Anytime we did a girl's night we made sure to have a new outfit on. It was kind of our thing! I needed this night

bad as hell. I just wanted to have a good time and get some drinks in my system.

A little after 7pm I dropped Jaxon off with my parents. I wanted to leave her with Derrick but he was not home. I called him and he didn't answer. Not giving a fuck, my parents told me they wanted her. My mama had not seen Jaxon since she came home. You would think my mama was gone for a year instead of a weekend. Her and Jaxon were inseparable I think it was because my baby looked so much like me. Me and my mother are very close. I'm truly blessed.

I came home to get dressed and noticed Derrick car was in the drive-way. I rolled my eyes at the thought of seeing him. I have not told him I got a call from the condos. I was scheduled to pick up my key tomorrow morning. I wanted to be moved in by next week. I walked into the house and took my shoes off. He had Dru Hill-In my bed song playing on the Alexa speaker. I laughed and shook my head. Derrick is such a fucking drama queen the shit is ridiculous.

With my shopping bags in my hand I went to the kitchen to get a snack. Derrick was sitting on the stool eating some cereal and in his phone. When I came in he gave me a look and put his phone face down next to him. I went put my bags down and went to grab me some yogurt and fruit. Derrick got up and turned the music down.

I don't know if he thought I was about to join him but he was sadly mistaken. He walked back in the kitchen and I couldn't help but notice how good he looked. Being good looking and sexy was never a problem for Derrick. I just wish his outsides matched his insides. Putting some strawberries in a bowl I grabbed me a spoon and was headed up-stairs. Before I walked out he stood up and tried to help me with my bags.

"You're having a girl's night out?" He asked giving me my bags.

"Yeah. Much needed." I put my yogurt and spoon inside one of my bags so I could have a free hand.

"Boo please don't fucking leave me. I won't make it without you and I am being for real. I was thinking we could go on a vacation. Just me and you British. Let's go to Hawaii or Puerto Rico for a whole week. We can clear our heads and get shit straight. Just drop all our problems at Atlanta airport." He grabbed my hand and smiled at me. I smiled back.

"Drop all our problems at the airport huh? And pick them bitches back up when we touch back down. Naw, I'll pass." I slid my hand out of his and walked up-stairs.

I tried not to cry but the tears fell without hesitation. I heard him turn his music back up. This time he played Dru Hill- We're Not Making Love No More. I turned my nose up and stripped out of my clothes to take a shower. I stepped in and let the hot water hit my body. The water felt therapeutic hitting me all over. I grabbed my favorite Pretty as a Peach body wash from Bath and Body Works.

Lathering my mesh loofah, I washed my entire body. After rinsing off I stepped out and began to dry off. I walked to my bedroom in my birthday suit. Grabbing my Pretty as a peach lotion I put some of it all over my body. I straighten my hair and wore some up in a ponytail and the rest down. My outfit required little jewelry.

I put on my white hoop earrings and white go charm bracelet. Me, Ashley and Kori all have matching best friends charm bracelets. I popped the tags off my clothes and got dressed. I was feelin' myself to the maximum tonight! I had on some light wash jeggings that had big rips on the side.
They fitted my thick frame like a missing puzzle piece. I picked out a black sequin bodysuit that was low cut in the front. I grabbed my black ankle strap Givenchy heels and turned my bedroom light off.

I walked down-stairs and saw Derrick laying on the couch. He had his basketball shorts on and a t-shirt. I slipped on my heels and looked myself over in the mirror again. Satisfied I opened the door to leave.

Walking to my truck my phone alerted me I had a text. I thought it was from Ashley or Kori. It was from Derrick. He was telling me to have a good night and he loves me no matter what. I placed my phone back in my purse and got in my truck. I just needed to get to my girls and some shots.

*

I pulled up at the spot Kori told us about. I felt a sense of relief because I didn't see police cars everywhere. Usually Kori ass had us at a spot that was so hood you need a gun just to get out your car. This place seemed hood but the kind where you can get a little ratchet and still have some dignity. Ha!

I found Kori and Ashley's car parked so I parked next to them. Walking in I noticed there were some fine men. Wouldn't mind sampling a few for myself. Tee Grizzely- No Effort song was blasting and everybody was rappin' along to the lyrics. The place was really nice with black and grey all over. There were booths and bar stools everywhere. I loved there was not D.J. Just a huge jukebox where you put dollars in and pick your songs. I saw hookahs on the tables and that excited me.

"BRITISH!" I looked around for Kori and Ashley loud asses. Only them too will call my name that damn loud! I spotted them in a booth with three hookahs on the table.

"Y'all loud asses! Hey bitches! This is a nice spot Kori." I greeted them with hugs as I slid in the booth.
"Yea I know right. One of my callers told me about this place. We got your favorite hookah already waitin' for yo' ass boo. After we do these then we are on to some shots!" Kori yelled over the music.

If weed was not in my hookah then I wanted ice, milk and mint in my hookah. Makes it smooth. Before you drop your mouth at the fact that I smoke weed. Relax, I don't smoke all the time. Probably about three times in a year you will catch me blazing. And never around my baby girl. No weed tonight though!

"Do you see all these fine ass men in here though bitch! I saw a few of them fuckin' you with some stares." Ashley joked to me. I shook my head while I was smoking my hookah.

"How the fuck you lookin' at niggas when Ty has you locked down." I started laughing. Ashley guarded herself from feeling Ty. Me and Kori told her over and over he was the real deal. She is so damn stubborn. I did notice that she has been with him almost every day since Jamaica.

"Whatever hoe! Ty is cool but we are not together. He does him and I can do me." Ashley shrugged her shoulders. She started smoking her hookah. Me and Kori smirked at each other. Anytime Ashley shrugged her shoulders she was lying.

"British don't need no eye candy anyways. Terrance ass is enough to fill her sweet tooth." Kori slick ass threw that comment in. I stopped smoking and looked at her. Ashley was cracking up. I couldn't help but smile at the mention of his name.

"Look at this bitch blushing and shit!" Ashley pointed at me. Her and Kori ass fell out laughing at me. I could not help but laugh as well.

"Fuck y'all hoes! Terrance and I are just friends who like to hang out," I said while taking a puff of my hookah.
"And fuck." Ashley acted like she was coughing when she said that. Kori started giggling.

"Umm we have not done that." I looked up at them when I notice they were quiet as church mouse's.

"Wait a minute Brit. You have not given him some pussy yet?! Damn British I think Terrance may be in love with you," Kori said and Ashley nodded her head.

"Whoa. Let me stop y'all right there. Me and Terrance have already agreed not to let things get complicated. He hasn't even met Jaxon. We are just hangin' and keeping each other company. No feelings involved on either of our end." They both just stared at me like I was a damn science project.

"Bitch why you scratch the back of your neck and flip yo' hair? Yo' ass lying but we will leave you alone for now," Ashley said with a smirk on her face. Kori had the same stupid smirk.

I waved my hand at them. We smoked our hookahs while sitting in the booth laughing and talking. You know how black people are. We will have a good time laughing and talking about people.

"Come on let's dance!" Kori said sliding out the booth. Me and Ashley followed.

As soon as we hit the dance floor we were tearin' shit up. You'd a thought we were in a Future music video. The jukebox was bumpin' Mike Jones- Drop gimme 50. No matter how old this song gets. When you play it in a club watch people dance and go crazy. The dudes started flocking around us trying to get on. This one fine guy with braids kept eyeing me.
He walked over to me and started dancing behind me. I didn't mind lil' nigga had to be about 22. Too young for my blood. He was dancing on me good as hell though. I could feel him brickin' up on me against my ass. That shit made me laugh. Music switched up to Chris Brown- Privacy song. We decided to go back to our booth and have some shots.

"Bitch I am going home with some dick tonight!" Kori yelled while licking her lips.

"Yo' slut ass." I teased her. We ordered two rounds of shots and started really turning up. Ashley and Kori held there liquor well like always. My light weight ass had was drunk after three shots. Kori had her eyes on a dude who was at the bar.

"I'm about to go over there and get his ass y'all. Watch a bad bitch work!" She slid out the booth.

Me and Ashley cheered her on and took another shot. Kori was fine as hell and got any nigga she wanted. Her confidence and personality made her even more attractive. Niggas ate that shit up. Me and Ashley watch her flirt and whisper some shit in dude ear. They talked for a minute then Kori walked back over towards us with wrinkles in her forehead.

"Damn bitch! I never seen you fail before. What was wrong with him?" Ashley asked. Curiosity was on her face as well as mine.

"Girl, he asked me if I was Kori from the radio. I told him yea. This nigga says, you Ronny's girl. You off limits ma! Then asks me if Ronny knows I'm in here half-dressed and dancin' on lames? I got mad and walked away." Me and Ashley looked at each other a broke out in laughter. We both were laughing so hard. I fell over holding my stomach in the booth. Kori had her nose turned up ready to fight us.
"Y'all some giggling hoes!" Her phone started ringing. I knew it was Ronny because of the ringtone. Mariah Carey- Touch my body. Bitch was a huge Mariah fan! Her eyes bucked out big as hell. When she answered she tried to have a sweet voice.

"Hey my island man. Ronny, I am not half dressed! I don't appreciate you tellin' people you claimin' me and shit. We never talked about being official you in Jamaica and I am in Atlanta." I don't know what he said to her but this bitch started blushing and biting her lip.

She put up her index finger telling us to hold on. Sliding out the booth she went towards the bathroom while still on the phone. Me and Ashley were cracking up. Never thought we would see the day a nigga would tame Kori ass. We decided to order three new hookahs.

A few minutes later Kori came back smiling from ear to ear. She slid back in the booth and put her phone in her purse.

"So, I take it Ronny is your man?" Ashley asked smiling like I was. Kori jokingly rolled her eyes.

"Maybe. Nosey hoes! I'm happy y'all find my life funny but I will be getting the last laugh." Kori took a shot and started puffing on her hookah.

Me and Ashley were laughing at her pouting. Kori hated drinking with us because she said we giggled like kids. It only made us laugh harder. The night was fun as hell with the shots, hookahs and good music. Not to mention the fine ass me. We decided to order some wings and burgers. All of a sudden, a crowd formed on the dance floor.

"What the fuck is going on?" I asked looking around. Kori short ghetto ass stood up in the booth hoping to get a look at the action. When she set down she had a huge smile on her face.
"What bitch? What's going on and why the fuck are you smiling so hard?" Ashley asked her.

I was still trying to see what was the hype about. Then I almost stopped breathing when I saw Terrance and Ty walk through the crowd. They were looking good as fuck! I loved how neither one of them didn't have to have to be flashy to look good. Terrance had on a grey Adidas track suit with white Adidas high tops. Him and Ty's watch was blinding everyone in a mile radius. Ty was simple also in some black jeans with a white Polo shirt. Kori punk ass was cracking up.

"Did I mention I told Ronny I was not alone. Of course, him being a good friend and all. He had to let his boys know!" Me and Ashley grimed the fuck out of her. I mouth the word bitch which only made this girl laugher even louder.

"What's good ladies," Ty said as they approached our booth. Terrance was looking at me like I was a fucking treat. I couldn't take my eyes off him either.

"Hey big brothers. Come on and sit down with us. We got more than enough room," Kori said still laughing. Ashley moved over so Ty could sit next to her. Kori got up so Terrance can sit next to me.

"Come here British." His deep sexy voice called out to me. Like a magnetic pull I slid out to see what he wanted. He let Kori sit down first, me next then himself so he could be on the end. Like always he was all over me. He had his arm around my waist.

"What's good Yummy baby," he whispered in my ear. I had yet to speak, my words were lost. I felt like somebody took all the words I knew and put them on the back of a milk carton. Yea my words were missing.
"Why the fuck y'all out here half naked and shit? Ash you dancin' with niggas like you ain't got one. You want me to fuck everybody up in here?" Ty looked at Ashley with this crazy look in his eyes.
Nigga looked a little loose in the head. She rolled her eyes and looked away. Ty put his finger under her chin to make her look at him. He whispered something in her ear that made her bite her lip.

"What's up with you sis? You think you could fuck around because bro in Jamaica? When he put his bitch out for you he locked that pussy down." Ty looked at Kori and said. All of us laughed while Kori gave us the hand.

"Why you so quiet Yum. Did you think you could clown and I wouldn't know? Where the nigga with the braids you were dancing with? I don't see the little nigga no more?" He started acting like he was looking for him.

Then he looked back at me with that sexy as mean face. His deep chocolate skin had me wanting to strip and swim in it. I love his mini curly-fro and white teeth. Swear when he smiled at me his teeth sparkled.

"It was only a few dances. We didn't exchange numbers. All of us were only dancing and having fun." I looked at him and said. He did a light chuckle. Bringing me closer to him he whispered in my ear.

"You might be a little confused because I have not introduced my dick to your pussy. I'm on chill mode now Yum. But if I get a call about you wild'n out again shit not gone be so chill. You off the market yum. And not because you got that wack ass crushed bullshit on yo' finger." This nigga grabbed my hand and took my ring off. When he put it in his pocket I looked up at him with an attitude. The look he gave me made me fix my damn face. I'm tellin' y'all he looked at me like bitch I dare you trip on me.

"Kill all that shy shit too. You know damn well yo' manly burpin' ass ain't shy." He laughed in my ear. I laughed as well and hit him on his arm.

"Aww y'all are so cute together. Terrance, you got my girl all glowing," Kori said smiling. I kicked her foot under the table.

"Don't kick me Brit!" Ashley and Ty was laughing. Kori stuck her tongue out at me and blew me a kiss.

I could feel Terrance burning a hole on the side of my face. I already knew he had that sexy smirk on his chocolate face. We chilled and smoked for the rest of the evening. We had a

$300.00 bill when we left. Of course, our men took care of it. I liked all of us being together.

All we did was laugh and crack jokes. It was like a breath of fresh air for me. The past three years drama was all I endured. My girls were themselves and there was no tension. Whenever Derrick and was around my family or friends. There would always be tension and a lot of silence moments. We left the spot a little after midnight.

"You better be lucky yo' ass sobered up. You know I would have driven yo' ass home." Terrance was in front of me while I leaned on my driver's door.

"I already told you I can drive just fine even if I am buzzed." I looked at him smiling. That's all I did whenever we were in the same room together. Hell, just the mention or thought of Terrance I was smiling.

"I told you I don't give a fuck. That shit was before me now it won't happen again. Fuck over here Yummy." He grabbed my waist with one arm. Slamming me into his strong body he hugged me so tight. This was one of the things I found sexy about him. When he touched me, it wasn't just to cop a feel. His touch had confidence in it. Like I was his and always will be.

"I thought I told you don't make me wait long for a kiss. Fuck wrong wit'chu?" I playfully rolled my eyes and kissed his soft lips. Terrance lips were so sexy with a hint of pink. He had that sexy ass dip in the center of his top lip. My God! My God! I stayed hot for this man. We kissed with his hands all over my back. Then my hair and ass.

"Get yo' ass in that truck before I take you with me," he said against my lips. I pecked him again and got in my truck. Kori left already and Ashley left with Ty.

Turning down my block I saw Derrick's car gone. I didn't even bat an eyelash at the fact that he was gone. I walked in my house and kicked my heels off. I still was in a trance from the sexy King brother. After I showered I put on a tank top and a thong. Climbing in my soft bed I buried my body in the covers. Ever just lay in bed and just move your legs around the soft sheets.

It's the fuckin' best! I grabbed my phone and went through pics of me and Terrance. Yea we took selfies all the time. A lot of them were of him sleeping or us our on dates. I only had a few that were rated R. He only had a lot of me sleeping as well or some of me laughing. As if he knew I was thinking about him. My phone went off with a text from him.

Terrance: Are you thinking about me like I am thinking about you.
Me: Yes I am. I didn't want to leave you tonight.

He responded quick as hell.

Terrance: You want me to come get you?

If I didn't have to take Jaxon for pictures in the morning I would have.

Me: No I have something to do in the morning. I want to see you tomorrow though.
Terrance: Whatever you want Yummy baby. You know that shit.
We texted for the next hour until I fell asleep. I knew I was going to dream about Terrance King sexy ass. Lord I hope I don't have to wake up and change my sheets.

(A Dream Is a Wish Your Heart Makes)

"Come here Yummy baby. Get yo' sexy ass over here." Terrance was sitting up in the middle of the king size bed. We were at our usual suite at the Four Seasons.

I could not stop staring at his chocolate muscular body. He looked like a milk Hershey in his white jeans with not shirt. He had them unbuttoned. I could see his dick trying to break free and get to me. I slowly walked over to him in nothing but a black thong.

"I have been patient long enough British. I need to feel yo' insides." Never taking my eyes off his I straddled him.

Terrance wrapped one arm around my waist. He took his other hand and caressed the side of my face. Biting his lip, he put his hand on the back of my head and brought my lips to his. He kissed me with the passion of a starving artist. Our tongues danced and I was moaning like he was already dicking me down.

"I wanna feel you Terrance. Please I need it now baby." I never even talked this way with my husband.

My body did not even feel like it was mines anymore. I felt like my body and soul belonged to Terrance. Without words, he ripped my thong the material rubbed across my clit making me moan loud. We broke our kiss to pull his pants down. His dick sprung out of his boxers like a Jack n' the box.

He leaned forward with me still straddling him. I was so wet I felt my juices run between the crack of my ass. Positioning himself between my legs he tongued me down. Terrance didn't even have his pants all the way of before he slowly slid in me. My back arched from pain and pleasure. Derrick's dick was a nice size but this dick was on another level!

"Don't tighten up on me Yummy. Let me in that muthafucka baby." I opened my legs some more. He was grinding his hips sliding in more and more. Before I knew it, there was no more pain. Pleasure took over my body and my pussy felt like it was forming to fit his dick like a pair of good ass jeans. Terrance was kissing all over my face, ears and neck.

"Sssss Terrance you feel so good baby. Don't stop fucking me." He looked in my eyes and had that sexy as smirk on his face. Leaning down while not missing a stroke here started sucking on my titties. That drove me crazy because he knew how to suck and pull on my nipples. I felt my orgasm build up more and more with each thrust.

"You not going back to him British. That shit is over now that I'm in this pussy. Say it Yummy, say you're staying with me forever." I couldn't even find my words because I was on the verge of cummin'. Terrance set up and put my legs in the crook of his arm. I couldn't take it anymore, I came all over his dick.

"Ughhhhh God Terrance! I'm cummin' baby!" All that could be heard was my pussy creamin' as he still stroked. Sweat was coming down his chocolate face making his skin glisten. He let my legs down and put his face in my neck. I was loving every minute of this amazing dick he was putting on me. He started putting passion marks on my neck and titties which turned me on.
"Fuck girl. This pussy is so damn good." A couple more strokes and I was cummin' again.

"Mmm hmmm I'm cummin' baby." I moaned in his ear. This time he came right along with me.

"Daddy with you baby. Arrghhh Fuck Yummy!" Still inside me after we both came we started making out. I did not want him to move from his position. I pulled away and looked in his eyes.
"Yes, I am staying with you forever Terrance." He smiled big as hell at me. I smiled back as I climbed on top of him. Not even bothering to clean up, we fell asleep just like that.

I woke up with the sun beaming in my face. Cracking my eyes open I noticed I was in my bedroom. I smiled while still laying on my back. I knew I would dream about Terrance because he was on my mind tuff. I felt something wet under me and realized I came in my sleep.

Then I felt heat, like body heat. I slowly turned my head and saw Derrick sleeping next to me. I peeked under the covers and saw both of us ass naked. My heart dropped while beating fast at the same time. What the fuck! How the fuck! No! No! No!

"Derrick get the fuck up!" I leaped out the bed. He set up just as startled as I was.

"Boo what's wrong?"

Terrance "Terror"

"I want this nigga brought to me alive! All who he has working with him I will leave for y'all to dispose of them. But bring Sleez to me! This nigga is not only takin' from my pockets, but y'all shit to. The mouths of y'all families and all who depend on you to feed them. Respect has been beyond taken from us! I do not fuck with my name being thrown dirt on. Anybody who even mentions Sleez name from here on out kill they ass! I don't give a fuck who they are. And to make sure y'all droppin' bodies I want pictures of each person. Either with a bullet in their head or their throat slit open. I wanna see white meat and brains. Or I'm comin' after y'all. For now, every muthafucka is suspect." I looked around at every nigga and bitch in our King Dynasty crew.

They all were nodding their heads in agreement. We were in another one of our warehouses having a meeting. Because Sleez tipped the police off and had our shit raided. I stopped all operations for a while. Even though money still flowed for me and mines. I wanted our crew to think shit stopped so the hunt for Sleez would intensify.

"Fuck outta my face!" I yelled at them. I watched all of them exit the warehouse. Me, Ty and Mike stayed behind.

"Mike put your boys on Sleez grandma and auntie. Don't fuck with them just watch and see if he gets at them. If he does snatch his ass up but don't harm his grandma and auntie. Cool?" Mike nodded his head that he understood. We dabbed each other out and left out the warehouse.

"Aye bro why the fuck did I have to show my ass on Ashley. Crazy ass woman called herself gettin' drinks with some nigga. My homie who owns the bar called me telling me my bitch on a date. Some lame as bank worker nigga." I couldn't help but laugh because I never seen my baby brother sweat a bitch before. Like this nigga was real life pissed.

"Damn bro! So what yo' ass do? I ain't see shit on the news so I know you didn't drop no blood." He shook his head.

"Naw, I let her go on her date. I parked outside her house and waited for her to come home. Dude called himself walking her to the door and getting a kiss. I popped up out the bushes like a lunatic and walked up on them. Bro dude almost shitted his pants! Nigga took off before I could even get a word out! Thank God I wasn't a robber because he straight left Ashley for dead. Nigga ran like he had the runs comin' out his ass!" I couldn't help but fall out laughing at my crazy ass brother.

"Yo' bro I would have loved to have been there! You ain't locked Ashley's ass down yet?" I said through my laughs.

"Nigga that's mines all day. Ashley just bull-headed and think I am gonna dog her and Aron like her baby daddy. I told her I am far from that bitch ass nigga. This is just a way for her to stay in control. She feels like if she acts like she doesn't care then she won't get hurt. I shut all that shit down. Bet she won't be going on anymore dates. Her and Aron are mines for good! I punished the fuck out them walls though." He laughed and we gave each other a five.

"That's what I'm talkin' about bro. I'm on my way to see British ass now. Well, she don't know I'm coming but I am. She been on some other shit for the past three days. I think I am ready to snatch her and baby girl. I'm over this sneakin' around shit." Ty smiled at me looking like a fuckin' creep.
"Nigga I knew you were feelin' British ass more then what you said. Talkin' about you just need to hit. Naw nigga yo' ass in love. It's cool bro! The shit feels good don't it?" I looked at my younger brother and he had a straight face. Nigga was serious. I

couldn't lie, the shit did feel good. Only problem is the woman I wanted was not available.

I had no idea if British felt the same. The worst thing for me is getting my feelings hurt. Couldn't tell you how many time I wanted to kill Sheena. The only thing that saved her and that nigga was the baby she carried. Kids don't ask to be put in fucked up ass situations They be innocent in the matter.

"Yea nigga it does. I just hope she feels the same." Me and Ty talked for a minute then I jumped in my truck.

Pulling up to British store I was impressed. The store was nice as hell! She had Slay written big in cursive purple letters on the front. I loved how driven she was. Atlanta was filled with people doing hair, nails, selling clothes etc.

British came into a competitive filed and worked her ass off. That shit turned me on big fucking time. So many women out here have they hand out. Can't tell you how many bitches tried to trap me. Me and my brother's nut was golden to these thirsty bitches.

When I walked in the music was playing loud over the store. Women were all throughout the store. They were either trying on shoes. Looking through clothes racks. Or coming out of these rooms with curtains. I'm assuming those were the dressing rooms. British layout of the store was nice as hell.

You could tell her favorite color was purple and she liked glitter shit. I noticed a few eyes was on ya' boy. A nigga can't even front on how fine these women were. Atlanta had hella bad bitches. It felt like they were all in British store.
"Hi! I'm Toya welcome to Slay. Can I help you find anything today?" This fine thick ass redbone approached me. She must be one of British employees.

"Yes actually you can. Where is your boss?" She smiled at me.

"I am the store manager. Is there something I can help you with?" She kept her smile on her face and folded her arms.

"Naw baby girl I need yo' fine ass owner. Go get her for me. Tell her that her nigga out her." I smiled and bit my lip. Saying I was British nigga felt good as hell.

"Umm ok one moment." She walked away confused as hell. I'm sure all her co-workers know she is married.

They asses probably confused as hell but I don't give a fuck. I wasn't about to explain shit to nobody. I finish looking around the store and noticed some eyes on me. British definitely made sure every woman she hired was fine. They didn't hold a candle to my sexy ass baby. But they were all thick and bad as hell. I felt like that was a smart move on British part. Eye candy bitches were definitely money makers.

I noticed redbone came back from the back. Wrinkles formed on my forehead because she came back alone. Seeing how annoyed I was she approached me and told me British would be down. A few seconds later I saw Yummy walking towards the front.

I felt my ass smile at the sight of her. As usual she looked sexy as hell! British had this long skirt on with a tight top that showed a little belly. The skirt flowed down so long she had to hold a little of it up. I loved British style of dress. To me nothing was sexier than a woman who could dress.

"What are you doing here? How did you even know I worked today?" I wish I had a picture of how big she was smiling. I thought she would cuss my ass out for popping up. Then I called myself her nigga. But she didn't react that way at all.

"Don't worry about that shit. Why have you been acting funny with me lately? What the fuck is up?" I was serious now. I really wanted to know why she been distance. Usually we would text and talk all day on and off. Now she was texting me short responses. Whenever we were on the phone she would rush me off. I didn't play that shit so here I am.

"Come on in my office." British grabbed my hand and guided me towards the back. Being in contact with her made me soften up a lot. I watched her ass move in that skirt. Her hair was in a side ponytail. I loved how she could wear kid hairstyles but still look grown as hell.

We got to her office door labeled Boss Lady. Of course, her door was purple and black. Walking in she had metallic and purple color scheme. Closing the door, she stood in front of her desk not looking at me. I hated when a person couldn't look at me. I felt like only deceitful people did shit like that. I stood in front of her looking with my arms folded waiting on her to talk.

"Terrance, I apologize if you think I have been acting weird. I just have been busy working. Soon as things settle down at work I will be back to normal." I looked at her spit bullshit to be. British thought I didn't know her because we were not together every day. But she couldn't be further from the truth.

"You wanna run that bullshit by me again? I know when you are lying. You get to moving your hair and rubbing the back of your neck." I walked closer to her keeping eye contact.

"Talk to me but only come correct. Stop fuckin' playin' me British." I rarely ever call her by her real name. But this shit she was bringing to me was insulting to a niggas intelligence. British wouldn't even look at me. I put my arms around her waist and made her look at me.

"The other night when we went out. I came home and texted you for a while. When I went to sleep I woke up with

Derrick next to me. Umm, we were naked. I don't even remember sleeping with him." She kept her head down while she was talking. When I tell y'all I was ready to burn her store down. With her and every bitch in here still in it. I know I had a murderous look on my face. I pulled away from her and stood there for a minute. I had to get my feelings together. Technically--- NAW FUCK THAT BULLSHIT!

"So nasty community dick is what you into? Ok I see how shit really is. I don't give a fuck if y'all still married or not! The nigga is dirty and still fucking around on yo' stupid ass. You stayed in this fucked up situation because you wanted to. I came along and filled in all the shit that bitch ass nigga was lackin'. How I'm feeling right now British it's best if I stay the fuck away from you." She had tears falling down her face.

I promised to myself that she would never cry sad tears from me. As much as I wanted to grab her ass up and love on her. I was hurt like a muthafucka and prideful. I walked out her office slamming her door hard as hell. I heard the mirror she had hanging on the door and wall shatter. Fuck this shit! Fuck love! Fuck feelings! Most of all fuck British!

*

Sitting in my truck I was parked in my drive-way. To mad to get out I rolled me two fat ass blunts. Putting my Aux cord in my phone I played some Al Green. Growing up in my house me and my brother knew all the oldies hits. I blazed up one of my blunts and took a hit. Call me what you wanted I was sad as fuck. Part of me wanted to pull up on British at her house. Snatch her and baby girl out of there. Bring their asses home with me and never let them go. My pride was kicking my heart ass. The more I smoked the more I felt like fuck that bitch British.

I smoked and listened to some heartbreak music. Rose Royce- I Wanna Get Next To You song was hittin' a nigga in the gut. I leaned my head back on my seat and let my high take over. My cell phone ringing snapped me out of it. I hurried up and answered it. I'm not gone even say who I thought it was.

"Yo." I spoke into the phone. It was my head chef at my restaurant. His ass was yelling his ass off in my ear.

"Wait, Thomas hold on man stop yelling." He calmed down enough for me to understand what he was saying. His words fell on deaf ears because I just know he was not saying what I heard.

"How the fuck did that happen?! Ok listen I am on my way now!" My high felt like it faded away.

I rushed the highway in full speed. The thick smoke in the sky was seen before I even got to my destination. It after 8pm so the night was setting in. Fire trucks were outside and so was the emergency trucks. The police were all over the street trying to keep people back. I hoped none of my employees were hurt. Walking up to the front of my restaurant I was stopped by an officer.

"Sir I cannot let you through. You need to stay back with the rest of these people." I mugged his fat ass.

"Get yo' fat ass out my way! This is my fucking restaurant!" My employees must have heard my loud ass mouth. They came all running to me dirty as hell.

"Boss the place just went up in flames in a blink of an eye! We were having our usual good Friday night! Then you heard glass break and smoke was everywhere!" One of my assistant managers Sally told me. She was crying bad as hell. I looked at my employees and they were all dirty as hell from the smoke.

"It's ok calm down. Fuck the restaurant, that shit can be repaired. Was anybody hurt?" Scanning all my employees everyone looked to be accounted for.

"We are all fine boss. Everyone got out fine. The hard part is putting out the fire. Boss, I swear it was not a kitchen accident. I run my kitchen stern I promise. No one left anything by the burners or anything." Thomas had a look of shock on his face. I shook my head with a smirk. Thomas was Cuban with a heavy accent. Whenever I came around for some reason he felt intimidated. He would talk fast as hell and explain every detail.

"Thomas it's ok man. However the fire started no one is in trouble. No one is out of a job or anything. This can be fixed. Meanwhile all of you will be taken care of until I can get this rebuilt." They all seemed to calm down. I meant what I said. I had good ass employees who worked hard. Most of them had families and were in high school.

"Everyone go home and let me handle things from here. I will be in touch with all of you tomorrow morning." I shook the hands of my employees and looked at my restaurant. I was pissed off but I know these things happen. Money was not a problem in the matter. Shit I had more money than I could handle. Getting my business back up and running would be no problem.

The fire fighters informed me they would be in touch with me in the morning. After handling shit with the police and fire fighters. I left out of the police station tired as hell. It was after midnight and I just needed to get home. I was ready to fuck the shit out of my $ 17,000 bed.

Pulling up to my drive-way I decided to park in my garage. After all that happened today the shit with British stood out the most. I needed to stay far away from that woman. If I even see her again I'm liable to kill her husband. Shit sounds crazy but I felt I deserved British as my woman. While I walked in through my garage door my phone ringed. I looked at the caller I.D. and it said Leslie Parker. With furrowed eyebrows, I answered the phone.

"Fuck is this?" I waited for the caller to speak. All I heard was heavy breathing and what sound like sniffles.

"Yo who the fuck is this?" I said again losing my patience. Just as I was about to hang up the caller decided to speak.

"I'm not fucking stopping. King me bitch." The line went dead. Frozen where I stood I balled my fist up. I swear on my life two things were going to take place. One, I was going to kill Sleez the worst way possible. He was beyond disrespectful and fucking with innocent people's lives. The second thing is making British mines. Both things were way over due and it is time for me to collect.

Derrick

I woke up with a terrible ass headache. Getting drunk on an empty stomach might have not been the best idea. Getting off my couch I looked around and was happy I was at home. I had no idea how the fuck I got here. Last thing I remember was being at the strip club with Eric. I looked out my window and saw my Maybach in the drive-way.

Clearly I drove myself home. I normally could drive while drunk. Last night Eric and I met some nigga name Sleez. He had a V.I.P section with bottles and bitches. He saw we had our own V.I.P section. Deciding to put the bottles and bitches together we got white boy wasted. Sleez had some pills going around. Eric popped every now and again.

It was never really my thing but lately my ass had been stressed. British and Jaxon had moved out two weeks ago and I was sick about it. The fucked-up thing is she didn't even tell me. I came home and her shit was gone with a note on the counter. Jaxon room remained the same. I was so fucking confused because we were just making love.

British came home from her girl's night out. I went to the strip club with Eric and came home horny and drunk. I took my chances and went into British room. She must have been tired as hell because she didn't lock the bedroom door. British looked so sexy sleeping even with her scarf on. I pulled the covers back showing her sexy body. Once I climbed in the bed I thought she would have woken up.

Whatever she was dreaming about had her lightly moaning and smiling. Her ass was horny as I was. I figured she was dreaming about me and all the dick I have given her. When I touched her thigh, she opened her legs. I smiled and made love to my wife for the first time in a while. In the morning, I woke to her screaming for me to get up.

British looked at me like I was a ugly ass nigga. Like she met me in the club, fucked and regret in the morning. She started talking all this shit about me being dirty. Saying she didn't know where my dick or mouth been. I grimed her ass and left out the bedroom. The next hour I heard her walk downstairs and slam the front door.

I went back up to our bedroom and this woman changed the sheets. British really thought I was a dirty dick ass nigga. Then a few hours later she came home. Without saying a word to me she took Jaxon and went upstairs. I went through her purse and saw papers from the clinic.

This stupid ass woman really went and got an STD test. I wanted to kick the bedroom door down. I mean yea I slipped up a few times but I was a clean nigga. I never had an STD before. For my wife to treat me like so crackhead offended me. I did what I normally did when I was mad. Left and linked up with Eric.

Now two weeks later her ass in gone. I couldn't believe this shit was happening to me. I tried to track her phone but British had it wiped clean. Oh but you can best believe this was not the end. I am never giving her a divorce. Looking in the mirror I felt broken.

I know I wasn't perfect but British did not even try. We should be on vacation laying on some tropical island. A getaway could have cleared our minds. Hell, I wouldn't mind picking another state and making it home. All these options we had to save our marriage and she chose to walk.

Not only was my heart hurting but so was my ego. Sometimes British has a way of making me feel like I am beneath her. Like she was perfect and didn't make mistakes at all. I know lots of men who did worse shit then me. They still had their wives and children under one roof.

My love for British was real and nobody could tell me different. To walk away from me without saying shit made me feel less than a man. After moping around for about an hour I got dressed and grabbed my keys. I knew what I needed to ease this shit.

*

"Ughhhhhhh fuck Derrick!" Fuck this pussy big daddy!" I was rearranging Treasure's guts. Her ass looked delicious slamming against me. Sweat was dripping off my forehead and onto her ass cheeks.

"Throw that shit back bitch!"

Slap! Slap!

Hitting both of her chocolate ass cheeks she started creamin' everywhere. Treasure pussy was good as fuck. The only thing I had to work with her on was giving head. Her gag reflexes were sensitive. I liked my shit to disappear in yo' mouth. I put my whole hand over her face and went hard. Treasure liked ruff nasty sex which turned me on. Pulling out I turned her over and fucked the shit out of her missionary style.

"Oh my God Derrick! Don't stop fucking me! Keep fucking me." This was just what my ego needed.

I bit down hard on her shoulder to prevent from cummin' now. Looking down at her she made some of the ugliest faces. To be so fine her face could form into some ugly expressions. Shit almost made me laugh while fucking her.

To prevent that I popped one of her titties in my mouth. I could suck on Treasure's titties all day like an infant. They were soft as hell and perfect size for me.

"Spit in my mouth big daddy! You now I like that shit." See what I mean. This bitch was nasty as hell. I did what she said and spit in her mouth. She opened up and took all of it. Shit made my dick grow inside of her. I licked all over her face leaving traces of spit. Treasure was moaning so loud and I felt her juice up with my strokes. I couldn't take it anymore as I felt my nut build up.

"Fuck bitch!" I shot my kids in the condom I had on. Breathing hard as hell I rolled over on my back. Treasure hoped up and went to the bathroom. I heard the shower on so in and joined her. After washing up and getting my dick sucked I was getting dressed.

"Your leaving?" I was putting my wallet in my pocket. I looked up at Treasure and she looked sad as hell.

I knew she was feeling me but I had nothing to give her. Aside from dick and head I was useless for her. I could tell the way she looked at me that she wanted more. On a better day I would trade Niecy in for Treasure any time. Treasure did what I asked without question or hesitation. Almost like a good submissive.

"Yea I have to have work today. I will be back later though so cook some food. I got a taste for some meat loaf. Fry my cabbage with some mash potatoes and corn. Ok?" she nodded her head. I knew she wanted me to stay. Knowing what would make her feel better I gave her a few kisses.

"You good? You need some money." Shaking her head no I kissed her again. Finally, she smiled and I dipped out.

I know y'all feel disgusted with me. I can explain how this happened. Treasure was at the strip club the night I found out British left. I was fucked up and she drove me to her house. Baby girl cleaned up my throw up and gave me a bath. For a minute, I felt like the man I was. We slept in her bed and I didn't touch her. When I woke up she fixed me breakfast and washed my clothes.

I was grateful but had no intentions on fucking. The next day I ran into her at Wal-Mart shopping. She saw I had all TV dinners in my cart and offered to cook for me. I accepted and went back to her house for dinner. Before I knew it, we were fucking after eating. I have not stopped since. Fuck was I supposed to do? I was a man with a broken heart and fucked up ego.

Treasure was fine, thick, can cook and wanted me. She never asked for a cent from me. all she wanted was Derrick with all my flaws. I know she wanted me to be hers but my heart was with British. I was still in love with her. The more she stayed gone the more I wanted her to come back home. I had a plan on how to do this shit now. I was sloppy with cheating on British in the past. I kept hanging out in the same spots.

Having the same routines and going to the same hotels. This time I was going to leave these clubs and random hoes alone. I was only going to fuck around when I go on business trips. You know what I mean? Keep the shit away from home. Treasure already told me as long as she gets her time she was good. Any other hoes in Georgia I was not fucking with. I also would always make sure I strapped up. No slip ups this way.

Driving to McDonalds my phone went off. I would have looked at right then but my stomach was empty. I needed a big mac, coke and a strawberry cream pie. When I got my food, I set down to eat. My phone went off again only this time I pulled it out to look at it. It was Eric talking about work. The next text made my stomach drop it was from British.

Wife: Derrick it has been two weeks. We need to talk.

I could not help but smile hard as hell. I set there and read the message over and over. I knew British would miss me. A marriage was not something easy to just throw away. Like I said earlier, I was not perfect. Things were not always bad between us. I remember how we would go on dates and trips. When I built our house, British was so happy she cried. Snapping out of my thoughts I texted her back.

Me: I would love to talk British. Do you want to meet now?

Wife: No, I have a store meeting. 5 ok for you?

Me: Perfect

Leaving McDonalds, I was feeling good as hell. I had a plan on getting my wife back. I was going to start doing shit different. My business was doing beyond well! Today we were putting more work into this club we were building.

Walking into my office my assistant gave me my messages and my coffee. I took a sip and opened my office door. My shit was high up over looking Atlanta. I liked color so I kept my walls white. I had pictures of all the historical buildings and statues on my walls. My office furniture was orange and white. Going through my messages I saw one from Daniel King. He wanted to meet me and Eric in a few weeks.

We had been only working with his assistant on the club. I never had a client I had yet to meet but I wasn't tipping. The money was right so I figured I'd meet them soon. Going to the basement of our building my team was down there. We spent a few hours going over the details of the club. Everything from the ceiling to the floor had to be special ordered. Didn't worry me because I was not paying.

The clients obviously had money. Eric made a graphic design of a walkthrough of the club. The shit looked good as hell and made me excited on finishing. I went back to my office to finish up some paper work. No matter how my personal life was fucked up. I made sure work was always perfect.

Besides my wife and daughter. Money was my happiness. It was the reason I was able to live my lifestyle. The reason bitches came to me. the reason strippers loved my ass. While working my assistant buzzed into my office.

"Mr. Noel. There is a Niecy on line one for you." I was surprised because I had not heard from her.

"Thank you Bridgette. I'll take it." I picked up my office phone.

"What's good Niecy?"

"Derrick this is crazy as hell. You really not going to have anything to do with your child? I am seven months pregnant and you have not been around." I looked at the phone because she was on some other shit.

"Niecy, I made myself clear. I do not want a child with you. You told me you would be good without me, so be good lil mama." I hung up the phone and had her number blocked from calling.

I was not about to deal with that shit. If you say you are good without me being around then do that. As far as I am concerned Niecy or her child did not exist. I wasn't heartless. I just know British would never come home. Not if another woman was having my baby. My office door opened and it was security.

"Mr. Noel we have a problem in the lobby. There is a woman yelling for you. She is pregnant and we don't want to be ruff with her." Anger ran through me. I cannot believe this bitch man. I jumped up and hurried to the elevator. Before I even got to the bottom floor I could hear her loud ass.

"I am not fucking leaving until DERRICK NOEL comes downstairs!" The elevator doors could not open fast enough. This bitch was being beyond messy and at my place of business. Hell naw!

"Well look what acting a fool will get you. So, it takes me to get ghetto on your ass for you to see me?" She was still raising her voice. People were already standing around watching. This shit was making me mad as hell. I hated a scene and Niecy was for sure causing a scene.

"Niecy what are you doing? Do you understand you can be arrested?" I said calmly through gritted teeth. This bitch started laughing.

"You think I give a fuck about getting arrested. I'll tell everyone I am your baby mama. You see there are already people watching this shit. Derrick I am not going away and neither is your son." I looked down at her growing stomach. Something made me feel different when she said son. I shook that shit off and handled her.

"Niecy, you need to go. Now! I don't know what the fuck you are trying to prove but this needs to stop." I looked security.

"Get her the fuck out of here. If she comes anywhere near the building I want her arrested for trespassing." I walked back towards the elevator.

"Derrick I swear you will pay for this shit! How could you do this to your son?!" I stepped on the elevator not even looking at her. I cleared my head of this bullshit. The only thing on my mind was getting my wife back. Nothing else matters.

*

I was sitting at the bar in Applebee's. British said she wanted to meet here. At first, I felt some kind of way. I wanted to meet her at the house with no distractions. I just wanted her to hear me out and understand. This separation has gone on long enough. I watched as the doors swing open.

British walked her fine ass in looking around. My wife had a beauty that a blind retard could see. She had a long sleeve floral dress on that tied in the front. It was loose but you could still see her shape. The front had a slit that showed her right leg. I had to fix my dick that was now hard. I waved her to come towards the bar.

"Hey D. How've you been?" She gave me a half smile while sitting across from me.

"I been ok. Working like crazy to finish this club. How has Jaxon been?" No way was I going to let her know how I really was doing. Like I told y'all before, my ego was bruised.

"Jaxon has been fine. That's what I wanted to talk to you about. Derrick I know I left without you knowing. But I left you a note and told you Jaxon is available for you any time. Why haven't you checked on her? I have called and texted you about her and you don't respond. Your ego is that messed up you can't spend time with your daughter?" She set back in the chair with her arms folded. This is the shit that I was talking about. British acts like she is fucking perfect. It's always me who is the bad guy.

"British my intentions were not to neglect Jaxon. I mean I just have had a lot on my mind and on my plate. See there you go again pointing out my flaws. Did it ever occur to you that I am fucked up over you leaving? You walked out without telling me shit leaving me in our home alone.

I don't want to split custody of our daughter. I want us as a family! You know that shit." At this point I was angry as hell. The fuck she wanted me to pick up my daughter like a custody case. I loved British but she was out her rabbit ass mind.

"All I am hearing is I in every fucking thing you said. It's always what Derrick wants. What is best for Derrick. Who the fuck is this person in front of me?" I shook my head at her.

"You are a piece of work British. Getting my hopes up with thinking we could be back to the way things were. Why the fuck are you playing with me?" I was trying not to get loud. I hated a scene.

"You know what Derrick, fuck you. Until you become a man and own up to all your bullshit. You will never be ready to be a father let alone a husband. Continue not being around your daughter if you want to. She will never go a day without being showed love. You already lost me! Don't lose Jaxon as well." She got up to leave but I grabbed her arm. I would never hurt my wife but this was getting out of hand.

"British I am tired of you walking away from me. Do you not see how fucked up I am over this shit? Why do you want to keep hurting me so fucking bad?" I looked around and there were a few eyes on us. I let her arm go and she rubbed it.

"I have asked myself that question so many time. Good-bye Derrick. Be in touch when you want to see Jaxon." She turned around and walked towards the door.

I set back down mad as hell. I was two seconds away from calling my wife a bitch. I just needed to breath and realize who the hell I was. Every woman I have ever wanted I got. Rather it was my approach or her approach. I have never been rejected before. Who the fuck would reject me? The more I sat in my thoughts the more I was hurt. Now my ego and pride is bruised by British. This was not the end of us no matter what she says.

British

I have been in my condo for almost a month now. I was loving every second of it. One of the perks of living alone. You can decorate anyway you want! I was a girly ass woman so I went crazy. Jaxon was a girl which made me really decorate how I wanted to. My bathroom was pink and black Paris theme. I had my living room gold and purple like I always wanted to do. Today Kori was coming over to swim in our indoor pool with me and Jaxon. Ashley had to work in her shop today.

It was the first week of September and the weather was still nice. The outdoor pool is more crowded than the indoor pool. I was in Jaxon bedroom putting on her swim suit. I brought her the cutest pink and yellow one-piece. It had ruffles all around it and her little chucky self-looked so cute in it. I was not a fan of babies or little girl's in two-piece swimsuits.

Call me old fashion but I just didn't like it. After getting her together I went to my room and changed in to my swimsuit. I have not gone swimming since Jamaica. Speaking of Terrance (Ha!) I really missed him. I knew he would feel some type of way about me sleeping with Derrick. I just didn't think he would lash out like that. Even though he tried to hide it I saw hurt I his eyes. I never wanted to do that to him at all.

The fact that his ex-cheated on him made me feel I had done the same. Though we were never a couple part of me felt we were. I texted him a few times but he did not reply. I knew it was because of him being hurt and upset. I never thought you could miss someone so much.

I missed our movie nights and laughing with him. We had no shame in doing embarrassing shit in front of each other. How can you fall for someone but belong to someone else? This shit fucked with me all day and night. Even when I try to distract myself Terrance still was on my brain. Today I just wanted to relax with my baby and take her swimming.

"Bitch where my baby at?" I heard Kori shout as she turned her key letting herself in. All of us gave each other keys to our places. It was supposed to be for emergencies only but as you can see it does not apply.

I walked in the living room and Jaxon almost jumped out my arms at the sight of Kori. Of course, she wasted no time dropping her purse and picking Jaxon up. I shook my head at them because they just seen each other yesterday.

"You ready for some swimming Jaxxy bear? Come on so we can get it in! Then after that we going to Toys R Us!" Jaxon giggled her ass off like she knew what Kori was saying.

"Umm excuse me punk. Who said we were going to Toys R Us? And damn I don't get no hello?" I playfully rolled my eyes and turned my nose up. My neighbors from the condo across from me were walking out their door as well. They were two gay guys.

"You are so needy. You need love to boo? Come to mama." I smiled at her punk ass. Kori hugged me while holding Jaxon.

"Thank you. I feel much better." We laughed and started walking towards the pool.

"Excuse me!" We both stopped and turned around. It was my neighbors walking towards us.

"We just want to say you guys are a beautiful couple. With a beautiful little girl. We are thinking of adopting ourselves. You are goals for us!" They hugged us and walked away. We waited for them to pull off and we broke out laughing.

"Bitch I am not going anywhere else with you in public. Niggas might want to holla but think you my woman and shit." Kori teased while still cracking up.

When we got to the pool I was happy it was only two people swimming. Kori set Jaxon up on her floating device. My baby looked adorable in the floating princess crown.

"So, I heard you on your radio show with Larenz Tate and Kofi Siriboe. I cannot wait for us to go see that movie they are in. Girls Trip is going to be so good! Jada Pinkett Smith is lucky as hell she gets to kiss Kofi fine ass," I said while moving my arms in the water.

"Girl they both are even finer in person! That was some sexy ass two hours. You know I don't have no filter when I talk. The segment we did with the answer a question or take a shot was fun as hell. The phone lines were going crazy with callers' girl. I am happy y'all enjoyed it as much as I enjoyed doing it." We laughed and talked some more.

Kori took Jaxon under the water a few times. I made sure my baby was familiar with the water from birth. I wanted her to know how to swim. You know some of us black people are not swimmers.

"Derrick still has not been too see her?" Kori asked putting Jaxon back on her float bed.

"Nope. I have called and texted. He keeps saying he want us both home.

I never thought I would say this. But Derrick is acting like a whiny bitch. I am so mad at him it don't make no sense. I don't even recognize him this way." I had to calm myself down because I was getting worked up. I was just so disappointed in Derrick's behavior.

"Calm down boo. Right now, Derrick is hurt and does not know what to do. You never left him before. His ego and pride is probably fucked up and he is pouting now. I am not team Derrick at all. But I don't think he will just tap out of Jaxon's life. Meanwhile, you just keep doing what yiu do best. Which is taking care of you and Jaxon." We hugged and I felt better.

"So, let's talk about Terrance." Kori came from up under the water with this bullshit. My heart dropped when she said his name.

"British what did you expect when you told him you slept with Derrick. Even though y'all are not an item. Terrance still thought of you as his. I feel where both sides are coming from. I am more on your side. I think Derrick picked the perfect time to slip in and get some pussy from you. I don't blame you for getting tested either. Derrick has community dick and only God knows where it's been." We both started laughing. This is why I loved being around my girl's and family. They would make me feel good and forget about the bullshit in my life.

"Girl I miss Terrance so bad it's crazy. I just want his big ass arms to wrap around me. I have texted and called him but no response. I guess I should expect that uh? He bet not have another girlfriend." Kori shook her head while laughing.

"Whipped ass! And no, he has no girlfriend. I was over Ty house with Ashley and Terrance showed up. He tried to mention your name all slick and shit. The man misses you to girl, bad. You know Ty is having a little kick back tonight at his crib. You should come and get yo' ass out the house. I know your parents will keep Jaxon for you." I shook my head fast as hell.

"No way bitch! I do not need to see Terrance and he has been dodging my calls."

"Girl Terrance is in Jamaica with Ronny. Come on Brit get out the house." I agreed and Kori started dancing.

Deep down I wanted to see Terrance. Guess we really were done for good. We played in the pool some more. After we were done Kori went home to get dress for Ty's kick back. My parents said they would keep Jaxon for me. After getting me and Jaxon dressed and her packed. I headed out to drop her off and go to Ty's house.

*

I pulled up at Ty's huge ass house. This was my first time coming to his home. Ashley told me about how nice it was but damn! His drive-way had to be about a mile long. His brick mansion had blue shutters on it and six garages attached to it.

I knew Terrance and his brother had money but oh my goodness. I would love to see what car was in each garage. I probably would feel like I was on Deal or No Deal game show. I parked my car and walked up to the door. There were three big ass men standing by it.

"Um hi. I am here for—

"You good British. Gone on in." The biggest one looked at me and said.

"They told you my name?" He smirked at me.

"We been knowing who you were. You Terror's woman." I could feel the dumb look I had on my face.

I just walked into the house. Usher- No limit was playing loud. Ty's house was gorgeous. Black and cream was his colors all through the house. I smiled when I saw some of Aron's shoes in the corner. My girl really had a good guy and I was happy for her. Speaking of my girl's I scanned the room looking for them.

I saw some people go downstairs so I went as well. It was a huge ass game room. There were two 70-inch Tv's mounted on each side of the room. Pool tables and arcade games were in the room as well. I saw Ty sitting in a recliner chair so I walked over to him.

"Hey Ty. Where is Ashley and Kori at?" He got up out his chair and put his blunt down.

"What I tell you about that Ty shit. Hey sis, give me love." We hugged. I laughed because him his brother and Ronny towered over me and my girls.

"My bad, let's start over." I cleared my throat.

"Hey big brother. Where are my besties at?" He laughed and picked back up his blunt.

"Her pretty ass up-stairs with Kori. She was fixing me a plate of food. When you see her ass tell her daddy hungry." I was about to walk away and go find them when Ty called my name.

"Aye sis, fix shit with my brother. And don't be lookin' at none of these niggas either. Yo' ass off limits." I shook my head and headed up-stairs. Ty's kitchen was just as gorgeous as the rest of his house. It was all black with chrome appliances. Just like Ty said Kori and Ashley were in the kitchen.

"Hey boo! I am so happy I made your ass come. You are looking good tonight Brit." I smiled and hugged her and Kori.

Ty had all kinds of food on display. Fried and bake chicken, ribs, macaroni and cheese. He had greens, corn bread, sweet potatoes, ribs, string beans and waffles. I hurried up and made me a plate.

"Ashley my big brother said come bring daddy his plate," I told her while tasting some of the good ass macaroni. Ashley blushed and rolled her eyes.

When she came back from giving Ty his food we set I the kitchen bar and started throwing down. We talked a little about Ashley and Ty. This bitch was still giving him problems about becoming her man. I understood where she was coming from. I just didn't want her to be so guarded that she missed out. But I loved how much patience my big brother was with her. That's how I knew he was the one for Ashley.

While we were laughing and now drinking some wine coolers the door opened and in walked Terrance fine ass. My heart started beating fast as hell and my stomach was in knots. I hurried up and shot Kori a mean ass look. This bitch wouldn't even look at me. He looked so fucking good in his True Religion faded jeans.

His matching shirt was fitted hugging his muscular body. My mouth watered looking at his sexy ass arms. He must have just come from the barber shop. He was looking extra daddyish! He had some red and black Lebron James high tops on. I had to regain some composure. I felt like I was watching The Best Man movie.

Remember when Morris Chestnut character Lance was introduced. Mmm hmm! When Terrance walked all the way in some yellow bitch with blonde hair was with him. I felt like someone took my heart and poked holes in it.

"Who the fuck is that bitch?" Kori said but only so me and Ashley could hear. I knew Kori was not scared of shit! She was waiting to see what I wanted to do.
"British you know damn well that is not his woman. This is his way of lashing out because he is hurt. You know we would have told you if he had a bitch," Kori said. Ashley nodded her head.
"Hell yea we would have. Brit, I have seen Terrance everyday sometimes all day. His ass never even talked on the phone. This bitch is just eye candy." Ashley said. I felt a little better because maybe they were right.

"And I am sorry for lying to you. I really just wanted you to come out the house. Oh and I secretly wanted you and

Terrance to make-up." Kori hugged me and kissed me on the cheek.

"I know boo. I am not mad, anymore bitch." I smiled at her. I got up to throw my plate away. Terrance had made me so nervous my appetite went away. When I turned around he was walking in the kitchen. I had to catch my breath from leaving my body. He hugged and greeted Ashley and Kori. His ass acted like I was invisible.

"Big brother you just not gone acknowledge my girl?" Leave it to Kori ass to say some shit.

"What up British," he said the shit so dry I wanted to throw water on it. He didn't even look up from his plate he was fixing. I did not give that punk ass greeting a reply.

"Ashley where is the bathroom." When she told me I took off up-stairs.

When I made it to the bathroom I had to breath in and out. I was mad and annoyed. Showing up here with a fake Diamond from Crime Mobb. Then giving me a dry ass hello. Washing my hands and drying them, I gave myself the once over in the mirror. I am happy I was looking good tonight. I loved my bodysuits so I was rocking a blue mesh one.

I had some light color tight jeggings on with my blue and gold wedges. Pretty much all my clothes were from myself. Unless I wanted to rock my expensive shit. I dried my hands and opened the bathroom door. Soon as I started walking I ran into a hard chest.

"Oh excuse me. I am so sorry." I looked up at the cutie I bumped into. He was very good looking with some deep dimples.

"It's cool mama. I'm the one that should watch wear I'm going. What's your name?" I half smiled and said.

"British. Nice to meet you." He kissed the back of my hand. I had to snap out of it. No way I could talk to anybody here. They all knew Terrance and Ty and that was to messy.

"I'm Levi. You are fucking beautiful British. Can I get your number and hit you up sometimes? I would love to take you out." I tried not to blush at his compliment. As cut as he was my attention was on a certain asshole downstairs.

"Levi that is really sweet but it's not a good time for me at the moment. I'm sorry." He licked his lips and nodded his head.

"I understand mama. Maybe our paths will cross in the future. Have a good night." He winked at me and walked into the bathroom.

When I walked back downstairs I saw a few bodies in the living room watching Paid in Full. I went to the basement because I heard Kori's loud ass mouth. When I reached them her and Ashley were playing pool. I went over there and joined them. We were really good at this game. My dad taught us a few years back. Some of our girl's night out were at a pool hall.

"I'm playing against the winner," I said as I sat down on the stool next to the pool table. Kori and Ashley began playing. Kori was whooping Kori's ass at first. Then Ashley knocked the socks off and won. Me and Ashley played next and she whooped my ass as well.

"Bitch you getting' lucky tonight." I teased and stuck my tongue out at her.

We opened up some more wine coolers and chilled out. Ty was being extra and would not let us smoke. While we were chillin' I looked across Ty's huge ass basement and saw Terrance sitting on another recliner. He was playing the game with some other dudes over there. His bitch he brought with him was sitting on the arm of his chair. I could not tell my face not to show emotion. Kori and Ashley saw what I saw as well.

"Just say the word Brit and we got you." Ashley said not taking her eyes off them. I snapped out of my stare.

"Naw, fuck him and her." We decided to play another game of pool. Kori and myself played. Ashley was all booed up with Ty's ass. While we were playing Kori got a phone call and I knew it was Ronny. This bitch had a smile on her face a mile long.

"You just gonna leave in the middle of our game?" She put her index finger up and went up-stairs. I smacked my lips.

"I'll play you mama." I looked up and saw cutie from the bathroom standing behind me.

"Ok cool." I set up the pool table. I could feel his eyes on me but I did not make eye contact back.

"Why you avoiding looking at me British? You nervous or some shit." I looked up at him with a serious face.
"Why would I be nervous? I'm good Levi." I broke the set and we began playing.

"You sound sexy saying my name." I smirked and continued playing.

"So why is it not a good time for a nigga to take you out?" He asked while shooting my 9 ball.

"I am in a situation with someone. We had a fall out but I am not sure it is over." I could see Terrance while I talked to Levi. Levi's back was facing Terrance. Blondie rubbed his back and whispered something in his ear. Then this trick kissed his neck. Fuck this bullshit.

"Actually, Levi the situation I spoke of is over. I just really am focusing on me and my daughter right now." He slightly turned his head towards Terrance. He chuckled and kept talking to me. He must have known something was up but didn't care. We continued our pool game.

"You good as hell girl! We should go to Mr. Cues one day." I laughed at how smooth he threw that in the conversation.

"Maybe?" He walked up close to me, he moved my hair out my face.

"I promise you will have a good time." Just as I was about to answer I saw Terrance walking towards us.

Looking like a totally different person then I was used to seeing. For some reason, he looked like he grew a few inches. His muscles looked bigger and his face looked like he was going to war. Reminds me how the Hulk gets when he gets angry.

"Yo' Levi what tha fuck you doin' nigga?" Terrance asked looking dead into Levi's eyes.

"Talkin' to this beautiful young lady. What the fuck you doin'?" Ok y'all. Is it wrong that I was turned on by both men at the moment? I mean clearly Terrance was sexier and just better. But the way Levi had not one intimidating bone in his body made him sexy as well.

"This me right here muthafucka! You bein' real disrespectful right now. You got two seconds to get up out my woman face. And one of them gone." He balled his fist up. Levi put his pool stick down and stood there. Hell naw, nobody was about to die in front of me.

"Hold up y'all please don't do this. Levi this is the situation I was telling you about. That's why I said we couldn't go out." I turned to Terrance who still had his eyes on Levi.

"Terrance, I am not you woman. Your bitch is over there waiting on you. I been trying to talk to you for a few weeks now.

But you ignored me so we don't have anything anymore. Kill each other when I leave." I walked away from them going upstairs. Kori and Ashley saw the whole thing and followed me.

I hugged and kissed my girl's goodbye. I told Ashley to tell Ty I am sorry about the drama. She waved me off and said it's fine. Getting into my truck I heard my phone go off. I took it out my purse and saw it was a text from Terrance.

Terrance: Say what you wanna say. I am not about to let another nigga have you. If I gotta drop bodies then so fuckin' be it!

I shook my head and deleted the text. I was so tired of my men problems. After today I am never seeing Terrance again. Good-bye!

*A month later**

Today was another shipment day at my store. Of course, that was when my lovely best friend Ashley show's up and offers to help us. This bitch thinks she is slick, she loves being the first to get her hands on our shipment before the public.

"So, have you and Ty been good?" I asked Ashley while she opened one of the shipment boxes.

"Girl yes, we went to dinner last night. I was so happy we both lived in Georgia, speaking of Terrance. Have you heard from him." She smirked. I looked at her and shook my head laughing.

Me and Terrance had not spoken in two months and I was going crazy. I missed his handsome chocolate face. I missed his voice and his aggressiveness. I miss watching movies and eating junk food with him. I was myself every time I was with him. I had not fucked Derrick since that night. I only played with my toys thinking of Terrance. That shit was getting old quick. Ya feel me!

"Bitch don't be slick! We had to stop doing what we were doing. I am still married and still love my husband. And what about Jaxon? I have to think about her and having a family is best," I told her while dressing our mannequins up in some of our hot new pieces.

"British I hear you and you know I am rockin' with whatever decision you make. The only thing is I just think you are holding your marriage up alone. I want to see you happy and at peace rather it's alone or with someone." Ashley had a serious expression on her face. I felt myself fighting back tears.

"I know boo. I am trying it's just I am so confused on what to do. I do miss Terrance like fucking crazy." I admitted.

"Well he has been asking about you all the damn time. His ass tries to play it cool and casually mentions your name. He misses you girl, I think you gave him a Jones." She started laughing while trying on shoes.
"Bitch that is not helping us by trying on the damn shoes." I teased her.

"I am coming from a consumer's point of view bitch." I just shook my head at her.

"Derrick has been trying his hardest to get back right with me. I really just want him to step back. Me and Jaxon are settled in the condo and I am loving it." I looked at her and she was smiling big as hell.

"Oh my gosh bitch I am so proud of you. Even if you do not divorce him I am just happy you are doing this fucking step. B Derrick has been a class-A dick to you and he needs the game switched up on his ass. You know me and Kori got you." She hugged me. I loved both of my babies.

"What about you, why are you giving Ty a hard time?" I had to get serious with my her for a minute because I had a feeling Ty was perfect for her and Aron but she was scared to take that chance.

"I don't know, I think he feels he is ready for me and Aron to be in his life but that's now. What about in a few more months? What about when Aron becomes sick from a cold and he keeps us up late? Or when Aron starts potty training and he has accidents around the house? Parenting is not all cute and fun. He thinks this is what he wants now. He can go home whenever he wants." I can look at my girl and tell that she does not mean none of the shit she just said.

"Ashley, Ty is not Alan. Neither was Chris or Josh. You can't keep doing this boo, Ty is the real deal. I know I am the last person who should be given you man advice but I have to tell you how I feel. Even you do not believe the shit you just said to me, give him a try boo. He has more than proved himself. You guys have been seeing each other for months now. He even popped up on yo' ass when you went on a date. You are going to have to take this chance sooner or later whenever you do want to start dating. The same way you tell me Kori and you will always be here for me it is the same for you boo, we got you and Aron." She started getting emotional so I hugged her.

"Gone and take the shoes on the house this time." I knew that would cheer her up.

"Thank you Brit. Love you girl and thank you for everything." We started putting up all of the shipment which did not take long at all since it was not very busy.

"Do you feel like coming to my shop with me? Scrooge called and said there is a customer who is requesting me to cut his hair. He said he told the guy he was trained by me but he did not want to hear it." She told me while placing her cellphone back in her purse.

"Well take it as a compliment that he wants the baddest barber to hook his shit up," I told him smiling. Ashley was the shit and she needed to give herself more credit.

"I guess you are right bitch," she said as we walked out the store. My team knew how to count the drawers and lock up. I come in every morning and check anyways.

**

I loved coming to Ashley's shop because it reminded me of how hard my girl worked to get where she is at. Her business partner Scrooge she met while in Barber school was on the same dream she was on and they clicked off back.

His skills were not on her level but he was just as good and so were her other barbers she hired. Ashley's shop was like a sports bar but for getting your haircut. She had pool tables, flat screen TVs and a bar. We walked in and her receptionists was making an appointment with a customer on the phone.

"Ashley I am so happy you are here, this dude was trippin'. He says he is not leaving until you come and hook him up. he is fine as hell but I think he is lowkey obsessed with you." We both looked at her like she was crazy because she actually had some fear in her eyes.

"Ok Lilly thank you. I will handle it from here." We both walked around to Ashley station and sitting in her chair looking handsome was Ty crazy ass on his phone. When he saw Ashley, he smiled showing his white straight teeth. I could not help but laugh and so did Ashley.

"Why the fuck are you scaring my staff? Are you crazy?" she jokingly said to him standing in front of him with her hands folded.

"Look I told them I wanted the sexiest, talented owner to cut my shit. They were trying to tell me to come back. I had to show my ass a little but don't trip I will tip all your staff before I dip. Come here baby girl can I get some love?" he embraced her and I could not help but smile hard because they were so cute together.

"What's up British. You know you got my big brother's head fucked up right?" I rolled my eyes at his comment.

"Hey Ty." That was all I could say. The mention of his brother gave me butterflies in my stomach and I did not need that shit right now.

"Come on so I can cut your hair and get you out my shop. I am supposed to be off today," she said to him while getting her clippers out.

I watched them flirt and crack jokes while she cut his hair. I could look at my best friend face and tell she was so smitten with Ty. I loved every minute of it. While they were talking and making plans for this weekend my phone started vibrating. I opened it and saw a text from Derrick.

Derrick: Baby I picked up Jaxon for you and we are at the house. Can we talk please???

Me: Yes give me a minute.

"Ashley, I am about to head home and I will call you and Kori later on three-way. Ty take care of my girl and my nephew or I will cut your ass." I stood up and hugged Ashley then hugged Ty.

"I got baby girl and my Jr. You have my word on that. They good, get shit together with my brother and drop that husband before he drops him for you." I had to laugh and shake my head at his comment. I low key was turned on thinking about his brother coming to stake claim on me.

Pulling in our drive way I looked at our beautiful home. I remembered Derrick being so happy when we moved in and started living our lives. Now I did not even want this house because it held more bad memories then good. Walking in I saw Jaxon chubby self in her play pin kicking and giggling at her toys.

"Hey fat mama, come here mommy missed you." I picked her up and kissed all on her chubby cheeks. Jaxon was not even one yet and already had a head full of curly black hair and curly baby hair all around her head and neck. My baby was a chocolate baby doll and I was obsessed with her.

"Hey B. I brought you some lunch if you have not eaten yet." Derrick stood there looking good with his work clothes on. He wore navy blue slacks and a light blue button up shirt.
"Thank you Derrick. Why did you pick her up from my parent's house?" I was a little annoyed because he always did this. When I do not move the pace, he wants me to move he will step in and make himself fit back into our lives.

"I just wanted you to be able to come straight home from work. She is falling asleep in your arms; can you lay her down and we talk." I nodded my head yes. I kissed Jaxon and laid her down.

"What's up Derrick," I said to him while sitting on my kitchen stool.

"British I cannot live like this. You are all I knew for seven years. Now you up and left and took Jaxon with you. I'm in our home alone and feeling empty. I need and want my wife by my side and my daughter. I know you are not the type of woman to keep me away from my child. I want to live in the same house as my daughter and my wife." He looked at me with sincerity and remorse. I felt myself breaking down looking at him and seeing how miserable he looks. I snapped out of it quickly. I had seen this look before and I wanted no part of it.

"Derrick I am happy with my decision. All I ask is that you respect it. Focus on being a father and a good man. Get close to our baby girl and stop making excuses. You can build a relationship with her. Just because she is a girl done not mean she doesn't need her father.

"British will you be my date for the grand-opening tomorrow night? The club I built is ready and having a huge event. I need my wife on my arm. After that whatever decision you make I promise to respect it." He grabbed my hand and kissed the back of it.

"Ok, I can do that. But Derrick my mind is made up." He held his hands up and was smiling.

"I just want to take you to the grand-opening. Have a good time out with you." I agreed to his date. I ate my lunch then me and British headed to our new home. Derrick was feeling some type of way about us leaving. He had no choice in the matter. Nothing was making me change my mind on moving out. I was happy, for the most part.

Terrance "Terror"

"Where the fuck that fool at!" Me and my brother walked through Sleez apartment but he was not there. This bitch ass niggas death was long over-due. I felt like he kept slipping through my fingers. My crew did what I instructed and killed anybody who mentioned his name. My clean-up crew was making bank off of us.

"Calm down bro. We will locate his ass. It's not like we don't know all his business. We know his family and all his properties he owns. That nigga will resurface." Ty told me while I was kicking shit over in Sleez apartment.

"You right bro but this shit is stressin' me. Bodies building up and still no sign of this fuckin' crackhead." I tipped his whole refrigerator over. I was pissed the fuck off.

"Nigga calm yo' King Kong ass down. Gorilla ass nigga. Bro you know who the fuck we are! We will get his ass. We need to get ready for tonight. All of our crew knows Sleez and knows we are looking for him. Shit gone be smooth bro let's just get lit tonight," Ty said as we walked out Sleez apartment.

I did need to calm down. Truth be told it was not just this Sleez shit that was fucking with me. I was missing the fuck out of British. The shit was nutty as a mental patient. I missed her face, smile, touch and her voice.

I even missed her manly ass burps and sloppy eating. Every time I thought about calling her I pictured her fucking her husband. I never even met the lame ass nigga. But for some reason I just saw her sleeping with him. I had to calm down before I drove myself angry. Me and Ty stood in front of our trucks.

"You bringing Ashley to the grand-opening tonight?" I don't know why I asked that stupid ass question. I was just trying to see if British fine ass would be there.

"Yo' nigga this is a big night for us. Hell yeah I am having my woman on my arm. You need to stop playing and get British ass. That slip up she had with her husband was not shit. That nigga saw an opportunity and took it. You and I both no he ain't been dickin' her down. She was with you every day sometimes over-night. Get rid of yo' pride nigga." Ty always has to bring this shit up. Even though I knew deep down he was talkin' true shit. I was just trying my hardest to leave her alone.

"Naw nigga I'm good. British all married and shit. I fuckin' want that girl bad as hell and if her husband tries to stop me I will kill that nigga. After the kick back at yo' crib. I have not seen or talked to her. I think it's best we let shit die." My brother nodded in agreement.

"I hear the lies you spittin' nigga. I'm gone pretend I believe you and just agree." Ty pounded my fist and he hopped in his truck. I needed to head to pick up my cuff links for my suit. A few drinks and some bad bitches was just what I need.

*

"Damn nigga this shit is tight as fuck. I told yo' ass having pops handle this shit would work out." Ty told me as we entered our club.

I wanted us to check out spot out before the party. I could give a fuck how much people was looking forward to this grand-opening, if I was not feeling the atmosphere of the club then I was going to cancel that shit. Ty was right through; the spot was everything we wanted. Our color scheme was black and gold with wrap around booths and Victorian furniture.

Even our bathrooms were marble and glass like we wanted. Me and Ty took the elevator to the fourth floor where our offices were at. We both were pleased with the outcome. Ty's office was burnt orange and cream and my shit was red and black. We both had full bathrooms and two stripper poles in there as well.

"This shit is fire Ty, come on let's head out so we can get ready," I told him.

*

Pop a Perky just to start up (pop it, pop it pop it)

Two cups of purple just to warm up (two cups, drank)

I heard your bitch she got that water

(Splash, drip, drip, woo, splash)

Slippery, 'scuse me, please me (please)

Arm up, or believe me, believe me (believe me)

Get beat, cause I'm flexin' 'Rari's (skrt)

You can bet on me (skr, skr)

Migos song Slippery was booming from the DJ booth. It was a little after 10pm and our club was beginning to pack up with people. Me and my brother had our interview with the press outside on the red carpet when we cut the ribbon. Looking at Ty with Ashley on his arm was having me in my feelings.

Don't get me wrong I wasn't hating on my baby brother hell him and Ashley looked good together. I just wanted British on my arm like that. The shit pissed me off every day because she did not even attempt to reach out to me. I know the phone work she is the one with the situation, not me. We were sitting in our VIP section over-looking the entire club.

"Aye nigga this shit is going to bring us bank roll of profit." My brother yelled to me through the music. I was smoking a blunt and I dabbed him up in agreement.

"What's up mon!" We looked up and saw Ronny walk in our section in all white with Kori on his arm.

"What up nigga, when you touch down?" I asked after hugging him and Kori. Her and Ashley linked up and was hugging each other.

"We touched down this morning nigga," he said as we all took a seat.

"What you mean we?" Ashley said what we all were thinking.

"I sent for my boo to come see me for a few days ago," Ronny said with excitement in his voice then he kissed Kori. We all started laughing and me and Ty gave him some props.

We started partying our asses off. MY security guy was making sure nobody was stepping in our section. I noticed a baddie with an ass like a horse was trying to get in, needing some eye candy I allowed her yellow fine ass in. I'm usually a chocolate fan myself but she will do, while we were dancing and drinking I noticed the other VIP section across from us had the reserve sign up.

"Aye who else booked a section up here?" I asked my brother.
"That's for the architects who build this for us. Mama and pops met with them and was pleased with their work." I nodded my head and went back to my eye candy. I did not even know this bitch name and didn't care. She was going to keep me company at this party then suck the joy out my dick later.

"Oh shit. Nigga keep yo' cool and remember this is our spot," Ty said to me as he looked over my shoulder.

I turned to see what he was talking about and I saw British headed up to our section. She looked good as fuck in this grey dress with slits on both sides exposing the sides of her thick frame. There were slits in the front to showing a little cleavage, she looked so sexy. I could not help but notice we matched.

I was a rocking grey and burgundy three-piece Brioni Vanquish suit. The lame nigga who was holding her hand must have been her husband, British was so busy looking around she did not even notice us up here. I know damn well this is not the nigga that build our club. What the fuck!

"You good bro?" My brother asked me and before I could answer I saw another familiar face. My bitch ex Sheena, what the fuck was she doing here.

"What the fuck is Sheena doing here? I'm about to bounce that bitch." I finished the rest of my blunt. My eyes were stuck on British as they came closer. Then I noticed the nigga on Sheena's arm was the hoe ass muthafucka I beat up. I leaned in and caught Ronny and my brother up on what was going on in case some shit popped off. As mad as I should be I was excited to see British again.

"What's up fellas. I'm Derrick Noel of Noel and Knight Architect. I hope you are pleased with the outcome." We stood up so we can shake his hands. His punk ass boy kept his distance while Sheena eye fucked me. British looked at me like she wanted to run and hide, I could not help staring at her fine ass.

"Nice to meet you bruh. Yea we are pleased with the outcome. Actually, we are not all strangers. I whopped your boy ass for fucking my ex fiancée some time back." I looked at his boy in his eyes and he just shook his head. I smirked at his hoe ass. Derrick looked back at his boy then at me with raised eye brows.

"Umm how do you fellas know Kori and Ashley? It's a small world because these are my wife best friends." He grabbed British hand.

"Boo I am so sorry, come here. This is my wife British." She half smiled and spoke to us. I stepped in front of her and shook her hand.

"Nice to meet you British. You are very beautiful." I looked at her and her pretty brown ass blushed and looked away. Her husband arched his eye brow and looked at her then at me. I looked at him back just waiting for him to say some shit to me. *Yea nigga I am taking your wife and child from your hoe ass!*

"We all met in Jamaica and my brother's hit it off with Ashley and Kori. British was a bit reserved but she loosened up after a while." I kept my eyes on her then back at her lame ass humping partner. I can tell he was pissed off.

"Is that right? She is always quiet as hell when I am not around. You know how wives are. Well you would have." This bitch is trying to throw curves at me. I chuckled at his comment.

"I'm only familiar with the way *your* wife is." I winked at British. This nigga tried to step closer but Ronny and Ty jumped up.

"Come on y'all let's not do this in front of the ladies and it's bad for business on all of our parts," Ty said squeezing my shoulder. I was still locking eyes with British bitch. He nodded and they headed to their VIP section. Kori and Ashley hugged British and they set back down next to Ronny and Ty.

"You foolin' nigga, control yourself bro. If you want her you know how to get her but here is not the place," Ronny said while he poured me a shoot. I almost smoked that nigga when he called her baby, that's my fucking baby.

"Goodness I had never been so scared. Big brother I am rooting for you but if you make British scared of you then she will bag off," Kori said with Ashley agreeing.

"That's the last thing I'm trying to do. But I am coming for her so let her ass know that. Her and baby girl are mine." I took my shot and set back to chill out. My little baddie I had jumped right back on my dick.

She started rubbing on my shoulders while sitting on my lap. Shots increased and so did the blunts. I looked downstairs at the club and people were turning up. We had to have some of the baddest cage dancers in Georgia. The DJ slowed it down and played a few slow jams.

Baddie in my lap was grinding on my dick but my focus was on British thick ass. She kept looking my way as well. Sheena watched me like a hawk as well. She was giving me nasty ass looks because she knew I wanted British.

I missed the fuck out of my Yummy and I was done playing these games. I want her for the long run and I always get what the fuck I want. I noticed her husband kept touching her and the shit was pissing me the fuck off. I pulled my cellphone out and decided to text her.

Me: Take the elevator to the top floor and meet me in my office. It is a red door

Yummy-Yum: No! Stop texting me!

Me: I am asking you nicely. Don't make me snatch yo' ass up.

She read my text and ignored it. "Get the fuck up," I told baddie sitting on my lap. I stood up and adjusted my suit. When British saw me stand up and head her way her eyes grew big and she hurried up and texted me.

Yummy-Yum: OK Terrance damn!

I smirked when I read it and went to the elevators. On the way, I saw Sheena's nigga in the corner all on a bitch. I laughed and shook my head. Stupid bitch downgraded for real. I stepped onto the elevator and headed towards my office.

British

I do not believe this shit! How come every time me and my husband decide to have a date night some shit goes down?! I'm cursed, yea that has to be it. A bitch is cursed! I do not know why I thought tonight would go smoothly. I figured since me and Terrance reached an understanding about ending things we could behave civilized. How fucking wrong was I!

Out of all the clubs for Derrick to build it had to be the guy I had a rendezvous with. I can't front, Terrance was looking so damn good in his suit. That chocolate skin in burgundy and grey matching my dress was turning me on. I needed to thank his tailor for making that suit fit his muscular body.

I almost shit bricks when he stepped to Derrick and made those shady comments. Derrick is not a fighter or a street nigga. He's not a punk but he is not Terror. Then to put icing on the cake Eric girlfriend was Terrance ex fiancé. I knew I never liked that bitch.

Derrick use to always ask me to hang out with her. Me and my girls tried to take her shopping with us but we just did not click. Especially her and Ashley. That bitch thought I did not see the way she was looking at Terrance.

Sheena better stand her ass down. And the little yellow bitch he had sitting on his lap. Listen to me sounding jealous over someone who was not even my man. Now here I am in another jam, having to sneak away from my husband so I can go talk to Terrance.

"Umm Derrick I am about to go use the bathroom ok." I whispered in his ear and stood up.

"Ok boo I'll be here when you get back." He said as he finished his champagne.

I walked past the bathrooms and went to the elevator and took it to the top floor. Just like Terrance said his door was red with his name on it. I took a deep breath and opened the door. Terrance office was gorgeous but I noticed I could see the entire club so that means that can see me.

"Don't trip it's a one-way mirror. We can see them but they cannot see us." Terrance stood up from his chair and walked towards me. I could feel my breathing change. Damn I missed this man.

"Did you have fun in your dick measuring contest with Derrick?" There was humor in my voice but I was so serious.

"You think I give a fuck about your husband? I miss you Yummy." He was so close to me I could smell his delicious breath. He put his arm around my waist pulling me closer to me. I closed my eyes being that close to him.

"I can't stay away from you yum. I know shit ended bad between us and I'm to blame. I just lost my cool when you told me about fucking him. That shit fucked me up but you rightfully were not mines. I apologize for that. The shit at the kick back though I am not sorry for. I didn't even know you were going to be there. But I be damn if I watch a nigga on you. I'm still debating if I should Levi your husband or not.

When I saw him talking you I wanted to snap. I meant what I said about you being mines. This ain't no fuckin' game British. Your punk ass husband almost got handled tonight too. You and baby girl are saving his life right now. I miss the fuck outta you though baby." He pressed his lips against mines. I could not resist his soft ass lips.

Terrance kissed me like no man has ever kissed me before. I never would have thought I would crave another man besides Derrick. Terrance was all I thought about for weeks. No matter what I do I just can't shake his fine ass. Finally pushing away from our kiss, I had to come back to reality.

"Terrance, I did not plan on sleeping with Derrick I was sleep and he came in while I was having a dream. The shit sounds crazy but it's true. We have not had sex since and before that it was even longer. I do miss you I just think it's a lot going on right now and----

"Come to my house tonight Yum. I can feel and see that your body needs daddy. You been missing and thinkin' about me to I can see it in your eyes." I could not even say anything. He had me loss of words. As if on que the DJ played an old school jam from R. Kelly Your Body's Callin.

I hear you callin', "Here I come baby"
To save you, oh oh
Baby no more stallin'
These hands have been longing to touch you baby
And now that you've come around, to seein' it my way
You won't regret it baby, and you surely won't forget it baby
It's unbelievable how your body's calling for me
I can just hear it callin' callin' for me

This nigga was singing the lyrics in my ear sounding just like R. Kelly himself. Somebody come ring my panties out! All I could do was smirk and grip my bottom lip with my teeth. All the time me and Terrance have hung out he never mentioned he could sing. Come on British open your mouth and talk. There goes my words on the back of a milk carton again labeled "Missing".

"I will let you know ok. I need to get back before he starts looking for me." Terrance would not let go of my grip.

"I am going to text you my address. Have your sexy ass at my shit tonight. Ok?" I do not know why I agreed to this but I get lost like a little girl when I am with him. I feel so protected, sexy and wanted whenever Terrance was around me. He kissed me one more time before her let me go. Walking out of his office I rode the elevator back down when my phone went off. It was Terrance texting me his address.

"About time you came back boo. I thought I was going to have to come find you," Derrick said when I came back.

I noticed Sheena kept looking at me like she had a fucking problem. I ignored her ass though because these are not the type of problems she wants. Derrick kept squeezing my thigh and rubbing on my arm. I knew he was drunk and he would want to fuck after we leave here.

He was in for a rude awakening. Even if Terrance was not here I still did not plan on sleeping with Derrick tonight. It was getting close to midnight and I was having a good time. Me and my girls got on the dance floor to show off. Terrance texted my phone and told me to stop letting Derrick touch me. I told him to get the yellow bitch off his lap. How the fuck are we both acting jealous and we do not belong to each other.

I started getting tired so me and Derrick left along with Eric and Sheena. I am so happy we did not all ride together because that would have been a tension filled car ride.

"British thank you for being my date tonight. You were the finest woman in there." I blushed and looked out the window.

The ride to my condo was quiet. I felt bad because Terrance was the only thing on my mind. I was debating with myself if I should go to his house tonight. Part of me missed him. But the other part was telling me to stay away.

A very small tiny ass part. We pulled in my driveway and Derrick turned off the car. He just set there looking straight ahead. I looked at him with a confuse face because he looked like he was holding his breath.

"B I need to ask you something. Did you and that nigga who owns Kingdom fuck while you were in Jamaica?" He wouldn't even look at me. I set there in shock but I guess I shouldn't be because of their dick measuring contest they had.

"No Derrick, I did not fuck him in Jamaica." Technically I did not lie because we didn't have sex.

Terrance only tasted my pussy. Derrick looked at me for a moment. I knew he was looking for signs of deception. I guess he was satisfied because he smiled and got out the car. I opened my door and stepped out and Derrick stopped me. He leaned me against the car with his body weight on me.

"British I want to come in and make love to you. I miss my wife baby and I need to be with you." He tried to kiss me but I turned my head.

"Derrick I do miss you but--- My sentence was cut short when I saw a figure walking up my walk way.

"What the fuck are you doing here?!" Derrick roared at Niecy. I felt like I was dreaming because I just know this bitch was not at my condo.

"Doing what your bitch ass couldn't do." She looked at me and gave me a folder.

I opened it and almost dropped to the ground when I saw ultra sound pictures and a positive pregnancy test. She even had forms that showed proof of her doctor's visit. I looked at her big ass belly. I have no idea how I fucking missed it. I looked at Derrick with so much hatred and anger.

"Baby I can explain this shit--- I punched the fuck out of him making his nose bleed.

"B you broke my fucking nose! How are you going to listen to this bitch over me?" He yelled letting the blood drip down to his suit.

"I am a bitch now?! Well here take your punk ass money because this baby is coming." She threw a wad of cash is Derrick's face. I walked up to her and punched her in the face so hard she fell backwards on my lawn. I do not give a fuck about her being pregnant.

"The both of you can have each other. It is a never ending of heartbreak being with you and I can't take it no more." I took my ring off and threw it at him. I walked to my truck and pulled off. Leaving all drama with Derrick behind me.

*

I followed the directions from my GPS and it brought me to a beautiful gated brick mansion. My mouth hit the floor when I saw how long the driveway was. Terrance was getting more than just a few bank rolls. Between him and his brother their houses needed to be on MTV Cribs. I parked my car and slowly took my seat belt off. Me and Derrick lived in the suburbs around beautiful homes. But these homes looked like buildings. The front door opened and Terrance stood came out to meet me.

"Hey Yummy baby. I'm happy you decided to come." I loved when he called me Yummy. It just does something to me.

"Hey to you too. Thank you for inviting me." We hugged and walked in his house. The outside does not do the inside justice at all.

"How many bedrooms are in here?" I asked him while we walked passed the kitchen and into the living room.

"Eight bedrooms, nine bathrooms, a man cave, basketball court and pool and jacuzzi in the back." My eyes almost fell out my head. We both set down on his couch. It was so comfortable and big, the cushions felt like they were a pillow top.

"Your home is gorgeous Terrance." I looked his body over and my heart started beating fast. He had on some grey basketball shorts and a grey beater hugging his sexy body.

"Thank you. I have not been here long. After my break-up, I needed a new start." I nodded my head then I thought about the condo me and Jaxon would be moving into. A new start was going to be just what we needed.

"Get the fuck over here. You all the way over there and shit. I have not seen yo' ass in a while. I have not touched you longer than that." He yanked me over up under him. I was turned on by how he handled me. Terrance made me so nervous my palms became warm.

"You invited me just in time. The night I had really made me put things in prospective." I was tracing his arm that was around my waist.

"If it was up to me this would be you and Jaxon's new home. But that will happen in due time. So, tell me what happened tonight." I really did not want to talk about it I just wanted to get lost in Terrance but I knew he would not let it go.

"I found out Derrick knocked up his side bitch. Then he gave her some money to get rid of it. I am so tired of that man breaking my heart. But like you said he did what I allowed." I did not want to cry but I could not help it. The tears came falling. He wiped my tears and held me tighter.

"British I do not want to complicate things for you. I never want you to leave one situation and jump into something else. But I can't hide how I feel about you. You had me at Ronny's beach party. We both wasted time with the wrong people. You got the shit right this time fucking with me. And I know for a fact you can be everything a nigga like me needs." I rubbed the side of his face were his soft beard covered it.

"Make love to me tonight Terrance, please bae." Those words just fell out my mouth but I meant every word of it.

"Mean that shit you speak girl because once I put this dick in that pussy it's mines. There is no going back to lame ass. It's me, you and Jaxon. I ain't the type of nigga to take a child away from its parents but you and baby girl will be here with me. Y'all will not be that nigga family anymore. You ready for that?" He looked at me with intensity.

I thought about what he said and for some reason I was ready for all Terrance had to offer. I was confused at first. But the one thing I was always for sure about was me and Derrick had been broken for a while now. The event tonight sealed the deal. I cannot deal with my husband having a baby outside of our marriage.

"Yes, I am ready for that. Just stay honest and communicate with me always baby." He pulled me up on his lap and kissed me deep and hard. I was knocked off my fucking feet with this kiss. He wrapped my legs around his waist and stood up with me straddling him.

We went upstairs in his huge master bedroom. His bed was so damn big a family of four could fit in it. Terrance helped me out my dress and gave me one of his beaters for me to sleep in. I went and took a quick shower and put it on.

My hair was wet so I let it hang and air dry since I knew he didn't have a dryer. I walked out and he was in the bed looking so good and chocolate. I pulled the covers back and slid in. His bed was so comfortable I could crawl in and never get out.

He had his TV on but it was on the Pandora app on Brian McKnight radio station. Terrance pulled me over to him.

"You gone stop that shit Yummy. Anytime we are in the same room you need to be on me. I don't give a fuck who we are around. I like my woman all on me because I will be all on you. You been dealing with that lame ass nigga so I am going to teach you how to be my woman." We started making out like teens and I was loving every second of it.

Terrance touch was so soft yet strong in the same sense. He moved his hands all over my thick body and through my hair. He knew when to add tongue and how to bite on my lip just the right way. My body felt like an inferno and I craved more. The music went off and the next song played Joe: All The Things Your Man Won't Do came on. Terrance started singing again in my ear making a river form between my legs. This man voice was so amazing I could listen to him sing all day.

Tell me what kind of man

Would treat his woman so cold

Treat you like you're nothin'

When you're worth more than gold

Girl, to me you're like a diamond

I love the way you shine

A hundred million dollar treasure

I'll give the world to make you mine

"How come I am just finding out about your beautiful voice? That is an easy panty dropper," I said to him while messing with his beard. I loved his beard.

"Baby, I do not need to sing to get a bitch out her panties. And I do not tell anybody I can sing because that is all they will want me to do. I'm a thug girl." He laughed showing them straight white teeth making me laugh in the process. We stared at each other for a moment. I saw so much truth and love in his eyes. I knew then I made the right decision.

"I'm falling for you Terrance, just don't hurt me." My voice cracked and he kissed me again.

"I got you British I put that shit on life. I'm ready to meet baby girl to. I am going to win her over like I won her mama over. I'm going to own both of y'all hearts." His comment made me smile hard as hell. I climbed on top of him and started kissing him. I know he loves skin on skin so I pulled his beater over my head so my naked body was on him. Terrance had already shown me his head game so I figured why not return the favor.

I started kissing his neck marking his neck with hickeys then down to his sexy chest and hard abs. He kept his eyes on me biting his lip the whole time. By the time I got between his legs Terrance dick as peeking out his boxers. I pulled it out and tried to hide my surprise when I saw his long, thick dick.

The shit had to be eleven inches. It was so pretty and chocolate and smooth. I took the tip of it in my mouth and licked it. My mouth was already wet when I saw his dick in my face. I took more of him in my mouth and to my surprise I did not gag. I started to get more comfortable and nasty with it. I had his whole dick down my throat and started hummin' on it. My mouth was working up so much saliva as I bobbed my head up and down I had my right hand stroking him.

"Shit! Daddy gone cum in yo' mouth if you keep this shit up." He was turning me on with his moans and the way he was gripping my hair.

I started to massage his balls while sucking faster and tighten my jaws. In no time Terrance came all in my mouth. It slid right down my throat. Pleasing him made my pussy so wet. I never felt this way with Derrick because I always would think of him with other women.

"Fuck girl! Yea you definitely not going anywhere with skills like that." He turned me over and climbed on top of me.

We started tongue kissing again and I was in heaven. I could not help but moan while we kiss. I never desired a man as much as I desired Terrance. He set up and bent my legs all the way back. Shit I did not know I was this flexible but I was comfortable as hell.

Between my legs were so wet I am sure he thought I came already. He rubbed his dick on my clit making me close my eyes and bite my lip. Then he slowly slid a few inches of him in me. I thought I was going to die. It was hurting because he was so thick and I was tight.

"Let me in Yummy baby, let daddy in yo' sweet honey pot." He leaned forward with my legs still bent back and tongued me down. While we were kissing he slid all eleven inches in and I went from pain to pleasure. He was stroking so good in and out of me I thought I was going to lose my mind. Terrance started sucking and lightly biting my nipples making me get wetter.

"Fuck you tight as shit girl. You are mines now British and I am never letting you go. I'm going to treat you right bae I promise you. Fuck you feel good." He started beating my shit up faster building my orgasm up.

"Shiittt Terrance bae! Ughhhh, don't stop fucking me!" He sat up without missing a stroke.

"Fuck! Fuck! British, damn you feel so good." He smirked at me and started sucking on my toes while he was fucking the shit out of me. I came so hard I shed a few tears.

"Arghhhh baeeeee I'm cumminnn" I creamed all on his dick and he was loving it.

"This yo' dick Yummy, come all on it." He let my legs down and tongued me down. Then he licked my tears and was kissing all on my face.

"I love you Terrance." I don't know if I was caught up in the moment or what but it was how I felt. He smiled and moved hair out my face.

"I love you to British. Tell me you here for good." He laid down and pulled me on top. I kissed him hard making his dick rise again.

"I am here for good bae." I kissed him again and slid down on his dick making both of us moan in pleasure. We fucked and sucked for the rest of the night until sunrise when we both passed out wrapped in each other's arms.

Sheena

What the fuck is really going on!? I was not supposed to get a chapter but I cannot keep quiet any longer. What the fuck are the odds I would run into my fine ass ex fiancé?

I know you may not like me but you only know one side of the story. I have always loved thugs, being a good girl from a Catholic school. I was very sheltered so naturally the good girl falls for a bad boy. I have had my share of thug love but Terrance is the fucking truth. He is more than a boss, he is like a fucking mogul or some shit.

Not only is he fine but he has a huge dick and killer head game. He treated me so good when we were together. I was spoiled rotten; the only thing is Terrance is all about his business. Sometimes he would stay gone for days yes! He would check in and leave me with stacks and access to all his trucks and cars. I got bored and all my friends had more than one nigga so I played the field.

When I met Eric at the strip club, I was not drawn to him. I wanted Derrick but he had a stripper bitch on his lap so I went for Eric. I never wanted to get knocked up by his ass. He started treating me like his woman within a few days. He even wanted me to hang with his best friend's wife British.

At first, I was all for it but once I linked up with her and her girls I saw we did not have shit in common. I love to turn up and have fun. They liked spa days and jazz lounges and shit. Kori gave me the hardest time with her funky ass attitude. Ashley really did not say much to me.

British acted like I put a nasty taste in her mouth from the beginning. We went shopping one time and I never wanted to hang out with her or her stuck up ass friends again. We would see each other here and there but we spoke and kept it moving.

I was always up front with Eric about Terrance and at first he was cool with it. Then I got pregnant and he started telling me he knew the baby was his. When he popped up to my job that day we were arguing because I wanted him to disappear. I would have gladly let Terrance raise the baby as his. But Terrance popped up with flowers and shit and caught me arguing with Eric.

Being dramatic Eric spilled the beans about me and him and Terrance beat his ass. I knew Terrance would be mad but I did not think he would drop my ass hard on my head. When the DNA came back with Terrance not the father I broke down. I wanted to be Terrance wife and have his babies. Terrance was protection not just financially but security. Being his woman gained you a lot of respect and haters from the bitches. Speaking of bitches, you should have seen the way Terrance eye fucked British chunky ass.

I knew they hooked up in Jamaica because of the way he threw shade to Derrick. I must admit Derrick held his own but he was no match to Terrance. Then when we went to our section he stared at her the whole time. They started texting and shit and then both disappeared.

British stupid ass husband was too busy turning up to notice. Not my ass, I paid attention to them the whole night. See I could deal with him just fucking her. But the look in both of their eyes was more than physical. For me and him to have been engaged and had a life together he did not acknowledge me once.

How the fuck do you turn love off as strong as ours was. I paid no attention to the bitch Terrance had sitting on his lap. I knew she was just eye candy. But this hoe British was going to be a problem. I felt bad for Derrick because he had already lost his wife and didn't even know it. Then all night Eric flirted with bitches but did not think I knew.

We get home and he tells me he needs to go back up to his job to finish some paper work for the club. I am far from fucking stupid, I knew he met a thot at Kingdom. Him and Derrick were born sluts and cheated all the time.

Even after I had this fools baby he still cheated. I know you probably thinking the nerve of me to feel a way about Eric infidelity when I played Terrance. But that has nothing to do with the price of tea in China. I didn't give a fuck though because I was working towards being Mrs. King. I will beat the brakes off British and her mutts if they stand in my way. Terrance still loved me and this pussy. He just needs reminding and I was going to refresh his memory.

Derrick

"Ughhh shit bitch swallow all my kids!" I was shoving my dick down this bitch throat. Her mascara was running from her gagging on my shit. I felt like I released all my tension down her throat.

"Damn Derrick it feels like you shut shot buckets down my throat." Treasure grabbed a napkin out my glove compartment. I was trying to catch my breath for that good as nut. I watched her clean my dick off.

"Are you coming in and staying?" Treasure looked at me and asked. She put that soft ass sexy voice on. I had never spent the night with Treasure before. I just always felt British was the only woman I wanted to wake up to.

"Not tonight. But I would like to take you to breakfast and spend the day with you. If your free." I know she was. Even if Treasure was not free she would have still said yes. This woman would do any and everything I asked of her.

"Ok. I can't wait Derrick. No matter how early you wake up just call me and I will let you in." She kissed me a few times on the lips. I watched her thick ass get out my car and walk up to her door. I waited until she got in and turned her lights on. Pulling off I headed towards the freeway.

The shit that happen after the grand-opening pulled me in a deeper hole. British had not reached out to me at all. I have not heard from Niecy stupid ass either. I wanted to fuck her up when she popped up at British condo. This bitch did all that yappin' about her having this baby on her own. But steady keep fucking up my damn life.

My worst fear was British finding out another woman was carrying my child. My wife looked at me with anger and hatred and that shit scared me. Usually British would look hurt and heartbroken. But this look was like of disgust. When she left I wanted to follow her.

If I was at her house where the fuck was she going? I knew Kori and Ashley were with their niggas for the night. Then I thought back to Terrance King the nigga who owns Kingdom. Something about him and my wife rubbed me the wrong way. I asked in the car if she fucked him and she said no. I know when my wife lies. She will rub the back of her neck and fuck with her hair. British didn't do any of that so I believed her.

But the way he stared at her had me wanting to beat his ass. Nobody was going to have British that was over my dead body. I thought in a few days British would have cooled down. But now it's been two weeks and still no word. I was getting impatient and annoyed. After that I felt like fuck it! My wife dipped on me anyways so I might as well get my nut off. I barley went home anymore.

It was lonely being in that house without her and my daughter. My ass been staying in a hotel suite. Now I am sitting in my room smoking and taking some shots. I went to my Facebook and found the person page who I was looking for. I messaged them and asked them to meet me at noon tomorrow at an outdoor café.

I did not even know if they would respond but to my surprise they did. We conformed our meeting. Finishing off my bottle and blunt I passed out fully dressed on the bed.

It was a little after noon and I was waiting for my accomplice to meet me. I hope she did not stand me up.

"Sorry I am late I had to drop my son off at my parent's house and they live in the opposite way," Sheena said as she took a seat across from me.

"It's cool just happy you showed up," I told her while taking a sip of my coffee.

"So, let's cut to the chase, you want to fuck or something?" she asked me almost making me choke on my drink. What the fuck is wrong with this bitch.

"What the hell are you talking about? Hell no I don't want to fuck you! You're my best friend bitch. What the fuck do you think this is?!" I looked at her with my nose turned up. I mean do not get me wrong Sheena is fine in a plastic way but she is Eric's baby mama.

"Oh, my bad. So why did you call me here?" she asked squeezing lemon in her water.

"I need some information on your ex Terrance King. My wife has been gone for almost two weeks now and I have a feeling she is with him." My heart broke every time I thought of British being with another man. Sheena started laughing.

"You are dumber than I thought. I have to give you some props though. I did not think you knew about the two of them. They eye fucked each other so hard at the grand-opening all night. Stevie Wonder could have saw something was going on. Look you are not going to be able to take down a huge tycoon like Terrance King. He has connections everywhere in every state. His parents are famous judges. Him, his brother and best friend have protection a mile long." She started back laughing pissing me off even more.

"Don't give me that shit! Anybody can be brought down to their knees. Look, just tell me where he lives or give me his number so I can go get my wife."

"I can't help you with that. When we broke up he moved and changed his number. Terrance and Ty are not they type of people you can just walk up to. They have killers everywhere and they will make you disappear and make it look like you moved or some shit."

"Well what the fuck does he do, I know it is not just run a club." I asked her getting annoyed.

"They sell drugs and weapons. When I say weapons, I mean shit that is not even on the black market. Mobs from all over the world are the King's clients and they protect them as well. You're out of your league." She grabbed one of the bagels from the basket that was at our table.

"I am never out of my league, he has money and so do I. Now you said they sell drugs and weapons, right? That along is serious jail time. Do they have a warehouse or something? I know you know more then you are telling me." I was getting impatient with her ass.

"Terrance never mixed me in his business. He made the money and I spent it. If you want your wife back you need to get to her not try and take Terrance down. When they fu—

"MY WIFE DID NOT FUCK HIM!" I said that shit louder then I meant to making people look our way. Sheena scoffed at me.

"Did she tell you that? And you believed her?! Look I can tell you are one of them niggas who does not like to face the truth if it will hurt you. I'm here to tell you if they did not have sex in Jamaica then they have had sex by now. Stop being naive it is unattractive for somebody so fine." She looked at me and licked her lips. Damn this bitch really is not shit.

I was done talking to her helpless ass. I stood up and put a hundred-dollar bill on the table and walked off. Talking to

Sheena's ass was useless and had me in my feelings. I do not care what anybody says, I know when British is lying and when I asked her if she fucked dude in Jamaica and she said I believed her.

Hoping in my Bentley I drove downtown to Atlanta police department. I was hoping to have more information but I figured I had enough to at least get an investigation started on Terrance King.

*

I arrived at the police department with enthusiasm in me. The detective I talked to told me to come in and have a sit down with him. I watched police escort some guys in with handcuffs on them, I stepped up to the front desk and waited for someone to assist me.

"Hello, welcome to Atlanta Police Department. Are you here to file a complaint?" The office asked me while eating a donut. I chuckled to myself.

"I'm here to see Detective Smith. I'm Derrick Noel me and him spoke this afternoon and he told me to come in." The officer went to the back and talked to a fat black guy. He put me in the mind set of Carl Winslow from the sitcom Family Matters.

"You can come on back his door is the first is straight ahead." I walked back there and opened the door. Anticipation went through my body.

"How are you doing Mr. Noel. I am Detective Smith, please have a seat." I set down in the chairs that were in front of his desk. He took a seat at his desk.

"Now the information you told me on the phone seemed a little far fetch. You see the police cannot operate without evidence, you know proof. So far you have the word of a bitter ex fiancé and that is all. You have no pictures, phone conversations, locations where you believe all this illegal activity is happening is taking place. Do you see why I cannot help you any further?" I nodded my head yes. Sheena comment she made about me being out of my league came to my mind making me angry. This nigga was not God.

"Well can you at least keep this on file and when I come back with some evidence a case can start building on them. You do know his parents are famous judges? Surely if this is linked to the press it will make them look bad."

"Mr. Noel the police department has an image to uphold. You want us to bring this to the media WITHOUT evidence? That is not how this works. I tell you what, keep take my card. When you have a lead or something comes up give me a call." I stood up and took my defeat. We shook hands and I left out his office. I felt like I wasted my time. I was going to get this nigga another way.

*

I pulled my car in the driveway and shut off my engine. I knew I could not keep avoiding my problems. Since British went ghost on me so I reached out to Niecy's ass. If she was not talking about anything I wanted to hear then I was leaving. I walked up to her door and knocked. She opened it with an attitude.

"Fix your fucking face girl," I told her as I walked in and leaned against the wall. She closed the door and stood in front of it with her hands on her hips rolling her eyes.

"I'm here so talk," I told her.

"I have been trying to talk to you for the longest and now you come. You have been treating me like shit! You let your wife put your hands on me when you know I am pregnant. Then you gave me money for me to kill OUR child!" Niecy started yelling and tears fell from her eyes. I was not a harsh nigga so I walked up to her and hugged her.

"Niecy, you showed up on my door step and you thought my wife was going to take that shit? Now I am sorry you got hurt but you cannot keep this baby. Do you really want to bring a child into all this drama?" She snatched away from me.

"Do not act like you are thinking of my wellbeing. You are only concerned about yourself and your precious wife. Well what about me? Derrick I am not getting rid of this baby. If I must do this by myself then so be it. You are a coward. You can stick and play all day until you satisfied. But when the shit catches up to you the first thing you try to do is throw your money around. Well this is something that is out of your control." She folded her arms and stared at me. I looked at her and for the first time I did not blame anybody but myself. Niecy was right, I needed to be a man about this.

"I apologize Niecy. If you want to keep this baby then who the fuck am I to tell you stop you? Just keep you and that mistake away from me and mines." I walked out of her apartment and slammed the door. Fuck that nobody was going to make me do anything I did not want to do. I left out of Niecy apartment with the intentions of closing that door. I was never fucking with her again. I needed to relieve some stress so I headed to my favorite spot...The Strip Club.

Terrance "Terror"

I pulled up to my brother Ty's house. I needed to get at him about some shit that was told to me. I was feeling good today as I have been feeling every day since British decided to become my woman. Every day I wanted to prove to her she made the right choice.

I knew her husband would not bow down without a fight. But if he thought he was getting her back he had another thing coming. Speaking of that lame ass nigga that's what I had to holla at Ty about.

"What up bro." I dabbed my baby brother up as I stepped in his living room. I looked around and saw toys everywhere. I had to chuckle to myself because I never would have thought Ty would settle down let alone with a chick who had a child.

"What's good man. Damn what Ashley cook? The shit smell good as hell," I said to him taking a seat on his couch.

"She made some ribs, greens, macaroni and cheese and some corn bread. Her ass be throwing down. It's a lot left if you want some." I declined because I know Yummy already cooked at the house. Ashley came down with her son on her hip.

"Hey big bro." she smiled and said to me.

"Hey baby sis. How are you and my nephew doing?" I asked her as we hugged and I dabbed little Aron up making him laugh.

"Good. I'm about to meet up with your girl now." Ashley said picking up Aron's Minion bookbag up and placing it on her shoulder.

"Where y'all off to?" Ty came from the kitchen with two beers.
"I'm meeting up with Kori and British to get our nails done. Then we are hittin' the mall since we are all off today." Ty looked at her like she was crazy.

"Why does he have to go with you to do all that girly shit? Leave my son here with me and we can find something to do." He took Aron out of Ashley's arms and grabbed his bookbag off her shoulder.

"I'm so used to taking him. You sure you will be alright with him all day?"

"Girl get out of here, we straight." Ty walked Ashley to the door. He kissed and hugged her and she kissed Aron and left. Ty put Aron on the floor and he started playing with his toys. I was in shock at how grown up my brother was acting.

"Damn nigga you really love her and Aron uh?" I asked taking a swig of my beer.

"Yea nigga that's my family right there. Ashley don't know it but she gone be Mrs. King and give me a princess." I nodded my head. I could not even begin to think he was moving too fast because I felt the same way about British and Jaxon.

"Look nigga let me tell you what's been happening. You know Demone Smith, one of the detectives on our payroll? Ty nodded his head.

"Well he hit me up yesterday and said a Derrick Noel came to the station. The nigga was making assumptions about me doing illegal activity. He said Derrick got his information from my ex fiancé. This hoe ass nigga wanted to take the shit to the media and expose our parents and everything. Smith warned us to watch our backs and make sure we are not being followed. And to keep an eye out for any suspicious activity. He said Derrick seemed like he was on a mission." My brother had the same look on his face as I had when I first found out. Murder, we both hate rats.

"Let's handle this nigga bro." He went to Aron and gave him a cookie.

"Now you know nothing would give me pleasure. But I have to think about Jaxon and British. My bae will bounce on me if she even thinks I killed him. We promised each other no secrets and lies. Derrick ain't shit to worry about. He thinks because he got a little change he can hang with us. But I can handle his ass." I already knew what I was going to do once I left my brother's house.

"I'm about to be out bro." I stood up and dabbed my nephew up and then Ty.

"A'ight bro. If you need me hit me up. I'm about to take little man to Chuckie Cheese." I smiled because I was happy for my brother.
Leaving Ty's house, I called a few of our people and got a location on Derrick. He was staying a hotel downtown. It was time for me and him to chop it up man to man.

I walked into the lobby and up to the front desk. I used to fuck the manager here so all I had to do was smile at her ass and she had the room key ready for me. Once Liz gave me the key and told me the floor I headed to the elevators and took it to the fifth floor. Liz told me he had been staying here for some weeks now. Sometimes he would have a bitch with him or he would be alone. I did not care if he had a bitch with him or not.

As far as I was concerned I would body that bitch to if she thought for a second she was about to flap her gums.

I got to his door and knocked. I wanted to see if he would open the door. He yelled go away from the other side so I used the room key to let myself in. His room smelled like ass and corn chips. He had bottles and takeout bags all over the kitchen. I walked in the sitting room and his bitch ass was laid on the couch. He seemed to be alone. Just in case I went to the bedroom and to the bathroom to check and found nobody. I went back to the den and kicked the edge of the couch making him look up.

"What the fuck!" He jumped up with anger in his face. I smirked.

"Nigga did you think you were never going to see me? You been trying to fuck with me and cause problems and for what reason? Because you could not keep your wife? Look I will cut to the chase. That pussy is no longer yours my nigga. No matter y'all history or the quantity of time you knew her, British is mines now. Don't die over some shit that you can't control. I got her pussy juice all in my beard and she got my kids all down her throat. Bow out with some dignity." I kept my eyes on him and talked through gritted teeth.

He had me so vexed I was ready to explode on his ass. Not only was he a rat but I knew he still wanted British and that did not sit well with me.

"Once she knows who you really are she will bounce. British is not a girl who dates thugs. I will not have to come get her; she will run back to me." He smiled like that shit was funny.

My anger grew like wildfire. Before I knew it, I hit his ass in his face. He got a hit in on me making my lip bleed. I hit him again in his face. Then a hit to his ribs making him fall on the couch. I grabbed my strap from my waist and put it in his bloody mouth. I felt myself blackout from being so angry.

"Listen to me bitch, there ain't shit for British to find out because unlike you I do not keep shit from her. You never been a man only a little boy playin' dress up. You are also a rat. Learn your enemies' nigga. I got this fucking state in the back of my pocket. You think going to the police and trying to tell them shit about me and mines is going to do shit?! Recognize when you have lost, the only reason you are not meeting our creator today is because of your daughter. You ain't even taking the time out to inquire about her. You too busy trying to fuck with me and getting your dick wet. Don't trip though I got her and her mama and as far as I am concerned you can vanish. But if I find out again you trying to fuck with me or British I will kill your ass." I pulled my gun out his mouth and kicked him in the face before I walked out the room."

As I rode down the highway in my truck part of me knew this would not be the end of Derrick bitch ass. But I would have my people watch him. I would be waiting for his ass with a closed fist and a bullet with his name on it. Pulling in my huge garage I parked my truck next to my other seven cars and trucks and hopped out.

I opened the door that led to my man cave and took my shoes off. The smell of fried chicken hit my nose and I smiled. British kept a nigga full of good food. I walked to my kitchen to see Jaxon sitting in her high chair and British covering up the food. I went to Jaxon first and kissed her cheeks making her giggle and slob everywhere. This little girl won me over when I first saw her at British parents' house.

She took to me easily. I always believed kids could see if a person was good or bad. The fact that she smiled and let me hold her warmed my heart. After giving Jaxon some love I turned my attention to British. She looked so fucking good in her cut-up shorts and tank top. Her thick ass body made my shit stiff. I walked up to her and put my arms around her waist and kissed her neck, she smelled so good.

"What's up Yummy bae I missed yo' ass. What you in her cooking?" She smiled and blushed.

"Hey bae, I missed you to. I'm cooking some fried chicken, mash potatoes, corn and biscuits." She turned to face me and kissed me on the lips. I loved that shit because no matter how long we would be apart for the day. Whenever we link back up she always showed a nigga love and affection. I washed my hands using that fruity soap British put in the kitchen. I would have beat Sheena's ass if she did that shit when we were together. But my Yummy had a nigga gone.

I set down at the kitchen counter next to Jaxon. I took her out her chair so I could hold her. British hated when I held her all day, she said it would spoil her. But do you think I gave a fuck. She was my little princess and I was always going to spoil her.

"Boy, put her back in her chair. You always let those cheeks and dimples get to you. She is going to be rotten if you don't stop." She placed my plate in front of me. British food was so good I couldn't wait to dig in.

"What I tell you about that boy shit? And as long as I have arms I will always pick her up. She not even one yet she still a baby. You just hatin'. Ain't that right baby Jax." I turned her around and started tickling her making her laugh. Her pretty ass started playing with my chain I had on. British rolled her eyes and set down to eat.

"Baaby you can't eat and hold her." She started laughing while eating her food.

"Watch me." I cleaned my plate up and had seconds all while holding my princess. Once we were done I put her in her play pen with some toys. She gave me a sad look but just this once I could not give in because I had to talk to British about the run in I had with her punk ass husband.

"Come her Yum let me holla at you." She was sitting on the couch watching TV. She got up and followed me in the kitchen. I sat down on my kitchen stool and placed her on my lap. I was obsessed with her on me.

"You know we promised no secrets, right?" She nodded her head and I could see the fear in her eyes. I hated that shit, I knew she thought the worst because of her past.

"I got a call that Derrick went to a detective to try and build a case aganist me. Derrick had been talking to Sheena. She told him what I do and he took the information and went to the police. He didn't know half of Georgia police is on the King payroll. I went to pay him a visit and we got in a little scuffle. I did not kill him but I did beat his ass. I'm telling you because I never want to leave you in the dark." She looked at me and smirked and played with my beard.

This woman loved my beard especially when her pussy juice was on it. My fucking Queen.

"Thank you for telling me bae. I never want anything to happen to Derrick but he can't just do what he wants. I know I cannot avoid him forever because we have a child. I just want you to trust me enough when that time does come. I made the decision to be with you and I do not regret it. But in order to let him see his child I need to have a sit down with him ok." I looked at her and kissed her. British was hands down my weakness and if she needed me to trust her then I would. Besides if she and Derrick did do anything funny I would just pop both of them and raise Jaxon on my own.

"Any funny shit Yum I'm greeting both of y'all with a bullet and me and baby Jax are going to leave the country." She started laughing hard as hell. Her ass thought I was playing.

"Don't threaten me Terrance. Just trust me ok." She stood up because Jaxon started wining. I hit her fat ass booty making it thunder clap. She picked Jaxon up but she still kept crying. I hated seeing her cry.

"Come here baby Jax." She reached for me and instantly stopped crying. British shook her head and rolled her eyes playfully. We set on the couch watching TV until Jaxon fell asleep. Like always I got her ready for bed and rocked her to sleep then laid her in her crib. I called my decorator over so British could tell her everything she wanted in Jaxon room. The color was pink and grey and it had everything a baby needed.

With a walk-in closet full of clothes, shoes, diapers and wipes. I turned on Jaxon baby monitor video, kissed her and walked out.

As soon as I walked in our master bedroom I turned our baby monitor video so I could see my princess. British was laying in the bed reading her Kindle.

"Come take a shower with me Yum." She smiled and got out the bed and walked towards the bathroom. We both stripped out of our clothes and stepped in the walk-in shower and let the warm water hit us. I loved our showers together because they always turned into some nasty shit.

"You know I love you right? I am not ever letting you go. As long as I have air in my lungs I will always fight for you and Jaxon. Y'all have quickly became my world and I will kill whoever tries to take y'all from me." I looked her in the eyes and gently touched the side of her face.

"I love you to Terrance. I'm here for good bae. I love how you accept Jaxon and treat her like she is yours. It's so genuine and I love you for that." She started tearing up. I pulled her closer to me and kissed her. I made sure to speak volumes with this kiss. I needed her to feel secure. We showered and washed each other up. I wanted to fuck her crazy like we always did in the shower.

But tonight, I wanted to lay it on her in our bed.

Once we dried off I watched her lotion up her body with that girly shit. I loved when British hair was wet and it stuck to her back hanging just above her fat ass booty. The shit was a sexy sight! I had my towel still wrapped around my waist as I walked over to her. I turned her around and laid her on the bed. I can tell she was caught off guard because she had a stunned look on her face.

"I need to eat Yum." I spread her legs and ran my thumb across her clit then I replaced my thumb with my tongue.

She squirmed instantly. I started making out with her clit like it was a mouth. I inserted two fingers in her tight walls. Like always her shit gripped my fingers like a snug condom. I moved my fingers in and out while stile working my tongue. I knew the exact pressure she liked on her clit. I knew when to swirl my tongue and I knew when to suck on it driving her crazy.

"Ahh shit baby! Ughhhh." She arched her back like the golden arches bringing that pussy more and more to my face. British was not a runner from my tongue or my dick and I loved that shit.

"Cum for daddy again Yummy." I pulled my face away so I could say that to her. Placing both my hands on her ass cheeks and squeezing. I had my whole mouth on her pussy licking and sucking her shit like it was my last supper.

"I'm cumminnnnnnnnn SHIT!" she yelled loud as hell. I hope she did not wake my baby Jax. I licked her juices clean like it was some sweet Kool-Aid. I kissed my way up to her body and tongued her as down. British nasty ass kissed me sloppy while rubbing her hands on my beard getting her pussy juices all on herself.

"You my freak bitch Yummy. Only mines!" I flipped her over and she assumed the position. I took my stiff dick and slid in her making me freeze and her moan loud. British had the tightest, wettest, tastiest pussy ever. I started slow stroking her making her juice up more and more.

"Tell me this my fuckin' pussy Yummy! Who does your pussy and heart belong to?!" I was speeding up making her grab a pillow and put her face deep in it.

"Arrghh! It's your daddy shiitt all yours!" She moaned. I hit her juicy ass as it slammed against my pelvis.

"Hell naw, I want to hear out of your fuckin' mouth! Tell me what's mines" I slammed hard in her each word I spoke making her cream up all on my dick.

"Fuck Terrance baby! Ugh my heart and pussy is yours daddy shit!" She came again all over my dick I felt it hit my balls. I felt my shit built up. I pulled out and turned her over with her nut still all over me. I could not help myself I needed to taste her again. I licked and sucked her just for a few minutes then I slammed my eleven inches in her.

"Sssssss mmmhmm." British cried out with her eyes closed and biting her lip.

"Look at me British." She did as she was told. I leaned forward so I was in her face while still beating her pussy like a runaway slave.

"I'm going to love you forever Yum, I promise. Nobody breakin' this shit here ok." She smiled and nodded her head.

"What the fuck does that mean? That's not an answer." I held her legs up and fucked her faster.

"Ok babyyyy. I hear you" I laughed because she was beginning to cream all over me again. I rubbed her clit with my thumb making her orgasm last longer. I felt my shit building back up. So being the nasty nigga I was I started licking her toes while I came all in her while biting on her heel.

"SHIT YUMMY!!" I called out like a bitch. I felt like my energy level came all out of me as I laid on her.

"Terrance get your heavy ass off me." She hit my arm and I laughed.

"Shit, I'm sorry baby. You made a nigga legs give out." We both was breathing hard. I got up and went to the bathroom to clean up. I came back with a warm soapy rag and cleaned my bae up good.

"Damn girl, you the best Yum," I said to her as I laid down. I looked at the baby monitor and my baby Jax was still sound asleep. I can see her back moving up and down so I knew she was good. British climbed in bed and got all on me just like I like. I swear I cannot sleep unless some part of her was touching me or vice versa.

"I love you Terrance, you and that dick," she said laughing making me laugh hard.

"I love you and that sweet pussy Yum." She started laughing hard right with me. We talked for a little bit until we both drifted asleep.

In the middle of the night

Ring, Ring, Ring

My phone was ringing loud as hell, I rolled over and grabbed it on the night stand. Not even looking at it I answered it. Just to make it stop ringing before my baby Jax or British woke up.

"Somebody is about to die, who the fuck is this?" I roared in the phone. British was sound asleep and so was my princess when I looked on the baby monitor.

"Yo' Ronny got hit at his crib man! They killed six of his boys and he is in the hospital!" Ty yelled in my ear. I jumped up like springs was on my ass.

"What the fuck! Yo' get ready so we can hit the red eye." I was already looking for some clothes before me and Ty hung up. British woke up because I was loud and turned the light on.

"What's going on bae?" she looked at me with sleepy eyes. I did not want to alarm her but I had to tell her what was going on.

"Yum some nigga hit Ronny up at his crib. They killed some of his men and put him in the--- I could not finish before she jumped up and started crying. I know she was fond of Ronny but she was crying like they knew each other for years.

"Baby Kori is in Jamaica with him! She left day before yesterday to see him! Oh my gosh is she dead or shot!" she screamed while crying.

I felt helpless because I had no idea Kori was in Jamaica. Ty did not say shit about it either. I reached in my pocket and called Ronny's right-hand man hoping Kori was good and Lee was not one of the six that died.

British

I cried while Terrance held me in his arms and made a phone call. All I thought about was losing one of my best friends.

"Lee, nigga you good? Damn you were hit in the arm. Look was Ronny girl there with him?" He talked and I felt him let out a sigh of relief. He was hugging me so tight. After he talked a few seconds he hung up the phone.

"British, baby calm down. Ronny locked Kori in his panic room while him and his boys handled the nigga's who came in his house. She is fine, she is guarded by his boys at the hospital. Listen, me and Ty are going to Jamaica to see what is going on. I will call you when we touch down and every day I am there." I let out a long breath. He kissed me a few times.

"I'm coming with you. My parents will keep Jaxon just let me call them." I picked up my cell phone.

"British you are not coming with me. This shit is dangerous and I do not want you involved. I promise I am going to send Kori home safely." He looked at me and I believed him.

"I need you to stay inside until we get back. Ty is bringing Ashley here with you and y'all will be fully guarded. Anything you need let Mike know and he will get it for you. British I know how hard headed you can be so please listen to me. If anything happens to you or Jaxon a lot of people are going to die so please stay in until I get back." I agreed and hugged and kiss him. He went and kissed Jaxon and I walked with him downstairs.

As soon as hit the last step his front door opened. Ty came in with Ashley and Aron. I could tell Ashley had been crying. I hugged her and told her Kori was fine but she knew it already.

"I love you Yum, please do as I say." We kissed and he walked to the Uber waiting for them. Ty and Ashley kissed and said their goodbyes as well. Aron smiled at Ty when he dabbed him and kissed his chubby cheeks. Once they were gone I took Ashley to the guest room next to Jaxon's room. She put Aron asleep and joined me in the kitchen.

"I cannot believe this shit. I am so happy Kori is ok. My ass almost shitted bricks when they said some niggas came in Ronny's crib." Ashley said siting down on the bar stool.

"I know girl as soon as she gets here I may not let her out my sight." I jokingly said putting some wine coolers on the bar for me and Ashley.

"So, everything is going good with you and Terrance I see. I am really rooting for the two of you to work out." I looked at her confused.

"We are already together Ash. Why are you still rooting and we are a couple?" I opened my cooler and set next to her.

"Cause bitch I know Derrick is not backing down without a fight. I know how he gets to you with his words boo. Look I know he is still your husband and you know we are rocking with whatever British wants. I just feel it in my heart that Terrance is the real deal. I just think it will always be bullshit with Derrick. Things will not be all peaches and roses with Terrance but I do not see him doing none of the shit Derrick has done." I looked at my girl and felt loved and cared about.

"Thank you, Ash boo. I really do love Terrance and want this to work. I try not to be afraid because that is not having faith but I sometimes feel like this will get snatched from me. I am really happy and secure in my relationship. Something Derrick has not giving me in a while. The way Terrance looks at me, holds me and treats my daughter makes me love him more every day." We sat at the kitchen bar for a while drinking and eating junk food. All that was missing was Kori but I knew she was going to stay with Ronny until he was good.

Four days later

I just got off facetime with Terrance. He informed me that Ronny was shot three-times. Twice in the chest and once in the stomach. He has yet to wake up yet and Kori was right by his side. She called me and Ashley and cried with us on the phone. I wanted my boo to come home so bad but I understood her wanting to be there with Ronny I would do the same with Terrance.

Kori had so much vacation time saved up she used those days to stay in Jamaica. My boo has fallen in love. Me and Ashley were doing ok, aside from missing our guys we were enjoying being in Terrance huge house. We watched movies on his Firestick, played in his game room and went swimming in his pool.

Anytime we needed anything we needed outside the house Mike was right there to get it for us. He was like a huge teddy bear.
Today we decided to bar-b-que outside. We had the fence guard up around the pool so Aron could run around and Jaxon could crawl.

Ashley was working the grill and I was on Facetime with Terrance. He wanted to make sure Mike put the fence up correctly then he wanted to see Jaxon. He cracks me up because he acts like in a week she changed so much.

"I miss y'all. As soon as we handle this shit I'm coming home to my ladies' ok?" Terrance said to me looking so sexy in his sweats.

"We miss you too baby. I just want you to be careful while you y'all are down there. Come back to us in one piece please," I told him. Jaxon was trying to take the phone from me and kiss it because she sees Terrance face. I moved her away from the camera.

"Put my baby back in the camera so she can see me blocker. Me and you can have our camera alone time later." Biting his lip when he said that I giggled and picked Jaxon back up.

"Her ass keep getting' spit all on my camera trying to give you kisses." I laughed.

"Hey my baby Jax dada misses you to. Mommy is a hater uh?" She started laughing. I shook my head.

"Yum you do not ever have to worry about me coming back to y'all. That's always baby. Thank you for listening to me and staying put until I get back." I smiled at his sweet words.

We talked a little longer then we hung up. Ashley was facetiming Ty as well. Once we talked to our guys we went back to our bar-b-que. My phone went off alerting me I had a message on Facebook. I checked it and it was from a person who was not on my friend's list.

I opened it and almost dropped my phone in my pasta salad. It was from Derrick! I did block him from all my social media accounts but I guess I thought because we had a child together I would have heard from him much sooner. Then I had to remember men handle their feelings different from us women.

British I do not even know where to begin to apologize for my actions. I miss you and Jaxon. I need to see you so we can talk about everything. Please get back to me.

Love you always

Derrick

I knew me and Derrick could not avoid each other for long. I needed to sit down with him and talk. Me and Derrick are over but we still have a daughter together and have to co-parent.

"Damn that food was good. You put your foot in that pasta salad British. I'm about to take Aron up-stairs for a nap, hell I'm tired to." Ashley yawned while going up-stairs. I was happy because if her ass knew what I was about to do she would be so against it.

I picked my baby up and we headed up-stairs to pack her diaper bag. I was going to drop her over my parents' house and head to meet Derrick. Then I remembered the giant human wall outside the damn door, Mike. I came up with an excuse that I needed some things for Jaxon at Target. He had no problem with going. I took that opportunity to slip out the house.

Dropping Jaxon off I told my mom and dad I was going to my store to handle some inventory. Both of them had become fond of Terrance. Although my mother had her reservations about me leaving one relationship and going to another. She said when she saw us together we seemed in sync. Speaking of my bae I felt horrible sneaking around like this behind his back. I know he would be angry and disappointed but this was something I had to do.

I wrote Derrick back and told him to meet me at the park s we could talk. It took him no time to agree and now I am parking my truck at the park downtown. Even though it was a forty-minute drive from Terrance place. I knew I did not want Derrick being close to where I was laying my head just yet. I didn't have butterflies in my stomach, I had more of an anxious feeling. I could see him sitting at a table on his phone. I walked up with anxiety building in me like growing flowers.

"Hey Derrick." He looked up at me and stood to his feet.

"Hey B. Wow you look good. How have you been?" he asked me as I took a seat in front of him.

"I'm fine and thank you. We have a few things that we need to talk about." I wanted to cut straight to the chase with no small talk.

"Your right we do. Listen I just want to apologize for the last time we were together. I never brought Niecy or any other woman to our home. I have no idea how she found out where we lived. Also, I told her to get rid of the baby. All of this can be fixed and put behind us if you just give it a chance." I looked at him like he was a science project.

"Derrick how the fuck can we put all of this behind us and move on. First, how do you think because you told that girl to have an abortion we could just move on? As if the problem does not exist. Did you forget I was there when she threw that money in your face?! That is NOT a girl getting rid of her baby. That is a girl saying fuck you I am keeping my baby. I am far from stupid Derrick so stop sitting here like all our problems are fixed because you walked away from a woman carrying your child. There is no us anymore, but we do have a daughter. We need to co-parent. You're a good father please do not let our issues stop you from being that." I did not want to get emotional so I fought back my tears. I never thought I would say these words to my husband.

"Co-parent? Your talking like we are about to get a divorce. That's what you want! Why, so you can be with that drug dealing thug! No way in hell am I giving you a divorce and no way in hell is my daughter going to be around him! I am willing to walk away from Niecy and her bullshit so it will not cause problems between me and you. But you won't even give me an opportunity you just want to run off into the sun set with another man! I never thought you would be this person." He had the nerve to turn his nose up at me like he was in disgust.

"Are you fucking kidding me right now?! What man tries to bury his dirt because it is catching up to him? You did all this shit to us. You will not sit here and blame me like I just gave up on our marriage. Yo' ass never man up and took responsibility for your fuck ups. It's always everybody else fault! Mines, your increase in income, these loose bitches, Niecy! Derrick is the fucking problem, he fucked up! I cannot have your bullshit overflow me anymore Derrick. Every time I think we can move on I get hit with more of your bullshit. I am tired and even if Terrance was not in the picture I would still leave you. It has been too much hurt and lonely nights being married to you. Put your pride and ego to the side and be there for Jaxon, we are over. Take care of your unborn child, don't be this person. That child has nothing to do with its parent's stupid ass decisions." I stood up to leave but he grabbed my arm.

"British since you left I have not been the same. I go to work and go home. I am sorry I have not inquired about Jaxon but I been fucked up. And now my fucking wife is walking away from me to be with someone else. What type of bullshit is that? You're a coward if you walk away from me and file from divorce." Just as I was about to respond his phone on the table rung with the name Carla came across the screen.

That was the stripper bitch I caught him texting last year. I looked at his phone then look at him with a smirk on my face. I snatched my arm from him and walked to my truck. I could not wait until this weekend was over because first thing Monday morning I was filing for a divorce.

I went to my parent's house to pick up Jaxon. I was trying not to go above the speed limit but I had already been gone almost four hours. After meeting with Derrick's annoying ass, I went to check on my store. I set in my office for a while just clearing my head. I just cannot believe I am filing for divorce.

I have fallen in-love with another man and my husband was having a child with someone else. I did not give a fuck about Niecy and Derrick's relationship but I truly hope he would not abandoned his child.

Pulling into my parents round driveway I parked my car and stepped out my truck. When I put my key in and opened the door my mother's cooking hit my nostrils like a breeze. I had not had any of my mother's cooking in a few weeks so I knew I was bringing a few to go plates.

"Hey honey. You ok?" My mama asked as her and my dad set in the den watching CNN. I looked confused because I did not see Jaxon sitting with them or in her playpen. And their baby monitor was turned off.

"Umm Ma where is Jaxon?" I looked at them confused. As big as their house was I know they would never leave her in a room without turning on the baby monitor.

"Terrance came and picked her up. I gave him a bunch of to go plates as well." My mother responded. I felt my heart drop in my ass. I had to play it off like I already knew Terrance had her.

"Oh shoot I must have forgot." I let out a chuckle trying to sound believable.

"Baby love you have to stop working so hard and moving so fast. You are too young to be having memory problems." My handsome dad looked at me and said. I smiled at him.

"You right daddy. I am going to get out of here so I can go home and relax." I hugged both of my parents and left out.

Walking into the house I noticed Aron's toys were gone. I knew that meant Ty was back as well and he had them. I placed my purse on the table by the stairs. I looked in the kitchen and living room and nobody was in there.

I knew they were not in Terrance man cave. He smoked weed in there and did not want Jaxon inhaling any of it. I walked upstairs and looked in our master bedroom and it was empty as well. Jaxon room was next to ours and her door was cracked with her night light on. I peeked in and Terrance was sitting in the rocking chair with Jaxon in his arms. She was on her way to sleep but was fighting it. I smirked because my baby girl was so stubborn. Terrance never once lost his patience with her. He set her up with her back in the crook of his arm and began to sing to her. Instantly she became quiet and started sucking on her pacifier.

Can't forget the day,

That you walked into my life

It was just the kind of thing,

That was soo right on time

After all that love changes,

My heart had locked the door

Then that gurl released her magic

And made me love once more

Like the warm rays of the sun her sweet love

Keeps shining down on me,

Oh oh, only one turned

My life around and wit one kiss she set me free

I smiled so hard at their moment. My baby was closing her eyes listening to his soothing voice. I was so blessed that I had a man who not only accepted me but accepted my daughter as well. We were a package deal. Nothing would turn me off more than someone who would not accept me being a mother.

This world was filled with people doing harmful things to children. God showed out when he created this man. I began to fill bad about not keeping my word when he asked me to stay indoors until he came back.

I went to our bedroom and stripped out my clothes to take a shower. Terrance shower head felt amazing and I could live in it. I stepped out and grabbed my Cashmere glow lotion from Bath and Body works. I oiled my body up and put my Dove powder scented deodorant on. I grabbed my short silk robe on the back of the door and put it on. I put my wet hair in a high pony tail.

When I stepped out the bathroom Terrance was sitting on the bed facing the TV which was off. He looked so good with his Moschino jeans with matching white and blue t-shirt. I loved when he wore shirts that showed off his sexy chocolate physic. I set on the side of the bed feeling like a little girl about to get in trouble by her father. I could not think of words to say to him. I think we both felt the same because we set in silence for a few more seconds.

"Do you have any idea how scared I was?" He finally spoke but kept his back to me.

"Don't shit on this earth scare me. You knocked me completely off my square breakin' yo' word like that. Yo' ass had me ready to body muthafuckas for no reason." Terrance finally stood up and looked at me. I looked at him with sad eyes.

"I'm sorry bae. I got word from Derrick that he wanted to meet. My first thought was to get it out the way so I can work towards moving on. I didn't plan on breaking my word to you baby." I looked at him as he walked closer to me.

"British you and Jaxon have become everything to me so fast. I love y'all. The life I live sometimes makes me make enemies. The first thing I have to do is protecting the ones I love. You and baby girl are number one on that list. When I tell you to follow my lead that is what I mean. I know you have to handle shit with your husband. Trust me I want you to divorce that bitch nigga so I can marry you. But that could have been handled when I got back. Some shit has hit the fan and until me and my crew handle this shit. I will keep you and Jaxon protected but you have to trust in what I tell you. I would never control you baby so I don't want you to think that is what this is. I just want to always keep you and my baby Jax safe." I looked at his handsome face and I did not only feel loved but I felt me and my baby girl were cherished. I smiled at him and he bit his lip trying to hide his smile.

"You are trying so hard not to smile back at me baby. I really do apologize for breaking my word and I will not do that again." I stood up and touched the side of his sexy full bearded face. This man made my mouth water anytime he was around me. or came to my mind.

"I wanted to kick yo' ass when I heard you left then took my baby Jax with you. Yo' ass made me nut up on Mike. Ty had to get me to calm down. I figured Jaxon was at your parent's house I grabbed her and brought her home."

"How the hell did you get here so fast?" I looked at him with a smirk because I felt like he had a Superman cape under his clothes.

"Did you forget from Georgia to Kingston is only three hours. I am only fifteen minutes from the airport bae. With money, you can do any fuckin' thing. And I accept your apology also Yum. I went straight from the airport to you parent's house. I never want to come home and y'all not here." This time he flashed that gorgeous smile at me making me smile and wake up Mrs. Kitty down below.

"I love you Terrance. Thank you for taking care of Jaxon and putting her to bed. I know how stubborn she can be about fighting her sleep." I watched as he bit his lip and untied my robe. My body immediately responded to his touch and he placed his hand around my waist and pulled me to him.

"I love you more baby. That's my baby Jax. You don't ever have to thank me about anything when it comes to her or you." We looked at each other for a second. Like always our stare downs were so intense. It felt like we both saw each-other true selves.

"You know yo' ass is about to pay for breakin' yo' word. I am about to get balls deep in that pussy and you bet not tap out. Before I get to that my beard is feeling a little dry." He kissed me so deep I felt like he was going to devour me whole.

I loved kissing him because his hands roamed everywhere and he used a lot of tongue. Just like I like it. His strong as arms and big hands over powered me making me feel so secure. Terrance placed me on the bed like I was going to break.

He hovered over me looking at me with love in his eyes. His arms flexed as he leaned forward and bite my bottom lip. He smirked and kissed his way down my body until he was face to face with my love box.

Terrance "Terror"

"I CANNOT BELIEVE THIS MUTHAFUCKA!" I was pacing in my office at our warehouse like a raging bull.

"Calm down bro. I know you mad, hell we all are. But we will get this nigga and all of those rollin' with him." My brother Ty was standing next to me feeling just like I did.

"Boss man I have a lead on who in Ronny's crew were the snakes. We now have to figure out if there are any in our crew." Mike said while assembling some guns.

"Yea bro he is right. We have already handled Ronny's crew. What about our own? How the fuck do we know if any of them niggas dirty?" Ty asked.

"Sleez only had an issue with Ronny. He wanted to take over his shit but knew we would not let him. I believe our crew is clean. Just in case I am already on top of knowing if anybody is a rat." I assured them while taking the money out our counting machine.

"British told me she talked to Kori. Ronny woke up after surgery and is recovering well. Kori is on her way home. You know they asses gone want to get together. I told British she could do her thing. I'm happy the shit played out this way. Yo' between this nigga shootin' up Ronny's crib and stealing our shit. He has just signed his death certificate." With anger and rage in me I day dreamed about taking Sleez ass out.

"I feel yo bro we gone get that nigga. We got like twenty-minutes until them Russian boys come and meet with us. So let's get this money and weapons packed up." I stood up and we started packing all the product up.

Sleez put his plan in affect and waited until the right time to ransack Ronny at home. Of course, bro would not go down without a fight. Even after Sleez killed six of his boys. Sleez must have thought he killed Ronny when he shot him three times. Ronny had cameras all over his crib so we were able to watch the whole thing take place.

My boy was definitely in love because he made sure to put Kori in a safe spot with a cell phone and gun. The sad part was he had video monitors in his panic room so she watched the whole thing take place. Baby girl was a mess when we got to Jamaica but she refused to leave Ronny's side.

We were some blessed niggas to have these girl's in our lives. Anyway, knowing that some of Ronny's crew turned on him. We had no choice but to handle the rest of them. It was too much of a risk! We set it up for his crew to meet up in a warehouse. Once they were all in there we blew that bitch up like World War 2. Shit sounds harsh but the way I see it.

I let Sleez slide when I found out he was using and now look at this fuckin' mess. No more slides were going to be giving from us. This bitch ass nigga has done too much shit these past weeks. It's makin' my dick hard thinkin' about how I'm going to kill him. The only reason Ronny's boy Lee did not get it was because Sleez tried to kill him to. He lived by playing dead but not before shooting on of Sleez boy's in the head.

To make matters worse while we were in Jamaica Sleez hit our warehouse. This bitch stole the Russian's and Italian's shipment of weapons and drugs. We talked to the Italian's and they agreed because we have been in business so long they will let us handle Sleez. They wanted some form of his body part along with their product they brought from us. I agreed to those terms because he was going to die regardless. We checked all his spots and stash houses. All of them have been torched even the spot he thought we did not know about. I know Sleez thinks he has gotten one up on us but that nigga is a junkie before he is anything else. He will slip up and I will be there to catch his fall. Now we were down stairs in our warehouse waiting for these Russian boys to show up and see what they are talking about. They were not as aggregable as the Italian's.

"I hope these Russian's do not stop doing business with us because of this shit," Ty said with aggravation in his voice.

"I do to bro. But you know we not no begging ass nigga's so if they want to take their business elsewhere then so be it. We been fucking with them for five years." I don't care how cocky I sound. I love my bread like the next person but I would never kiss ass. Not for shit! Unless we talkin' about kissin' my Yummy's ass then I will pucker up. Ha!

Our truck just left to start the process of delivering our shipment to these African's we been fucking with for a minute now. Money flowed for the King's 24-7 so like I said if the Russian's wanted to dip they could. Mike cleared the warehouse out and came down stairs with me and Ty.

We heard a car pull up. I looked at the camera and saw a black limo pull up and I knew that was them. I opened the sliding door when I saw three men step out. One of them looked like Arnold Schwarzenegger big ass.

"The King brother's. Hello to you this wonderful afternoon." One of the dudes shook our hands. He had a thick ass Russian accent.
"Good to see y'all again. We can get started inside." I lead the way into the warehouse. Mike stood by the door and my brother stood next to me.

"Look I know your boss is pissed at his shipment being stolen. We are on that shit I can not only guarantee his order delivered. But we can also guarantee the muthafuckas heads on a platter. The disrespect was not just towards y'all but to us as well." I looked at him with a stern expression. I meant what I said about murkin' Sleeze and all who helped his ass do this shit.

"We have done business with you people for some time now. As skeptical as we were because of your tempers and trigger-happy fingers. Against judgement we proceeded to move forward. Do you know who did this?" The slim big nose Russian looked at me and Ty and asked. We were familiar with him because anytime we met with them he would always represent his boss.

"Yes, we do. That is why I want to handle the situation. If anybody is going to kill him it will be me. This is personal." They looked at each other then back at us. My brother and I made eye contact.

"Ok, we will let you handle it. You have also not lost us as a client. We would be a fool to stop doing business with the King's as much respect and rank as you have internationally." They shook our hands and began to leave.

"I appreciate that." I nodded my head. As they walked to the exit they stopped in their tracks.

"However, we cannot have this happen again. Do what you need to do Mr. King to assure your lion's den has no hyena's in it." In one swift motion, the Schwarzenegger lookin' one shot Mike in the head.

"WHAT THE FUCK!" Ty yelled. I bit my lip and we both pulled our heat out.

"I would not do that if I were you." Big nose dude said while shaking his head.

"There are targets on you." He pointed at us. Me and Ty looked at our chest and they were covered with red dots. I looked at my brother and we both put our heat down.

"Good. Now I am sorry about your muscle. He seemed like a good loyal man. BUT we had to make you understand. This is a serious matter that needs to be handled ASAP. We want all heads on a platter and our merchandise. Deal?" He looked at us with big smiles. I could physically feel me grow three sizes big from my anger. My brother looked like smoke was coming from his ears and head.

"Cool." That was all I could get out my mouth. They turned and walked out. The one that shot Mike winked at me. The big nose nigga started whistling as the waked back to their ride.

"No need to say anything baby brother. You already know." We both stood quiet for a second looking at Mikes body.

All these years he had been rollin' with us. Loyalty was a hard thing to come by. Especially in our line of work. But Mike was as loyal as they came. We were his only family after his pops died. I called my cleanup crew and they came right out. They were just as shocked as we were. They looked at Mike's body and said they would be respectful and handle with care. Rest easy my friend.

*

My drive home was quiet as hell. I didn't have any music on or my windows rolled down. I was blazing one of the blunts me and my brother rolled up. Right now, I just needed to get home and be with my family. I never was the type to stress myself out. I felt like that shit caused yo' dick to shrink.

But not only did I want to kill Sleez them Russians niggas had to pay as well. Fear did not live in my body. Unless your God or you name is Stonny or British. I had no fucking fear facing me.

Russians wanted a war then it is what it is. They had no reason to kill my nigga Mike. We were not even looking to shed blood with them. Now the shit was fair game and they were going to pay.

I parked my car in the garage and got out. Walking in the house I could hear Jaxon crying. That shit made me get wrinkles in my forehead. I hated hearing or seeing her cry. I still wanted a son but having a little girl made me feel good as hell. She did cute shit that melted a thug's heart. I don't see how her funky ass daddy could be away from her so long. I would go crazy if I did not see my child every fucking day. I don't play that court shit! Rather I was with the mama or not I was seeing my kid every day. Wasn't no sweat off my balls that Jaxon daddy was being a sperm donor. But I knew that shit bothered British and what bothered her I had to kill. Simple!

I went to our master bedroom and British was sitting on the bed. Jaxon was in her lap laying on her back. British was sticking some tube looking shit up her nose. The shit looked weird like a ball with stick on the end.

"What the fuck you stickin' in her nose British!" I was mad as hell. Jaxon was screaming at the top of her lungs. Her little pretty brown face was soaked with tears.

"I'm cleaning her nasty ass nose. This makes it easier to get her snot and boogers." She held the funny looking thing in the air showing me.

"It does not even hurt. She is just being dramatic." British was about to stick that shit back in her nose.

"Hell naw! How the fuck you know it don't hurt her? Is you the one gettin' shit stuck up yo' nose?" I grabbed Jaxon off British lap. Jaxon laid her head on my chest and cried.

"It's ok princess Jaxx. Shhh it's ok baby." I rubbed her back while sitting on the bed. Jaxon calmed down and was slowly closing her eyes. British smacked her lips.

"Both of y'all are so annoying. I'm cleaning her nasty nose when she wakes up." She got up and put the booger thang in the bathroom.

"No the fuck you not. You not sticking that weird shit in her nose." I went and laid Jaxon in our bed. Because of the shit that happened today. I just wanted my Queen and Princess in the bed with me. British came back from the bathroom and I noticed she had her pajamas on. Nothing special by far. She loved Winnie the Pooh and he was all over her pajama pants. She had on no bra with a black tank top on. Her hair was in a ponytail on top of her head.

The shit turned me on to see her so comfortable with me. British told me her husband hated her coming to bed in shit like this. She always had to wear negligees and silk robes and shit. Don't get me wrong that shit is sexy as hell. Especially if British thick pretty ass is in the shit. But damn after a long as day sometimes a woman just wants to be comfortable. Sweats or silk my Yummy was sexy as hell and I loved her either way.

"Oh baby I made Mike a German chocolate cake. He went through the other one I made for the house. I figured he needed his personal on," British said with humor in her voice. I just started taking my clothes off. I tried to smile at her but that shit wouldn't even form on my face.

"What's wrong baby?" British walked towards me. I just dropped my head. Even though the life me, Ty and Ronny lived was dangerous. There was risk in doing illegal shit. However, I didn't think the shit would hit this close to home.

"Yum Mike got killed today. Shit went south at our meeting and they popped him one in the head." British gasped and held her chest.

"Oh my goodness. I liked Mike he was such a gentle giant. Are you ok baby? I know he was a good friend." She walked up to me and wrapped her arms around my neck. I hugged her back getting lost in her intoxicating scent.

"I'm good yummy. I just need to lay with you and Jaxon. I never lost anyone close to me before. Shit fuckin' with me." I took the rest of my clothes of and walked in the bathroom.

"Do you want a minute alone baby or do you want me to join you." I looked at her. Sadness and remorse was in her eyes.

"I need you to join me baby." British didn't hesitate coming out her clothes. I knew she already showered for the night. She was getting back in just to please me. My fucking Queen.

While we showered I told her the shit between me and Sleez. I didn't get to into details but I told her enough. Just so she could understand what was up. Ty said he was letting Ashley know what was up as well. After I put the bed guard up on Jaxson side I walked around to my side and climbed in. My body needed this and my heart needed my ladies in bed with me. British kissed Jaxson a few times on the cheek. The she turned over to give me some love. My bed was so damn big I didn't worry about British rolling over on Jaxon.

"Baby people are dying and getting shot. That shit is scary. Are you going to be ok?" She was laying on my chest. Her soft as hands was rubbing on my arms. My yum loved my big ass arms.

"I'm good baby. I can promise you that I am always going to come home to you. And I can also promise you something else." I tilted her head up to look at me.

"You and Jaxon will always be covered. No matter what on every level the two of you will be ok. That's the only way I will die. If I am protecting y'all." I kissed her soft lips. I don't know why I did that. I was brick hard and she was moaning lightly while we kissed. I sucked on her bottom lip. British kept her eyes closed when I pulled away.

"Come on girl. I was on my way to bed but you had to wake him up." We both climbed out of bed. I grabbed the baby monitor as we were leaving. I had my arms around her waist as we walked out the master bedroom. I told her to make a left and go in one of the guest bed rooms.

Sitting the baby monitor on the night stand I pulled British shirt over her head. Those sexy ass titties bounced like springs. My mouth attacked them muthafuckas first. British didn't know it but I was about to lose myself in her.

Derrick

For the past few days I have not been able to sleep. Even if I am beyond faded my ass still could not go to sleep. I have never had a problem going to sleep before. Shit every fucking night I slept like a baby. But these few nights I am lucky if I get two hours.

This shit all went back to British. If her selfish ass would just come back to me. Her being gone was now making me lose sleep. The only way to get my life back in order was to fix it myself. Waiting on these crazy ass women to do shit my way was not working.

After I had and sausage Mcgriddle, two hash browns and pancakes from McDonalds. I jumped in my Maybach and headed towards Niecy's place. I still did not want anything to do with this baby. But I knew how expensive kids can be. Her stripping income was not going to be enough. I figured we could work something out where I gave her some money every month. What person would turn down $3000.00 every month tax free.

The only deal was we were not to be in contact with each other. Even though British knew about the situation. I know she does not want to see me raise a child by someone else. What if he looks just like me. He is a boy so we would do father and son things together. British and Jaxon might get jealous. I could not have that shit. Doing this for Niecy would ease my conscience and maybe help me sleep at night.

When I parked her car, I saw her green Kia parked so I knew she was home. I walked up to her door with confidence and knocked. I heard some Keyshia Cole playing and I could smell cooking. Hell yea! After we talk she is definitely fixing a brotha a plate and maybe some head. When her door opened I was surprise a nigga stood in front of me. He was a tall slim Steph Curry looking nigga.

"What up. Niecy here?" I asked even though I could see her in the kitchen. This dude eyed me up and down.

"Who the fuck are you? Why you want my woman?" His little ass nostrils flared. This dude was a pretty and I couldn't take him seriously.

"I'm a friend. Calm down dude nothing like that." I laughed at his ass. I could see Niecy walking towards us.

"Nigga I ain't yo' fuckin' dude." He walked up on me. Not bagging down, I balled my fist up.

"Hold up! Not in my shit and not while I'm pregnant!" She turned and looked at me with annoyance.

"Derrick what the fuck are you doing here?" Niecy pointed at me.

"I just came to talk about our situation. Yo' dude trippin." I motioned towards Curry Jr looking ass.

"Derrick! Nigga get the fuck outta here! This baby is good over here bro. You can get the fuck on." He waved his hand as if he was shooing me away. I looked at Niecy not paying her dog any more attention.

"Niecy, I only came to offer you a proposition. I wanted to give you a sum of money—

"Nigga if you don't get the fuck on! You being mad disrespectful right now. Not only do they not need yo' money! They don't need you! Fuck outta here donor ass nigga" He pulled Niecy in the house and slammed the door in my face. Part of me wanted to knock that bitch down. But then I walked away counting my blessings. This was one door that I could close for good. I bet I get a full 8-hours of sleep tonight.

*

Juvenile-Back that azz up was booming threw the speakers at the strip club. Me and Eric were in our usual VIP section. I two bad hoes with fat asses dancing all on me. I felt like I was sleep walking. It was past midnight and I was tired as hell but for some reason I still could not sleep. I went home after Niecy's place and tried to take a nap.

My ass still tossed and turned like a person on fire. I tried music, putting on a movie. I even closed the blinds to make it dark in the daylight. Nothing! I finally said fuck it and went to work. After that me and Eric decided to turn up.

"Aye D your eyes are looking heavy as hell. You good?" Eric asked me while tipping a dancer.

"Yeah I'm ok. Lately I just have not been getting any sleep. I don't know what the fuck in going on with my body. I'm lucky if I get 2-hours," I said shaking my head.

"I think I can help you with that." Eric got up and singled for me to follow. We walked towards the bar.

He whispered something to the owner and I followed Eric to the back. Walking down some stairs I had no damn idea where I was going. We got to a black door and Eric knocked once hard as hell. Some white fat guy opened the door with an Ak-47 in his hand.

"Here for a pickup," Eric said. The guy opened the door and we walked in. The nigga we partied with last time was in the room. He was counting money and putting pills in a ziploc bag.

"What's good Sleez. You remember my boy D." We fived each other and set down.

"Yea I remember y'all crazy ass niggas. What can I do for you?" He asked sitting back looking at me and Eric.

"My boy can't seem to sleep. When his ass is up he has zero energy. You got something for that?" Sleez nodded his head. Getting up he went to a safe and opened it up. Taking out a pill bottle he gave it to me. The bottle was see through and I counted six ills in it.

"That will be a Franklin and a Grant please." He smiled at us. I pulled out my wallet and paid him the money.

"Any other problems you got?" He looked at me and asked.

"What all do you do?" He laughed.

"Anything but sexual. Unless the bitch is bad as fuck." I don't know why but a light went off in my head. I did have another problem. A big ass problem that even the police could not help me with.

"Yea I do have another problem. How much would it run me to have somebody handled?" Eric head turned towards me fast as hell. I was dead serious to. If this Terrance King nigga was who Sheena made him out to be. Then I knew Sleez was just the nigga to fix this problem. Sleez looked at his white boy and nodded his head. The next thing I knew he pulled his gun on me. Sleez had a gun to Eric's head.

"Nigga who the fuck are y'all? Did he send you geeky ass niggas to set me up?" I looked at him like he was crazy and so did Eric.

"Who the fuck are you talking about?!" Eric asked with his hands up and fear on his face.

"TERRANCE KING NIGGA! DID HE SEND Y'ALL!?" Sleez looked like he had foam coming from his mouth.

"No man. Look, Terrance is fucking my wife! They met in Jamaica and she is trying to leave me for him. I tried to get the nigga in trouble with the law but they were no help." Sleez and his white boy still did not lower their guns.

"Look I just didn't know what else to do. My wife thinks the nigga walks on water and shit. He is not about to just walk away with my wife and child. I'll pay whatever." I guess that must have snapped him back to earth. He slowly lowered his gun and so did his boy.

"All right. I believe you nigga. I can see the desperation in your eyes. I am having a little King problem myself. I want $50,000 cash in a bag. After the job is done then you can bring my money back here. Deal?" He held his hand out for me to shake it.

"Deal. I'll have your money with no problem. So you can know I am not on any bullshit. I can pay you half now and the rest when it is done." Sleez nodded his head.

"Oh, and keep my location a secret. As far as y'all know. My ass doesn't even exist." Me and Eric agreed and walked out. Shit my heart was in my ass. I know Eric was just as shaken up. "D, you sure you want to take shit this far. I say fuck it and just let the nigga have British. You don't see me trying to kill his ass after we fought over Sheena. This ain't us man."

"I am sure Eric. I think the reason I am not sleeping is because of British. I tried talking to her ass and she won't listen. Me and you both British man. She is just as square as us. Her ass is not going to be with no damn thug. Right now, she acting to dickmatized to listen to reason. I have tried all options. This is the only one. As money hungry as that nigga Sleez is. He is going to take the money and dip out. I'll have my wife back and Georgia will have one less thug to worry about." Eric dabbed me up and we went back to our section. I was about to have all my problem solved. My life was slowly getting back to normal.

We continued to party until I was fried out. At 3 am I was leaving the club. Eric went to a hotel with a bitch he met. Me on the other hand I did not want to go home or to my suite. I pulled my phone out and texted Treasure. I knew she was sleep but when she saw my name no doubt she would get up.

I told her I was on the way. Not waiting for her to respond I pulled up at her crib. Treasure had a cute two-bedroom house with a finished basement. Baby girl took care of her shit good. I remember one time I popped up she was outside working on her yard. Looking just like Mrs. Parker on Friday.

I walked up to her door and before I knocked she opened it. She was ass naked in some black pumps. Her braids hung down and she had red lipstick on. I licked and bit my lip eyeing her fine ass. She pulled me in by the rem of my pants. I pushed her door closed and wasted no time picking her up.

Treasure moaned and smiled at me. Even though I was not feeling Treasure the way she was feeling me. I still could not deny her beauty at all. I kissed the fuck out of her ass. Slamming her back against the wall her legs wrapped around my waist.

"Stay the night with me Derrick. Please big daddy I need you." Her words made me lose all train of thought.

That's all I wanted was to feel needed. My own wife had so much family and friends support. I knew she didn't need my ass. Any man desire from his woman was to feel needed. I knew right then and there. I was not going to stop fucking with Treasure anytime soon. I walked her to her room and laid her on her bed. No ruff nasty shit tonight. I wanted to show my appreciation to Treasure. No matter what she was always submissive to my needs. No questions ever asked she did what I said. Made me feel like a man.

I kissed and sucked on her neck making hickeys all over her. I marked every bitch I fucked. Kind of like a reminder of who was there. I loved sucking on Treasure's big ass titties. When you sucked on her nipples and pulled forward. They got hard as hell and looked like gorilla nipples. Shit turned me the fuck on! She didn't know it but tomorrow I was taking her to get them pierced. I made my way down to her wet pussy. Treasure was breathing hard as hell.

Looking up at her there was no ugly expressions on her face this time. She looked like she was in pure ecstasy. I parted her bald pussy lips and dove in. Her juices were sweet but had nothing on British. I am not going to lie I pictured this was British. I imagined it was British legs wrapped around my neck.

When Treasure moaned I heard British voice. When I slid my dick in and fucked the shit out of her. Every back-scratch Treasure put on my back was from British. When I let her get on top and ride my dick. I looked at her and I swear my hand before God.

I was looking at my wife from her face to her feet. You could not tell me I was not having my dick rode by my wife. British face looked so sexy while she was enjoying me. I set up and sucked on both of her titties making her moan. She started moving fast and I wrapped both my arms around her body. It was like I wanted to get wrapped up in her love.

I never been a moaner but she had me moaning like a woman should. After a few more rides I came all in British. I loved how she kept riding even after me and her came. I fell back and let sleep take my ass away.

British

"Stopppppp Terrance." I giggled while he was biting on my ear. I was trying to roll up my yoga mat.

I had just got done with my session following behind my Jillian Michaels DVD. I loved that woman even though sometimes I tap out. Ha! Anyways, I was trying to clean up but somebody kept messing with me. When I tell y'all this is the happiest I have ever been. It's been so long since I have had everything right in my life. Now I understand shit will not always be perfect.

But to deal with heartbreak, infidelity and lies on a regular is not normal. I always felt I couldn't walk away until I did everything to fix it. I was beyond ready to move on from Derrick. I felt like a fool staying and letting him keep hurting me. Now I have this amazing man who I truly love and am in love with. But right now, he is being so annoying messing with me!

"Boy would you stop." He had his hands around my waist. I knew he hated when I called him boy. I didn't expect him to do what he did next.

"AHH! Terrance stop before you drop me!" This crazy fool had me up in the air with one arm. He was much taller than me and I felt like I was high as fuck.

"What I tell you about that boy shit? Uh?" He raised his arm up higher. I started screaming hoping Jaxon did not wake up. Terrance was looking up at me smirking then he started tickling me.

"Stop! Stop! Terrance, I swear if you drop me I'm leaving you." What the hell did I say that for. He lifted me higher and tickled me more. I had tears coming from my eyes from laughing so hard. I was trying to talk but I kept laughing. Finally, he swung me in his left arm like I was a bag of groceries. I started hitting him in his arm and chest. He was blocking my hits and cracking up.

"You. Could. Have. Dropped. Me," I said between hits. I couldn't hide my smile tough.

Terrance was 100 times more handsome when he smiled or laughed. I never just played around before. Unless you were my girls or my baby girl. I never knew the shit I needed and lacked until I had them. I was done punching him and I tried to walk away.

"Get yo' ass over here Yum." He pulled me into his chest turning me on. I wanted this life with Terrance every fucking day forever. He just filled me up on every level. I was basking in his love and it felt so good.

"Now what was that shit you said about leaving me?" I looked at his sexy ass face.

"You know I was just playing with you baby. Can I have a kiss?" I went to kiss his lips and felt that same feeling. The heart dropping, wet panties and floating feeling.

"You hangin' with me when you take Jaxon over Kori's house." I nodded my head yes. I was still breathless from that kiss.

"That wasn't a question. I want my Queen with me all day today. Hell, every day. Come on let's take a shower so we can head out. I need to stop by the restaurant and Kingdom. We also need to go to Macy's and Nordstrom's." He hit my ass when I turned to walk up the stairs. He had his arms around me the whole time. Terrance was not playing when he said he loves to be all over his woman. I didn't mind at all when he was all over me. Wouldn't you let a fine big dick nigga be all over you? And he loyal, look at Gawd!

Turning the shower on I stepped in and closed my eyes. Terrance shower head came out turbo blast. Shit felt good as hell and like most women I loved my showers hot as hell.

"Shit British! You trying to burn the black off my ass! Hell naw baby I need some cold water mixed with this shit." I cracked up at his big grown ass scared of some hot water.

Once the water was just right he let his body get wet. I love watching water cover his naked chocolate body. I know to some this is weird to say. But Terrance body was gorgeous from head to toe. I mean that shit literally. His feet were always taken care of and clean.

Even his ass was sexy but he would kill me if I touched it. Terrance was facing me with his head back and eyes closed. He was letting the water wet his hair and face. I was gawking my ass off at him. He lifted his head up and caught me staring. He bit his lip and grabbed his hard dick. My God!

"You like what you see?" I nodded my head. He kept eye contact while stroking his dick and walking towards me. Quickly he lifted me up again the bench on the wall. We kissed with so much fire and desire in our mouths.

"Swear to God I can just love you until I die. And even after death continue to." His deep voice was low and heavy in my ear. My heart soaked those words up he spoke. The water was still warm hitting us. He looked down and rubbed his dick around my pussy. I was in intoxicated with hunger for this man.

"Still not long enough for me to love you Terrance." I looked in his eyes and said. He kissed me deep and slid his dick in me. Every inch was all in my pussy. I felt like his dick was about to come out my mouth. I put my head in his neck and bit shoulder. Terrance leaned forward and made eye contact with me. His beard was soaked and for once it wasn't from my pussy. That shit made me get wetter as he fucked the shit out of me.

"Fuck Yummy. Fuck yo' pussy so good. You give this shit to anybody else besides me I'm killin' they ass. Nigga or bitch bet not touch this pussy." He stuck his tongue in my mouth and went harder.

"Oh my goodnessssss Terrance baby! Arghhhhh I'm cummin' love." I came good as hell.

He still each of my legs in both of his hands. Still stroking he finally came all in me. I don't think we ever used condoms. I wasn't trippin' because I was on the depo shot. As a matter of fact, I'm due for in in another week. Terrance kissed all over me until he reached my sweet nectar. This man is just sent from heaven.

Finally done with our shower and drying each other off. I used my favorite peach lotion on my body. Deciding to keep it simple I wore my black fitted jeans with the knees cut out. My Burberry buttoned up blouse and low top Burberry sneakers. Putting on my gold hoops I checked my man out when he walked out his walk-in closet. He had on some grey sweat pants and matching hoodie with the hood on it. The word Jordan was written in big black letters on the side of the legs. It was also on the hoodie as well. Of course, he had black Retro 12.

"Yea big homie yo' ass lucky you are with me today wearin' grey sweat pants. Don't make me slap a hoe Terrance." He started laughing at me. I was laughing to but I was serious as hell. You can't hide a dick as big as Terrance dick. If a bitch even sneaks a peek I'm going HAM!

"Shut yo' ass up. Look at yo' tight ass jeans you got on. Huggin' all them sexy ass curves. That ass is protruding out them jeans. Looks like you will be slappin' hoes and I will be shootin' niggas. Black Bonnie and Clyde type shit." We both started laughing as we walked out the bedroom.

*

We had just left the restaurant so Terrance could check on the progress. Don't let anybody tell you money don't talk. You could get damn near just about anything if you have a lot of money. Just that fast Terrance restaurant was coming along. I loved how he looked out for his employees and still paid them. It really showed me his compassionate side.

We were in his black Lexus LX on our way to Lenox Square so we could go to Macy's.

Once we parked we got out and we hand and hand walking to the store. I knew I needed to hit up the perfume counter. I also needed to go to the baby section and get my fat mama some clothes. I needed to figure out a way to go alone.

Terrance always over did it with Jaxon in everything she got. One day I told him to pick her up some diapers. No lie this crazy man had a trunk full of Huggies diapers and wipes. As soon as we walked into Macy's the perfume hit my nose. That was my weakness right there. Besides clothes and shoes.

"I already know where we are headed first. Come on with yo' smell good ass." Terrance teased then kissed my hand.

I smiled but not at him. I saw the Gucci Bamboo perfume that I needed to restock up on. Terrance shook his head at me the whole time we were at the counter. I was like a kid in the candy store.

Getting my Gucci bamboo and Gucci Flora. I also got a bottle of Chloe Love Story. I knew Terrance was going to want to go to the men section. I figured this was my time to break away for Jaxon stuff.

"Baby you go ahead and look in the men section. I will be over by the bedding." I don't know why I thought he would agree.

"No, we can go to bedding together then hit up men's." His brows were furrowed when he said that. I laughed to myself because he hated to be away from me. My ass failed in my attempt to object.

"Umm no it's cool baby. You know how long I take looking at sheets. Go ahead and meet me in bedding. I'll still be there when your done in men." I tried to lie and play it off. I did not even know I was rubbing my neck until I did it. Damn!

"British why the hell you rubbin' yo neck? What the fuck you hidin'? I swear I will set it off and blow all Lenox Square up. Everybody in this bitch will die. What's up?" I could not stop my laugh from busting out.

"Ok Terrance. The truth is I need to get Jaxon just a few pieces. Baby every time we shop for her you over do it. Like a lot! I only need a few shirts and that's all." He smiled at me and kissed my lips.

"Ok I won't even interfere Yum. I will let you do your thing." I did the black girl mm-hm face. We will see.

Of course, I added up Jaxon stuff to be a little over $500.00. The shit was a never wining battle. I am throwing in the white flag. We paid for her stuff and headed to the men section. While we were looking at clothes. I saw three girl's walk in our direction. I recognized the one with the fake titties was Sheena. I didn't even know she had friends probably because I didn't care.

"Hey Terrance. So, what the fuck is this? Y'all a couple or some shit? You playin' house with another nigga's wife?" Her comment caught me off guard. I had to breath in and out and realize I do not want to go to jail.

"Aye Sheena get yo' slut bag ass away from us talkin' that bullshit. Tha fuck you even fix yo' mouth to say shit. Fuck on!" She turned her nose up and so did her friends.

"And how the hell you tried to act like you were better than me? You and I are the same boo-boo. Want our cake and eat it to." She high fived her fucking litter box bitches.

"You better get the fuck away from me with that shit. You just mad because you will never ride this dick again. But don't worry, I'll be ridin' that muthafucka all the way to sleep tonight." I dropped my bags and grabbed Terrance dick when I said that last part. Sheena was fuming.

"You better watch yo' mouth. Your two minions not here to have your back. It's three against one little bih." If Sheena thought that shit meant anything to me she is sadly mistaken. I could care less because I was out numbered. I was still going to beat her ass. Before I could step to her Terrance pulled me behind him.

"Shiitt! Any of you bitches touch my woman watch I lay y'all asses out. I don't hit women but I will knock a bitch out Tyson. Now like I said, Sheena get the fuck on. I promise you if I even hear of you or yo' ugly ass friends causing my woman any harm. I am killin' all of y'all and everybody you bitches love. Bible that shit and get the fuck on." Terrance voice roared all over Macy's.

He made me scared and the threat was not eve for me. Sheena and her girls walked away with so much fear in their faces. Terrance nostrils were flared and fist balled up. When they were out of sight all eyes were on us.

"Fuck y'all lookin' at? Continue shopping." As if God himself spoke the people went back to shopping. Terrance grabbed me and kissed my lips.

"Ain't nobody ever gon' fuck with you baby." He smiled at me and I smiled at him. Just that quick we went back to normal. Even though I believed his words. I had a feeling Sheena was going to try and test my gangsta again.

*

After shopping me and Terrance went to Kingdom so he could do some paper work. It was sexy as hell watching him take care of business. We went to New York Prime Steakhouse for dinner. We didn't do much talking because both of us were hungry as hell. Now we were back home and I was putting Jaxon clothes up in her closet.

I'm sorry let me rephrase myself! I was stuffing clothes in Jaxson closet and drawers because she has so much shit there is barley any room! Anyways, while I was in her room my phone went off. I looked at it and it was a text form Derrick. He said he misses Jaxon and would really like to see her. To say I was shocked to see a text from him was an understatement. I had no idea what to say.

I never wat to take Jaxon away from Derrick at all. Nor was I replacing him with Terrance. But damn how could you not want to be around your child. Especially a beautiful baby girl like my Jaxon. I decide to let him know he can see her tomorrow at 2. Putting my phone back in my pocket I finished putting Jaxon clothes up.

I walked down stairs where Terrance was laying on the couch watching TV. Jaxon was staying the night at Kori' house. Aron was over there as well. I went and laid on top of Terrance. He kissed the top of my head and rubbed my back. I figured since he was relaxed and full. I could slip in the fact that Derrick texted me. After we discussed it I could put some lovin' on my baby.

"What you gotta tell me baby. I feel yo' body tensing up and shit. You know you can talk to me about anything Yum." I looked up at his handsome face. Our eyes linked up and like always I felt calm.

"Derrick texted me and said he would like to see Jaxon. I told him I was free tomorrow at 2 and I would bring him to her. My baby has not seen him in a minute so I am not leaving her with him. The way Derrick has been acting I don't know what he is capable of. Terrance baby I need you not to come. You will pop off if Derrick coughs wrong and I don't want that around my baby." He licked his lips. Popping his bottom lip out is teeth hard as hell. I knew he was annoyed. I rubbed his face and kissed his lips. Just to assure him I can handle this situation.

"Ok Yummy baby. I will let you handle this but on one condition. You let one of my guys drive you and Jaxon. He goes in with you while the nigga has his visit. Don't worry about shit baby. Nothing will pop off while my baby girl is there. You won't even know my guy is there he will be that low key. You tell that punk ass nigga either he abides or you are leaving. Deal?" I smiled and nodded my head.

Other people may have thought Terrance was a tad protective. I didn't at all. I felt he loved hard and with everything he has. For the rest of the night we watched movies and ate junk food. We also sucked and fucked on each other! Then went right back to watching movies and eating junk food. Shit just repeated itself all night. Mmm!

Leave it to Terrance to be so fucking extra. This dude he picked to drive me and Jaxon to Derrick's house was far from low key. He reminded you of the big black guy form the movie The Green mile. He did not talk at all. Hell, he barely blinked. All he did was have a huge ass shot gun on him.

I thought for sure we were going to get the police called on us if people saw it. But I guess when Terrance said the Kings owned Georgia he wasn't playing. I really missed Mike a lot. At least he would throw two maybe four words my way. Black ass drove me to Kori's house so I could pick up Jaxon. Ashley was there picking up Aron. The two of them bitches thought the shit was funny as hell. The went to the black Escalade I was in and saw the huge shot gun on the front seat. Them hoes rolled over laughing. I did not find shit funny at all!

Seeing my old home brought back bitter sweet feelings. I missed my house because I personally had put my taste and touch on every room. Because the bad outweighed the good I was happy to have me and Jaxon gone. Black ass opened the door for me and picked up Jaxson book bag. I unbuckled Jaxon out if her car seat and put her on my hip. I couldn't wait for my baby to start walking. Black ass was no joke!

He had that shot gun in his left hand on display like the shit was normal. I just know Derrick is not going to let me in the house with this big nigga standing behind me. I knocked on the door and Derrick only took a few seconds to answer. He had a smile on his face until he saw a huge shadow standing behind me.

"Who the fuck is that?" He pointed at black ass but was looking at me. I rolled my eyes. I really wanted Jaxon to see her daddy.

"Derrick just ignore him. I don't know what you been up to or who you been around. I feel more comfortable with him with me. Can we come in or not?" Derrick looked at me and laughed. Then he moved out the way so we can come in. Black ass closed the door and stood against it. Shot gun in both hands. Jeez!

"You real funny B. I guess yo' new man gave you a body guard huh? You know what type of man I am. I have never physically hurt you." I did not even want to go there so I changed the subject.

"Derrick are you not going to speak to your daughter?" Jaxon had her Dr. McStuffins toy doll in her mouth.

"Can you sit her on the couch so we can talk? I mean damn I have not seen you over a month." I was getting annoyed.

"There you go again Derrick damn! Just visit with your child. She can't even get a fucking hello?" Getting mad he walked passed me and picked her up. I watched him hug and kiss her. Jaxon was too busy playing with her toy to notice. I guess Derrick was getting frustrated because he snatched the doll from here and threw it on the couch. Jaxon hit the roof.

"Aye what is wrong with her? She never used to cry this much? Jaxon, baby girl smile for daddy." He lifted her up and tried to play with her. That only made her scream louder and look at me. Now I am not going to lie, my baby is spoiled. She was even more spoiled because of Terrance. But she has never been a damn cry baby. If I am not in her nose then she is laughing. Jaxon didn't even cry when I combed her hair.

"D just give her back the doll. Sit down with her and play with her. She will stop trust me." He waved me off and started trying to rock her. Jaxon was fighting to break free. That was all I could take. I reached my arms out and grabbed her.

"So what the fuck! You have turned my daughter against me? You got her thinking that nigga is her daddy? Jaxon came from my fucking nut sack British! I'm her daddy not that thug!" I was not even paying him no mind. I was busy soothing my baby girl. She calmed down and closed her eyes. I laid her in the play pen that was left over here.

"Derrick she just has not seen you that's all. Nobody is replacing you ok. You did all of this shit! Now this is the outcome. Just be a better father to your children." I specifically said children in remembrance of the bitch he knocked up.

"B please come home. I miss you boo for real. All I do is go to work and come home. I have not even fucked with a bitch. I want my family back." I looked at him and tried to hold my laugh in.

"A lot has changed Derrick. Looking into your eyes I can see one thing." I walked closer to him.

"You're still the scum of the fuckin' earth. You would sit and lie to me about not being with anyone? Your neck looks like cheetah skin and since we both know you're not allergic to shit! That can only mean those are what? Huh? I can't hear you Sherlock!" I had my hand on my ear like I was listening for his answer. Derrick put his head down and didn't say anything.

"Exactly! Look, just visit your daughter. I don't care what you do with your life. Just be a father to Jaxon. Me and you will never be again." There, I finally said the shit out loud! And it felt damn good. Derrick chest was going up and down.

"You think that fuckin' thug is going to replace me! You fucking stupid bitch—" before he could finish Black ass got off the door we was leaning on.

"Aye nigga ease the fuck up with the name callin' and yellin'." That was the most I ever heard him say.

"I don't have to do shit! This is my fucking house. As a matter of fact, y'all can get the fuck out! Now!" Derrick was not hurting me by saying that. Me and my baby been put out of better places. I grabbed her bag and gave it to black ass.

"Hell naw! Leave her ass here and you can pick her up tomorrow." I don't know who the fuck he thought he was talking to.

"It ain't no way in hell I am leaving my baby with you. Not on that bitch ass attitude." I picked her up.

"Fine! Take her ass and get the fuck out! Don't come back! Oh, and tell yo' nigga to watch his fuckin' back. Got some shit waitin' on him." I looked at Derrick and he was rubbing his hands together laughing.

Black ass was about to step to Derrick but I pointed at Jaxon. He stopped and we walked to the car.

I was so mad at myself I wanted to knock my own ass out. Once again, I was dumb to Derrick Noel. I thought he really wanted to see his daughter.

Until my divorce is final I will not be seeing him anymore. I looked at Jaxon while she was sleep and smiled. This little person was my best blessing. I thanked God for her every day. I looked and saw black ass eyes looking at me through the rear-view mirror.

"You know I gotta tell boss man, right?" I nodded my head and turned to look out the window.

I had no idea my marriage would end so soon. I can tell you this much. I will never love for two again. Heading home I was in deep thought about a lot of things. I didn't even notice the black charger with tinted windows. Not until it pulled up on the driver side and rolled its window down. A loud as pop was the best way I could explain what I heard next. I could not even yell because I was in shock.

Black ass rolled over with a hole in his head. Glass was all over his face and his eyes were open. The truck started swerving and I looked at my baby girl. Hell no! She was not about to die. Shaken up I climbed forward and grabbed the wheel. Black ass was so big I had no choice as I climbed in the front. I opened the door and pushed his ass out. Firecracker sounds started and I found my voice then.

All I could do was scream and keep driving. Finally, the Charger turned down another street on full speed. I was so distraught I didn't even recognize where I was going. All I kept saying was to drive and don't stop. Was Derrick really serious about killing Terrance? Did I hurt him that bad that he wanted to kill me? And with Jaxon in the car? Jaxon!

Oh my fucking God! My baby is in the car and they shot it up! I turned in a driveway and hit the brakes hard as hell! I don't even care how or where I parked. Even though Jaxon was crying from the whole time. I think my fear pushed all sound out my body. Loud pops were all I could hear. Swinging open the back door I grabbed my baby out the car seat. I hugged and kissed all over here.

"WHAT THE FUCK! Baby, what happened?" I didn't even know I made it home. Having Jaxon in my arms and seeing Terrance. I broke down. He hugged me tight as hell with Jaxon still in my arms. Ty and some other dudes ran out with their guns drawn.

"It's ok baby. It's ok. I'm here Yum." He was rubbing my back like he does Jaxon when she is crying. Speaking of her she was breaking out my arms trying to get to Terrance. He grabbed her and she laid he head down.

"Baby what the fuck happened? Where is Black?" I calmed down and started talking.

"We were leaving Derrick's house and a black Charger pulled up on the driver side. They killed Black ass and then started shooting at us. I had to take the wheel so I pushed his body out the car and kept driving. I don't even know how I made It here. I can't believe he would really do this! Jaxon could have—" I couldn't even get my sentence out before I was balling again. Terrance took me into his arms and hugged me again. Ty came over and took Jaxon in the house.

"Baby who the fuck did this shit? Tell me and that's it for them." I didn't want anything to happen to Derrick. But he had no regard for my baby girl's life.

"When we left Derrick's house he said for me to tell you to watch your back. He said he had something waiting for you. But I didn't take his threat serious baby. Derrick is not a street guy. He is a square just like my ass." My tears kept coming down my face. I looked at Terrance and just like at the kick back. He looked to be taller and bigger. His fist was balled up and he was spaced out.

"Listen to me British. Please don't make me put my foot up yo' ass. Don't ever say you and Derrick name in the same sentence again. Second, I need you and Jaxon to stay here. I am about to have my boys pick up Ashley, Aron and Kori. Y'all stay here until you get word from me. British, you broke yo' word last time. Please baby don't do the shit for real. We promised no secrets so I am going to be real. Your ex-husband is going to die today. He had no care for you or my baby Jaxx life. So, I have no care for his. I love you baby and you will be my wife one day. We clear?" He looked at me and wiped my tears with his thumb.

"Yes Terrance. We are crystal clear." He kissed me so deep.

While we were kissing four black Tahoe's pulled up filled with big ass dudes. They all had weapons of all kinds. They walked in the house next to ours.

I was confused because there was a black young couple that lived there. Every single person in that rode in the Tahoe went in the house and closed the door. Terrance looked at me and winked. Ty came out with a blue duffle bag. He gave it to Terrance and they hoped in one of the Tahoe's.

"I love you and my baby more than life. Ok?" He said from the passenger side. I kissed him and rubbed his beard.

"We love you more baby. Come back to us." I couldn't help but cry. I cried about the whole situation.

"Always," he said as they pulled off. A Ford Flex pulled up with a white guy driving. Ashley, Aron and Kori got out. We hugged and I broke down again. Walking in the house I just prayed for Terrance and Ty to come back to me and my girl safely.

Terrance "Terror"

Fire, lava and all that other hot shit ran through my body. I cannot believe this lame ass nigga stooped this low. Now my ego and pride had been hurt before. But unless my family or my money was in jeopardy then I don't shed blood. Then to do the shit while your child in in the way! Oh yea, this bitch ass pussy was dyin' tonight. I had to have my brother take the wheel.

Driving was not something I needed to do at this moment. Just the thought if British or Jaxon getting killed. Shit made me want to rip the steering wheel off the truck.

"We peelin' this nigga cap back bro. Don't even worry about the shit. I killed Ashley's baby daddy over hurting her. So I know you murkin' this pussy nigga." I looked at my baby brother.

He never told me he popped Ashley's baby daddy. I knew this nigga was in love but damn. I honestly couldn't do shit but smile. I felt proud.

Before Ty could even stop the truck, I was jumping out. I saw the punk nigga's car in the parking lot. Ty was hot on my heels with a bat in his hand. I didn't need shit but my fist. Walking up to the door I kicked that bitch in. the entire door fell off the hinges. He was laying on the couch and jumped up.

"Wh—I knocked his ass out. He fell into the glass coffee table. He wasn't a small nigga at all. I mean he ain't have shit on me. But he still was solid. I stood up and waited for the nigga to get up and fight. He stood to hit feet and wiped his lip. We started fighting ol'school style right in the living room. I have to give it to the pussy. He got swing, but he wasn't a King. After he got a hit in on my ribs. He pushed me into the fireplace making all the pictures fall. Ty was doing what I wanted. Staying watch outside and letting us fight. When he tried to swing again I ducked. Making his fist collide on the brick fire place. I know the nigga hand had to be broke. I turned and hit him with all my strength in his face again.

This time blood splattered all over him and a little on me. I grabbed his collar and kept hitting him square in his face. I know his shit will be unrecognizable. When he fell to the floor I pulled my heat out and pressed it to his head. With blood coming all out of his face. Teeth missing and both eyes closed he spoke in a low tone.

"He still is coming for you nigga." He used some strength and spit blood in my face. I wiped it off. With the gun still pressed on his head I said.

"I will be waiting for whoever you *think* is comin' for me. You could have killed British and Jaxon you stupid ass nigga. That's why you dying tonight." He stopped breathing and put his hand up. Because it was quiet Ty came in and stood next to me.

"Fuck are you talking about. Sleez was supposed to only kill you. Not my wife and my daughter." Me and Ty looked at each other. I didn't know rather to still kill this fool or hug his ass. If he hired Sleez to kill me then that means he knows here he is at.

"I am going to ask you this one-time nigga. Save yo' own life and answer me. Where the fuck is Sleez?" I said through gritted teeth. Pussy boy told me he was staying in the basement at some strip club. He told me where it was at and then he blacked out. His bitch ass wasn't dead just unconscious.

Me and Ty threw him in the back of the trunk and pulled off. This time I drove because I had to make a little stop first. When I got to the stop I put the car in park. I looked at my brother while putting my silencer on my gun. He looked at me and nodded his head. I got out leaving him in the truck to watch pussy ass in the trunk. Walking to the side door I grabbed the key under the rock. I opened the door and crept inside. I saw the purple minivan in the garage so I knew someone was home. I also could hear the theme song to Golden Girls playing. When I walked passed the kitchen I saw who I was looking sitting in her rocking chair. She couldn't see me because her back was facing the kitchen. I walked in front of her startling her. I raised my gun and said.

"Blame your grandson for this." And I pulled the trigger. Putting a bullet between her eyes.

Walking to the back of the house towards the bedroom. I heard what sound like water in the tub. I opened the bathroom door and fired my second shot. Again, it went straight through the head. I called my clean-up crew and told them to come. I also told them to put the bodies in trash bags and keep them in the freezer. Getting back in the truck my brother dabbed me up and we headed to the strip club.

Pussy boy was still knocked out in the trunk. I ducked taped his hands, mouth and feet together. I told Ty to go around the back and stand there just in case someone tried to run out. Before I went in we made sure there was no other way to get out. Seeing there wasn't I made my way in the building.

There were only two cars parked out front. I figured there was not a lot of people inside. When I walked in there was a bouncer sleep on a stool by the door. I gave him a bullet to the dome. My silencer was still on so the gun shot made no noise. I grabbed big fella's body preventing it from hitting the ground hard. There was a dancer on stage and two niggas watching her.

Phew!

Phew!

Phew!

Lights out for them muthafuckas. The nigga behind the bar had his hands up in a surrender matter.

"The money is in my safe in the office. I can give you the combination just please don't kill me." He started crying. I laughed.

"Nigga I don't want your pennies. Is Sleez in the basement?" He nodded his head yes.

Then the stupid nigga made a wrong move. He tried to reach for his heat. I popped his ass in the chest and in the head. A glass broke but nothing to loud. I opened the door to the basement and walked downstairs. I heard music and moaning. *Fucking dumb ass nigga getting pussy. At least he will die getting' a nut.* I thought to myself. I kicked the door open and almost threw up in my mouth. Sleez was fucking a big white Vin Diesel looking nigga. I hurried up and shot him in the head.

Sleez took off to the back running naked as shit. Looking like an Olympic crackhead. I let him run because he was not getting far. I heard a loud thud and knew Ty had his ass. I looked behind the door and saw all the shit Sleez stole from me. The Russians weapons and drugs were still bagged up. Looked like they haven't even been touch. What the fuck was the point of taking the shit if you're not going to sell it?

This would have set Sleez up for life. Stupid ass nigga. I started bagging the shit up and putting it in the truck. My clean-up crew showed up and handled inside. Two of our other goons showed up and put Sleez ass in the trunk. I told them to meet me at out second warehouse. Pussy boy still was out and that's how I wanted it. I needed to handle Sleez ass first. Shit was long overdue.

Walking into the warehouse I saw the bodies that I dropped at the strip club. They were about to get shredded up or burned. I walked downstairs to the freezer and opened it up. My brother grabbed a bag while I grabbed the other. Coming back up-stairs I saw my goons dragging Sleez inside.

"Throw that bitch over there!" I threw the garbage bag next to Sleez and so did Ty.

"Terror don't kill me man. Look, I was just upset that y'all kicked me out. I been nothing but loyal to y'all." He had a knot on his head from where Ty hit him. His naked ass was scratched the fuck up from being dragged around.

"Nigga all the shit you did and you actually think you are going to live? I wanted to give you to Ronny and let him fuck you up. But if anybody is going to kill you it is going to be me. Let me ask you this before we start. Why the fuck have you been sittin' on all the weight you stole from us?" He wiped his tears and spoke.

"I was going to make it look like some other niggas stole it. I was going to kill some little dudes and bring them and the product back to you. All I wanted was back in bro. for real for real. That's all I fucking wanted." He started crying even more. Ty was cracking up along with the rest of our crew that was here. I didn't find anything funny. Shit was sickening to watch a naked crackhead crying.

"Why the fuck did you shoot up my truck with my woman and daughter in it? You could have fuckin' killed them." I grabbed his jaw hard as hell when I said that. So hard my nails made his skin on his jaw bleed.

"You taught us a long time ago that it's a dog eat dog business. Do what we have to do." He sniffed and looked everywhere but at me. I let his face go and opened the first bag. Ty opened the second one.

"You right I did teach you that shit. And I took my own advice." We both dumped the bodies out the bag. Sleez screamed like the bitch he was.

"Ahhhhh! No! No!" He crawled to his grandma and auntie bodies. He hugged and kissed them. Nigga was crying hard as hell. Now that shit made all of us fall out laughing.

"FUCK YOU TERROR NIGGA! FUCK ALL OF Y'ALL! YOU DIDN'T HAVE TO DO THIS SHIT! I DIDN'T EVEN KNOW THOSE TWO BITCHES WERE IN THE TRUCK!" That made me stop laughing right there.

I picked up the bat and hit Sleez in the head. Knocking his ass out instantly. I didn't kill him which is how I wanted it to be.

Two hours later Sleez woke up still naked laying on the concrete floor. He was shivering and shaking. He had dried up tears and green snot all over his face. Probably from screaming so fucking much. I had cut all his fingers and toes off. Then I burned the nubs so he would not bleed out.

"Well look who finally woke up! Welcome back my nigga. Since this is your last few moments I wanted to let you see something. Just a going away present from me to you." I stood out from in front of him.

Ty turned the machine on and started shredding Sleez grandma and auntie. I looked down at Sleez and he had tears coming down his face. That shit lit up my face with a huge ass smile. I wanted him to feel noting but pain and hurt. When he burned my restaurant down he could have killed my employees and everybody in there.

When he ran up in Ronny's crib he could have killed Kori. When he shot up my truck he could have. I hated that I had to take out his grandma and auntie. Just the way it is. When Ty was done I walked back over to Sleeze crying ass. I had a saw behind my back.

"Lights out nigga." I began sawing his head off. The shit felt good as hell with each cut I did. I owed a lot of people this niggas death. Manly my Queen and Princess and home.

When I was done with Sleez grimey ass I went back out to my truck. Pussy boy was waking up which was fine by me. I left Ty at the warehouse while I drove to my next destination.

When I got to pussy boy house it was after 1 o'clock in the morning. I didn't give a fuck if it was 1 in the afternoon with sunny skies. Anyone who saw me and even thought about doing some shit was dying. Period!

I opened my trunk and dragged pussy boy by his legs. He grunted through the duct tape. I drug him all the way to his door and walked in with him dragging behind. He had a screen door so no one saw his big door off the hinges.

When we got into the house I dropped his legs. I pulled my gun out and twisted my silencer on. He started that pussy crying and sobbing. I bent down and yanked the tape off his mouth. Then I yanked it off his hands. I left his feet tied up. I looked at his ugly ass and remembered my Yummy baby crying on the beach in Jamaica.

I rubbed by beard with the tip of the gun. He laid there quiet with nothing but fear in his eyes. Even if he couldn't see I still knew fear when I smelled it. I loved the look of fear. Shit made my dick hard! I knew I was crawling up in my baby tonight. I thought a minute then made my decision. I stayed bent down in his face.

"This is what you are going to do. Get in your daughter's life my nigga. You know she good either way but you are her donor. As a matter of fact, be in her life or don't be in her life. I will leave that decision to you. I won't even fuck wit'chu if you choose not to. BUT I will tell you what you don't have a choice on." I put the barrel of my gun so far in his mouth pussy boy gagged.

"You WILL give my woman a divorce. You and she will never be again. You fucked up my nigga. The shit is done. Over with. No fucking more. You will give her a divorce by my baby Jaxx 1st birthday. If you don't then she won't need one after all. Yo' ass will be dead. Either way I will make British my wife and unlike yo' stupid ass. I will know what the fuck I have. Do we have an understanding?" I pulled my gun out his mouth so he could talk. The nigga had two closed eyes and dried caked up blood all on his face.

"I will never give her a divorce." I nodded my head.

Phew!

Phew!

"Ughhhhh!" He grunted loud as hell. I shot him in both of his feet. I aimed the barrel back at his head.

"Ok! Ok! I will give her a divorce by Jaxon's 1st birthday!" He yelled loud as hell. I smiled and stood up. Without saying anything else I walked out of his house. There was no need to tell him what to say when he got to the hospital. Pussy boy didn't want to die so I knew he would think of something. Meanwhile, me and Ty have a 11-hour flight to catch to Russia in the morning.

Eighteen Hours later, Moscow Russia

That 11-hour flight was used for some much-needed sleep. Me and my brother slept the entire way. One of the many perks about having your own plane is not having to deal with people. Our shit was decked out with beds instead of seats. A full kitchen and bar.

We had a board room for any meetings we may have to have. We also had a king size bed for when we had a female with us. Ty never brought a woman on our plane. Sheena was the only woman I ever had on here. I couldn't wait to take my family around the world in it. I rented a black Land Rover while we were here. This trip was just a drop off then we were headed home. I missed my ladies and I wanted to just be up under them.

Pulling up to a long gold gated mansion I stopped so the camera could look at my face. Once I was cleared the gates opened and I drove in.

Ty was on the passenger side texting Ashley. We have been out here plenty of times and the shit never gets old. The mansion looked more like a castle to me. It was tan and gold with big ass gold statues all outside. These fuckin' Russians loved their gold. Parking my truck in front of the entrance me and Ty got out.

The doors opened and big nose and Schwarzenegger look alike came out. My pressure went up at the sight of them two bitches. Then three other dudes came out. One had on a long grey fur with gold rings on his hand. He had a matching fur ear muffs on as well. It was cold in Moscow so I couldn't wait to get back to Georgia.

"Terror, Ty it really is a pleasure to see you again. I must say I did not think we would be hearing from you. At least not this soon." He smiled at me and my brother. Just like the other two. His Russian ascent was strong. Wasn't shit to smile about for us. Not only was I freezing my nuts off but I hated being around those two muthafuckas that popped Mike.

"Are you joining us for dinner? We have quite a feast." The fur wearing nigga asked. Usually when we come here we drop at the entrance and dip out. Some big nigga would check shit or give us a message and we were on our way. We handled all my business that way. These muthafuckas were not our friends.

"Naw we are not staying to eat. We came here to deliver and leave. The truck already came and dropped y'all merchandise off. We came to give y'all the last of the delivery. I handed the blue bag to big nose. He unzipped it and pulled Sleez's body parts out. They all smiled and clapped. Weird ass fuckers.

"That's the person responsible for your delayed merchandise. Him and all that were involved are dead. The others were blown up and he was saved for last," I said to them while pulling my hat over my ears. It was cold as fuck!

"This will go great with tomorrow night's dinner. We thank you very much. You will get the usual call from us in 6-months. Eight million dollars apiece for you. And now gentlemen pah kah (goodbye). They turned and began walking away.

"We still have one more problem," I said with their backs to me. Me and Ty pulled or guns out so quick. If you blinked you would have missed it. I popped Schwarzenegger in the head and Ty popped big nose. A fuckin' 2 for 1 deal! At the moment who knew what would happen to us. I know I planned on keeping my promise to British and come home. My brother as well.

"FANTASTIC!!" The Russian dude with the fur started clapping and smiling. He stepped over his dead people's bodies like they were trash.

"Oh you have made me proud! I would have killed both of you had you not done this. I don't tolerate disrespect. And anyone who lets me disrespect them I do not want around. That shows a sign of weakness. My boys here." He pointed to the two next to him.

"They thought you two were not going to do it. I told him to have more faith in you people." I side eyed my brother and he did the same. Racist bitches.

"I knew you would not tolerate me killing one of your men. Plus, this big nose muthafucka was fucking my wife. He thought I didn't know but I always knew. We are about to eat her now in my secret beef stew. Are you sure we can't persuade you to stay?" Me and my brother had the same nasty look on our faces. Crazy muthafuckas eatin' people like the shit is normal.

"Naw we good. We gotta get back to the States. We will be in touch like you said."

"There is another three million apiece for the three of you. Just for taking this problem off my hands. And for my fresh meat. Again, I bid you farewell gentlemen." This time they walked in their castle and shut the doors.

"Let's get the fuck out of here bro. Crazy ass muthafuckas," I said to Ty as we walked back to our truck. I was happy as hell this shit was over with and we can head home.

Derrick

It had been four days and I was still in the hospital. Thank God my feet were in the healing stage and so was my face. I had to had 30 stiches all over my face. Two plastic surgery procedures on my nose. And I had ten missing teeth so now I wore false teeth. My eyes were slowly opening and healing up as well. I needed to be in a wheel chair for a few weeks. As much as I wanted to tell the police what really happened.

I didn't want to die at all and as crazy as that nigga is. He probably still would kill me from in jail. I just told the police it was a burglary gone wrong. They bought the story and took my statement. I could not fucking believe this was my life. All the good shit I have done in my life. I went to school and graduated. I stayed out of trouble and I made an honest living. So why the fuck do I end up in a hospital bed?! Shit just did not seem fair. After my nurse left with my breakfast I ate my food which was liquid eggs.

Oh yea, did I forget to mention. My fucking jaw is wired the fuck shut! I had a note pad and pen as my means of communication. I wrote something down and passed the pad to Treasure. Yea she was right by my side. She had called my phone when I was in surgery and they told her. She called Eric and he and Sheena had been down here to.

I wrote on the pad that she could go home if she liked. When she read it, she smiled and shook her head no. I set back in the bed and picked up my phone. I went on Facebook and the first status I seen was Niecy's. It said Elijah Nick Patrick born 7lbs 8oz at Piedmont Atlanta Hospital. That was where I was at. For some reason, I wanted to see if I could go see her. I wrote on my pad then buzzed my nurse. Treasure walked out the bathroom drying her hands.

"Derrick are you ok? What's wrong baby?" Just as I was about to give her my pad my nurse came in.

"Hi Mr. Noel. What can I do for you?" She smiled at me and picked up the pad. I could see Treasure rolling her eyes.

She swears my nurse likes me but I just think she was friendly. She was a fine thick snow bunny. Never had a white bitch before it might be kind of nice. Maybe that's what I needed. White women don't run their mouths as much as black women. Plus, they appreciate a good man when they have one. After she read my request she set the pad down.

"What I can do is page labor and delivery and ask if she checked in. if she has we need her permission for you to visit. I will be right back when I have conformation. Meanwhile your bath is in two hours. Luck for you my shift ends after so I will be administering you with that." She smiled and winked at me.

As she was walking out Treasure smacked her lips and pouted. I grabbed my note pad. I told her she is sexy as hell when she is mad. Then I told her I like my coffee black with no cream. Treasure laughed when she was done reading it and she kissed my lips. Treasure didn't say anything about Niecy because I had already told her that about that drama.

I wasn't worry about rather Treasure stopped fucking with me like I was with British. She either stayed or she left. No sweat off my balls.
About twenty minutes later snow bunny came back smiling big. I figured she had good news or she was just happy to see me. Hopefully it was both.

"Ok Mr. Noel. You have been approved your visit. I am going to get your wheelchair and we can be on our way." I gave her a thumbs up. I wrote in my pad for Treasure to stay here. I didn't want to upset Niecy.

When my nurse came back she set the wheelchair up. Even though I could get myself out the bed. I wanted her to help me anyways. These hospital gowns were thin so I knew she would see my dick print.

And as if on que she did and her cheeks turned red. Treasure was in her phone so she didn't notice. When I was good and ready we left out the room. As she pushed me I felt like we were going on a long journey.

Even when we got off the elevators we still had to go down so many halls. It was like Niecy was in another building or some shit. I could tell we were getting closer. I started seeing pictures with babies on the walls and cartoon characters.

Some woman must have been in some serious pain. She was pacing back and forth and a nurse was rubbing her lower back. The woman's belly was big as hell and she was crying. It made me think if British went through that with Jaxon.

We got to a door that had room 68 on it. My nurse knocked and slowly opened the door. I saw Niecy sitting up breast feeding the baby. Once I was all the way in the room my nurse locked my chair in place. I guess she was trying to give Niecy some space while she was breast feeding.

She put me in front of her bed but not to close. As my nurse explained to Niecy about my injuries I was writing in my note pad. The bathroom door opened and the Steph Curry look alike came out. He set in the chair next to Niecy's bed.

He nodded his head at me and kissed Niecy on the forehead. After she was done feeding him she gave the baby to her man. I still could not see the babies face. All I saw was a baby blue hat. I gave my nurse the pad and she gave it to Niecy.

I don't want to cause any trouble. I saw on Facebook you were at the same hospital as I was. All I want to do is see him. If that is ok with you.

"It's cool Derrick. You can see him. Baby let him hold Elijah," she said to her man. Dude got up and put the baby in my arms.

Once I was comfortable I looked down at him. Elijah opened his eyes a little and looked at me. I broke down hard as fuck. Not only did he have my complexion. But he had the same two dark shadows on his eye brows that I had when I was born. That let me know he was going to have my thick eye brows.

I didn't care who saw me cry I was overwhelmed and felt like shit. I missed Niecy's entire pregnancy. All my sons kick, ultra-sound pictures and gender reveal. I couldn't take looking at him anymore. I gave the baby back to Niecy's man and grabbed my pen and pad. I started writing as Niecy put our son back on her breast.

I could hear the TV playing ESPN sports highlights. When I was done writing I gave the pad to my nurse. She gave it to Niecy without reading it.

I don't need a DNA test to tell me what I already know. That's my boy Niecy and I do apologize. I still want to give you money for him but I need/want to be in his life. Please Niecy. I won't be on no creep shit. I just need to see my boy.

I saw tears fall from Niecy's eyes.

"That's all I ever wanted from you D. Yeah I was still trying to mess with you in the beginning. But once my pregnancy became further along I knew I just wanted you to be a dad to our son. If you can do right then I have no problem with you being in his life." Niecy passed the note to her man. He read it and nodded his head at me. I guess my beef was not with him or her. It was with myself because Elijah was in deed mines.

I stayed for a while and just held my son in my arms. He smelled good as hell and he was so cute. I could not keep my eyes dry and I thought about my daughter and son. I had not been a good father to Jaxon at all. To busy working or with bitches to spend time with my daughter.

Even though she was a girl I knew she still needed me in her life. Fathers play a big role in a child's life. No matter how independent a woman is that child still needs its father. The way Jaxon screamed and cried in my arms made me feel like a monster. I needed to get my shit together and be there for my kids.

Once Niecy said she was tired I gave the baby to her. My nurse rolled my back to my room. Before we made it to my door my nurse took my pad and opened it. She turned to the last page and started writing it. It took her a minute to write whatever she was writing. When she was done she gave it back to me and said in my ear.

-"Read it later." Then she winked at me. When she opened my door, Treasure was eating some Chinese food. I saw my lunch sitting on the table waiting for me. Once I was good and comfortable in my bed I drunk my soup and watched TV.

Treasure left because she had a class today. She enrolled in school to become a Medical Assistant while still dancing until she graduated. As I was watching TV I remembered the note my nurse wrote for me. I opened the pad and read it.

You have become my favorite patient. For that reason, you get a special sponge bath this evening. Here is my number also so I can give you these baths at home as well. – Nurse P.

My dick got hard thinking about her snow-white ass. My door opened and in walked my nurse with a sponge, a bucket and a smirk. Hell yea!

*

Two days later and I was finally able to leave the hospital. They made me take a wheel chair home but I was not going to use it. My face was getting better each day. Having money made me have a good ass plastic surgeon work on me. My nose looked regular the only thing annoyed me were the stiches.

But in another two weeks they could come off. I still was a handsome man with a lot of money. The wire was taking out of my jaw but I still couldn't talk. Well if I force some words you could understand me. But then I would sound like 50 cent in Get rich or die trying.

So, I decided to just still write in my note pad in order to communicate. Treasure was helping me get settled in my home. While I was in the hospital I had her call a maid service to clean my face. When me and British thug ass nigga got into a fight. We trashed the fuck out of my living room. I really appreciated everything Treasure had done while I was in the hospital. Eric was coming over later to bring me some meals.

Sheena cooked a big ass feast for Thanksgiving and he was bringing me the leftovers. I needed a home cooked meal now that I could eat some solids. I noticed Treasure still had her Jacket on. I told her she could stay the night if she wanted to.

This is the first time I have ever had another woman in my home besides British. I didn't have any pictures up of my wife all over the house.

I was more if an art type of man so I had paintings up everywhere instead. I wrote in my pad asking Treasure was she staying the night with me. When I gave it to her she did a light chuckle and gave it back to me.

"Derrick I just came to get you situated and then I am going home. This will be the last time I see you after today. Please don't call or stop by my place because I will not be there. I'm moving into a new place next week anyways. Look, I thought this could workout. Hell, I wanted it to so bad. But I am not about to get played the same way you played your wife. I don't think you have it in you to be a good man. At least not to a good woman who is good to you." She grabbed the notebook out my hand.

She turned to the last page and put in in my face. I could have slapped myself for not ripping it out. I left it in there because snow-bunnies number was on it. Treasure nicely put the folder back in my lap and walked out the door. I was a little annoyed she didn't let me explain but I figured fuck it. One less headache I had to worry about. I sent my snow-bunny a text and told her to come over tonight.

A knock was at my door and I figured it was Eric. I grabbed my cane and walked to the door. When I opened the door, a big brown folder fell on the floor. I picked it up and looked around but didn't see anyone. Closing my door, I set on my couch and opened it. My heart dropped when I saw it was divorce papers.

My marriage was really over. I lost my wife for good this time. All of a sudden, every wrong I ever did to her replayed in my head. All her crying, begging and pleading for me to do better. I let the shit fall on deaf ears. Her smile, her walk, her cooking, her love she had for me was all gone.

The worst part about this whole thing. She was giving it all to another man. After just sitting there for about two hours I got up and went to my kitchen to grab a pen. Sitting back down I looked at the papers and tears fell. I owned her this much so I signed them. Goodbye British.

British

As I left out the court house the December winter wind it my face. I felt like a big weight was lifted off me. My divorce was finalized and I could not have been happier. Derrick was entitled to pay spousal support and child support. I declined both payments leaving both our lawyers and the judge shocked.

Terrance or anybody else had nothing to do with my decision. I really did not want anything from Derrick. All I wanted was for him to give me my divorce. And since her did that my next thing I wanted was for him to be a father.

Derrick requested to get Jaxon every other weekend. I had no problem with that because he didn't ask for holidays I don't know why but I didn't question. Apart of me still saw some selfishness in Derrick and lack of care. I have no idea what problem he had with having a daughter. All I knew was the first time I see my baby unhappy all visits were off.

I saw on his Facebook how much he was with his son. They were at his house and I'm assuming Niecy's house from the pictures. He even had the baby around his family and office. He never and I mean never had Jaxon like that at all. He kept saying she was a girl and needed her mother. My stupid ass went along with it and continued letting him stay that way. Next month is when he will start getting her and I was going to give it three visits. If my baby was not use to him by then we would have a problem.

I saw Terrance pull up in my black Escalade. I smiled when I saw my sexy ass man. He had my baby girl in the back seat. I saw some Toys R Us bags in the back seat as well. I shook my head. Walking towards them I heard my name being called. I turned around and it was Derrick. He walked up to me with a calm but sad look on his face. I heard Terrance open the car door and get out. He didn't do anything but lean against the front of the truck with his arms folded. Derrick looked at him then back at me. He held his hand out for mines. I shook it and he nodded his head slowly and walked off. I guess that was his way of saying goodbye. I walked over to Terrance and smiled which made him smile big as hell to.

"Say hello to British Jones." I kissed his lips and he squeezed my ass. Turning me on all in front of the court house. We got back in the truck and I kissed my baby making her laugh. I looked at all the bags.

"Really baby? Why would she need all of this and her birthday is next week? You already invited a shit load of people. Jaxon has one friend and that is Aron. I told you we should just have cake and ice cream at the house." I was laughing at him and shaking my head.

"I ain't tyrna hear none of that stuff you talkin' woman. You only turn 1 once and she is having a damn party.

Now we about to go home so Jaxon can take a nap and I can make sweet love to my woman." He bit his lip and turned the radio on. Maxwell – Fortunate was playing and Terrance was singing along. He kept glancing at me and rubbing my thigh. How did I get so blessed to meet this sexy ass man? The way he loved me and my daughter was amazing and made me want him more. And when he sings! Mm! When he sings I get a tingle all over my body!

True to his word we arrived home and I fed both my babies. Jaxon was tired so her went and rocked her to sleep. I told him she was too big for that but I lost all battles when it came to her. After Jaxon was asleep we both took a shower together. Terrance kept telling me how much he loved. Like oil on dry skin I was soaking his words up. I felt it every time he says he loves me.

Clean and dried off we both were laying on the bed. We were as naked as the day we were born. I climbed on top of him and started kissing his hungrily. I wanted to show all my feeling through this kiss. I was beyond grateful for this man and wanted to keep him forever.

I went to his neck down to his strong ass chest. I licked over his nipples which I knew was his spot. He let out a small grunt as I worked my way down. His swollen hard dick as staring me in the face. Even though I could not deep that muthafucka. I sucked the hell out of it making my baby go crazy.

I reached over to the night stand. I brought this edible peach flavored massage oil from Lover Lane. Terrance watched me with seduction and lust all in his eyes. I opened it up and poured some all over his dick. I was biting my lip and looking in his eyes as I stroked his dick. He leaned his head back and closed his eyes.

"Look at me." I moaned to him. He did and I took as much as I could of his dick in my mouth. I never gaged I just could fit the whole thing in. I massaged his balls and I stroked his dick with my jaws. The edible oil was so good it was making my mouth very watery which I knew he would love. I squeezed my jaws tighter with each suck. Popping his dick out my mouth I went and showed some love to his balls.

"Ugh Fuck Yummy! You gon' make me nut woman!" I was about to put his dick back in my mouth. But Terrance snatched my ass up and slammed me on top of his dick. I cried out in pleasure while I started riding him. Terrance dick rubbed my clit over and over every time I rode him. I couldn't take this position. To keep me from waking up my baby he set up and tongued me down. I was moan loud against his mouth.

"Shut yo' ass up and ride this dick Yum. You bet not wake up my baby." I had my eyes in the back of my head looking possessed. All you could hear was squishy noises as I came all on his 11-inches.

"Arrgghhhhh Terrance baby fuck!" I could not stop bouncing as I prolonged my orgasm. Out of breath I slowed down and kissed his neck.

"Hell naw Yummy baby. I ain't done wit'chu. Turn the fuck over!" I did what I was told. On all fours, I thought I was about to get some more dick. Terrance dived face first and was eating me out from the back. I rode his face from the back until I came twice then he slid inside of me. I could do this forever and after death.

*

A week later

Today was my baby 1st birthday and I was overjoyed. It feels like I just had her yesterday. I remember being so sad because she was coming so close to Christmas. I never wanted people to forget about her because her birthday was December 24th. I walked downstairs and grabbed my keys. I had to come back home and grab her crown that I insisted on her having. I looked in our living room and shook my head.

We had a twelve-foot Christmas tree that me, Terrance and Jaxon decorated. We made a big night out of it with matching pajamas and house shoes. Our house looked like a winter wonderland with blue and silver everywhere. When I tell y'all we had Christmas presents all around the tree!

It was ridiculous how you could barely get in the living room to watch TV. Pretty much all it was Jaxson's! This girl had another room for toys and clothes only. Blame Terrance!

Getting to the hall we rented out, I saw so many luxury cars parked outside.

My family was here as well but a lot was Terrance family and friends. Each person had at least three gifts and Jaxon had so many damn cards. You would have thought this was a party for an adult. Terrance had Dr. McStuffin every fucking thing. He had two Dr. McStuffin moon-bounces, three long tables with Dr. McStuffin party favors. Three towers of cupcakes with every flavor you could imagine. The frosting was purple and pink. The same color Dr. McStuffin wore. There was a DJ and a 135-inch visual projector screen. It was on mute playing Dr. McStuffin show.

Oh, did I forget to mention we had a Dr. McStuffin character. Purple and pink balloons were everywhere and so was Jaxon pretty picture blown up on each wall. My baby looked so pretty in her purple leggings and pink chucks on her feet. I got a jean jacket custom made with her name and 1st birthday on it. It was bedazzled out all over. Her long, thick, curly hair was in ponytails.

Terrance had a special princess chair with her name on the back of it. Of course, she didn't sit in it one time. Terrance held her. And when it was time to sing Happy Birthday my baby wanted no part of it. She was partied out after only two hours.

So guess what his mean ass did? Kicked everybody out and took us home. He had some people he hired to bring her gifts home. All that damn money wasted on a baby who slept and wanted to be held all day. I didn't even say anything because Terrance would have thought nothing was wrong.

Once we got home I cleaned my baby up and put her to sleep. Tomorrow was Christmas and she had yet more stuff to open. When I finally got into bed with Terrance it was around 10 o'clock. I laid on him while watched TV. Terrance never had to remind me to be all over him. I never could keep my hands to myself when it came to him.

"You know you are the best Christmas gift I ever have gotten. And you are coming up against a lot." He chuckled as he rubbed my back. I looked at him and kissed his full lips.

"You are Christmas and New Years for me baby." I smiled at him. He started laughing and kissed me.

"You know that was corny right." He teased. I laughed at hit him in his arm.

"You always beatin' on me woman." He started tickling me and like always I was cracking up. I loved our nights like this. I could not wait to see what all God had in store for us.

Epilogue

British

"Aww British are you crying happy tears?" Kori asked while poking her lip out. I wanted to slap her.

"Hell naw! I'm crying because it is my wedding day and I look like a fat ass pig. You and Ashley lookin' all good out shining the damn bride. I feel like whale." I continued to wheep.

I didn't care how crazy I sound. Kori and Ashley looked good as hell in their maid of honor outfits. Hell, my bridesmaids looked good to. I wanted to fire all their asses! Don't get me wrong I had taste in picking out their dresses. Kori and Ashley had a grey fitted, long Dolce and Gabbana dress.

They looked good with the long split revealing their legs and their chest set up amazing. My bridesmaid's dresses were identical except theirs were lilac. They all looked good but the fucking bride looked like a blimp.

"Oh honey bear stop crying. You are 5-months pregnant what did you expect. You were just happy a second ago." Ashley was rubbing my back trying to calm me down.

"I know! But then all of you came in here looking like some sexy sluts. I wanna be a sexy slut to." I started balling my eyes out. Everybody crowded around me and hugged me.

"Girl stop crying. You are about to marry the love of your life in a few minutes. Trust me when he sees you he will not care about your belly. If anything, you are going to be more beautiful carrying his first baby for him. Ok? So stop crying." Ashley wiped my face and Kori fixed my makeup. She was right I needed to calm down. I was beautiful in my own pig like way. And my wedding dress was a custom-made Andre Leon Talley gown. It flowed down with beads on the end.

This was my first time in a wedding dress so I wanted to go all out. I decided against a vail because of my hairstyle. I got a sew-in for the first time ever and I loved it. I had deep wavy hair in and it was pinned to the side. My face looked like God himself beat it for me. I told Kori if she ever stopped doing radio. Her ass needed to be a makeup artist.

My nails and feet had Swarovski crystals on them and so did my bridal party. I was not one of them butches who wanted my bridal party to look a mess. Hell no! I needed my pictures to look good and that wasn't going to happen if my bridal party looked a mess. After I got myself together we all walked out the room. I hugged my girl's first since they had to walk out before me.

"I love y'all so much. Thank you for always being there for me and Jaxon. I just hope y'all don't give me hell when I help with y'all wedding." We giggled and hugged again.

That's right both of my boos were engaged. Ty proposed to Ashley Christmas day and Ronny proposed to Kori on New Year's. I was so happy for both of my best friends. I could not wait for them to have their weddings.

I heard Toni Braxton- I love Me Some Him began. My dad kissed my forehead and the doors opened for me. I had to fight hard as hell for the tears not to fall. I had never seen the church finished because everyone wanted me to be surprised.

All I had to do was pick what I wanted and my girl's and the wedding planner handled it. I was in owe! I picked to have my wedding at First Baptist Church of Decatur. I am even more happy of my choice. There were lilac and white tulips on her ends of the pews. I asked for them to be covered in white satin and they were. I have no idea how it was possible but I had my crystal chandeliers and heart instruments hanging. I even had my gold multi-colored candle holders everywhere giving the church the intimate lighting I wanted.

The light from the windows hit the chandeliers just as I imagined. Jaxon was in front of me looking so cute in her white and lilac dress. My baby was almost 3yrs old. She looked down the aisle and saw Terrance. He held his arms out for her. My baby dumped all the flowers and took off running towards him. Making everyone laugh at her including me. He hugged her and kissed her chubby jaws.

I looked down the aisle and saw my handsome husband to be. He looked so sexy in his charcoal and lilac suite. Ty and Ronny were right by his side looking handsome as well. The rest of his groomsmen were all looking good. Terrance had the biggest smile on his face as I was walking down the aisle. I looked at my dad and he was wiping his tears.

I squeezed his arm tighter and smiled at him. I had no idea how I was holding it together. When I got to the end of the aisle my father gave me away to Terrance. Him and my dad hugged and I stood next to my guy. The pastor began speaking.

"We are here today under God to witness these two become one. I have been knowing this young man since he was 5 years old. Him and his brother use to drive the girl's crazy at Sunday school. What an honor I have to see him become a husband. Proverbs 18:22 "The man who finds a good wife find treasure and receive favor." Everyone said amen and nodded their heads to his words.

"This lovely couple has written their own vows. We will begin with Terrance." He passed him the microphone and Terrance began speaking.

"I cannot believe it is me standing up here looking into the eyes of the most beautiful being I have ever seen. British before you came in my life I was so lost. I walked around hiding it from everyone around me. I was steps from making another woman my wife based on all the wrong reasons. The way me and you led to this moment, no one can ever tell me there is no God. Baby you have made my life so much more worth living. You and that little girl have given me something no one else on this earth can ever give me. The little one you are carrying for me shows me how selfless you are. I know I am a lot and so is Jaxon. Now you are about to have another one and I have never heard you complain." My bridal party started coughing and laughing. Everyone else laughed and I stuck my tongue out at my bridal party.

"Y'all leave my baby alone. But as I was saying I just thank you British for being an amazing woman, mother, and wife. In my eyes, you were always my wife. But I want to let everyone know how much I NEED and want YOU. I am so thirsty for you baby and will forever be. I don't give a damn who sees or what people think. I have your pictures all over the house because your beauty inside and out is fucking amazing and I wanna just drown in it. You will never look the way you looked when I saw you on that beach in Jamaica. I vow that shit to you baby forever. I love you and thank you for standing in front of me." I couldn't hold back my tears anymore. They fell like rain drops falling from the sky. He wiped them away and passed me the microphone. I sniffed and took a deep breath.

"I can't stand you for making me cry." I laughed and so did everyone else.

"This man right here came into my life and I wanted to punch him. He was rude and would not tell me his real name. I went to my girl's and told them and they told me to forget about it. I would not see you again while we were in Jamaica. I guess God laughed because we kept running into each other. I was someone else's wife. Even though I had one foot out the door. I still belonged to someone else. There was never any judgement from you. Although what we were doing was wrong in the eyes of God. Even though he is a forgiving God it still didn't make it right. Sounds crazy but I would not change anything. I was so scared of you from the beginning. You challenged me in ways I didn't know. You supported me and encouraged me in ways I never saw before. The way you love and touch me is in explainable. I never felt so much like myself then when I am with you. I hid so much of me when I was in my past relationship. I was only British when I was with my friends or family. You excepted all of me, every flaw. You excepted my baby girl without question. No one could ever tell you that she is not you daughter. I could not be more blessed. You saved me baby. I was in over my head in heartbreak, loneliness, sadness and confusion. I never felt any of those things when I was with you. It's me who should be thanking you. I had given up, I was willing to except what I was in. But you came and gave me a love that consumed me and I knew I wanted it forever even when I denied it. Thank you, Terrance King. I love you so much baby."

We stood there smiling big at each other. I could hear my bridal party crying and so were people in the pews. The pastor finalized our union and we sealed it with a kiss. I was now British Rena King! I loved every moment of it.

*

Next song Wifey played loud in the hall as the DJ introduced us as Mr. & Mrs. King. We came in and everyone was clapping and shouting. We walked towards our grand table that was for us and our bridal party. Me and Terrance chair had a glass K and Q on it for King and Queen. We ate the good ass food we had catered. It felt so good to have our family and friends having a good ass time.

All of us got up to dance when Yo Gotti- Rack it up came on. Me and Terrance cut our huge white, purple and grey cake. His ass mushed me in the face with some. But I got him back when he was not looking. We kissed and the photographer took great pictures I couldn't wait to see them. I threw my bouquet and one of my friends/bridesmaids caught it. Terrance took of my garter from around my leg and threw it. One of his groomsmen caught it. We continued to have a ball at our wedding reception. Jaxon was running around chasing Aron and eating all kinds of sweets.

Now it was time for my surprise for Terrance. He had no idea I was doing this for him.

Ty got a chair and put it in the middle of the dance floor. Kori and Ronny rude asses were clearing the dance floor for me. They were not nice about it but you gotta love them. The DJ gave me a microphone so I could be heard in the big ass hall. Terrance set down cheesing and of course holding Jaxon.

Ashley was able to get her from Terrance with some cake as a bribe. Ty came the big white box with a huge black bow on top of it. He set it in front of Terrance.

"Baby I have a gift that I want to give to you. I wanted to give it to you in private but I figured why not let everyone see. I just want you to know I love you and always will." He mouthed the word I love you more to me. Myself, Ty, Ashley, Ronny and Kori already knew what the gift was.

Terrance stood up smiling big as hell. Before he opened it, he kissed me. Then pulled the first side of the ribbon then the other side. When it fell to the floor he opened the box and balloons flew to the ceiling.

They were blue and white and had It's a boy on them. Everyone started yelling and clapping. Terrance put his hand over his face and started crying. Ty and Ronny clapped and patted his back he looked at me with a wet face and pulled me into his arms he was hugging and rocking me.

"Thank you baby. Thank you so much," he whispered in my ear. I told him you're welcome and we hugged and kiss.

The DJ announced it was time for us to have our first dance as husband and wife. Blackstreet- Joy song came on. I knew it was Terrance choice because he singed it to Jaxon and played it a lot. We danced and I felt like I was in a dream. Terrance sung in my ear sounding so damn good. My hormones were kicking in and I wanted some of my husband. He leaned forward and kissed me with so much love. Everyone in the room disappeared and it was just me and him.

"I love you Yummy baby." His deep voice was in my ear.

"I love you more Terrance." He smiled and started singing the second verse in my ear.

Goodbye to loneliness,
And so long to my heartache,
Now that joy has taken over,
And decided to stay
Her love lifts me up,
Like no other love before,
With every beat of my heart,
I'm holding on, hey

THE END

**This is not the end for the couples. They will be back and we will get to see drama with Ty and Ashley. We also have not heard the last of Sheena either.
Stay Tuned!! Thank you for all the love and support.**
-Londyn Lenz

Made in the USA
Middletown, DE
02 December 2017